ARSENIC AND OLD BOOKS

A Cat in the Stacks Mystery

ARSENIC AND OLD BOOKS

Miranda James

BERKLEY PRIME CRIME, NEW YORK

THE BERKLEY PUBLISHING GROUP
Published by the Penguin Group
Penguin Group (USA) LLC
375 Hudson Street, New York, New York 10014

USA • Canada • UK • Ireland • Australia • New Zealand • India • South Africa • China

penguin.com

A Penguin Random House Company

Berkley Prime Crime Books are published by The Berkley Publishing Group.
BERKLEY® PRIME CRIME and the PRIME CRIME logo are trademarks of Penguin Group (USA) LLC.

Library of Congress Cataloging-in-Publication Data

James, Miranda.
Arsenic and old books / Miranda James.—First edition.
pages cm.—(Cat in the stacks mystery ; 6)
ISBN 978-0-425-25729-6 (hardback)
1. Librarians—Fiction.   I. Title.
PS3610.A43A88 2015
813'.6—dc23
2014037644

FIRST EDITION: February 2015

PRINTED IN THE UNITED STATES OF AMERICA

10 9 8 7 6 5 4 3 2 1

Cover illustration by Dan Craig.
Cover design by Lesley Worrell.
Interior text design by Tiffany Estreicher.

This book is dedicated in loving memory of
Ernestine Pendergrast James (1923–2014),
one of the strongest women I've ever known.

ACKNOWLEDGMENTS

As with every book, I owe thanks to many for the support I receive during the process. My editor, Michelle Vega, never fails me with her unflagging support, encouragement, and excellent advice. The amazing and efficient team at Nancy Yost Literary, including their indefatigable eponymous leader, make the business parts of the process run smoothly.

The Wednesday night critique group—Bob, Julie, Kay F., Kay K., Laura, and Millie—share their opinions of the work-in-progress freely and constructively, and I appreciate their help. The Hairston-Soparkar family continues generously to offer their home for our meetings, and I am thankful to have such a pleasant place to work.

For technical information about archives, I thank my former colleagues M. J. Figard, MLS, and Philip Montgomery, MLIS, CA. Any mistakes in archival matters are my responsibility, not theirs. Lynda L. Crist, PhD, assisted with information about paper. Terry Farmer, PhD, and Joseph E. Figard, PhD, also generously shared their expertise in matters of chemistry. Again, any mistakes to do with chemistry are mine alone.

Finally, thanks as always to my two dear friends, Patricia Orr and Terry Farmer (double-billing this time), for cheering me on during the headlong rush of finishing each and every book.

ARSENIC AND OLD BOOKS

ONE

||||||||||||||||||||||

I checked my watch, then glanced at the clock on my computer. They both told me that it was seven minutes after one p.m. I resisted the urge to get up and pace around the archive office. Instead I turned my chair and looked at the large feline dozing on the wide windowsill behind my desk.

Diesel, apparently sensing my gaze, yawned and stretched. He meowed and rolled onto his side, head twisted so that he was staring at me almost upside down. He warbled a couple of times, as if to ask, *Why are you so restless, Charlie?*

"The mayor said she'd be here at one, and she's late. You know how that bugs me," I told the cat. "I'm curious to find out about these family documents she wants to talk to me about. The Longs have already given so many collections of papers to the archive, I have to wonder what they've been holding on to."

The cat calmly began washing his right front paw.

"You may not be curious, but I am," I told him. "It's not every day that I get consulted by such an august person as Lucinda Beckwith Long."

I heard a cough, and it didn't come from Diesel.

"I beg your pardon. Are you Mr. Harris?"

I swiveled my chair to face the office door, and I could feel the blush starting. The mayor stood in the doorway, her expression puzzled.

I rose from my desk and walked around to greet Mrs. Long. "Yes, I'm Charlie Harris, Your Honor. Please come in. I was . . . Well, I was chatting with my cat. It's a habit I have, you see."

Mrs. Long nodded as she extended her hand. "I quite understand. My husband and I have three poodles, and we talk to them all the time."

"Won't you be seated?" I indicated the chair in front of my desk. Mrs. Long, clutching a tote and a black leather handbag, moved forward. She set the latter on the floor beside her when she took her seat. Clad in a chic crimson suit with a white silk blouse and colorful scarf knotted loosely around her neck, she looked cool and crisp and ready to get down to business.

I had seen the mayor on several public occasions, but never this close. She was shorter than I expected, probably no more than five-three, when she wasn't standing on the spike heels I had seen her wear. Though I knew her to be in her mid-sixties, she exuded an air of youthful energy, as if she could barely contain herself. Even now I could hear her toe tapping on the hardwood floor of my office. I figured a mayor's life must be hectic, even that of the mayor of a small city like Athena, Mississippi.

Mrs. Long appeared to be assessing me as I waited for her to speak. Diesel hopped down from his perch and padded around my desk to approach the mayor. He sniffed at her bags and then attempted to stick his head in the opening of the tote. Mrs. Long touched his head lightly to discourage him. "No, no, kitty, what's in there is too old for you to play with."

The cat stared up at her and warbled as if to say, *Are you sure?*

Mrs. Long smiled. "He seems to understand what I said, like our dogs do."

"He's a smart cat," I said. "He's also extremely curious." As I spoke Diesel batted a paw at the tote bag. "No, Diesel, stop that."

The cat threw a baleful glance my way. He stood, made a circle around Mrs. Long's chair, and then came back to his perch on the windowsill behind my desk.

"Apparently he understands a firm *no* when he hears one." Mrs. Long laughed. "Our dogs aren't always so compliant."

"He isn't, either," I had to admit. "Depends on his mood." I waited a moment for the mayor to speak again. When she didn't, I decided it was time to steer the conversation toward the reason for her visit. "I believe you wanted to consult me about some family documents."

Mrs. Long picked up the tote and settled it in her lap. She delved inside and pulled out a large manila envelope. She leaned forward and placed it on my desk. A faint mustiness, overlaid with a whiff of mothballs, wafted out of the open end.

"Inside that you will find a volume of a diary written by Rachel Afton Long. I forget at the moment how many times a great-grandmother she is, but she was born around 1820 and died in the mid-1890s, if I am remembering correctly."

I stared at the envelope before me, my excitement growing over the thought of handling such an old document. "How many volumes of her diaries survive?" I pulled open a side drawer of my desk and extracted a pair of cotton gloves. If I was going to be handling a book that was more than a hundred years old, I had to be careful with it.

"Four," Mrs. Long replied. "I have glanced at them but I find the writing hard to read. From what I could glean, however, I believe she started the diaries a few years before she married my husband's ancestor. The last diary is dated around 1875." She shrugged. "I'm not entirely certain. The handwriting is small and cramped, and I got a headache trying to decipher just one page of it."

"I'll have a look at it," I said. I held up my hands to show that I was wearing gloves before I extracted the volume, sliding it carefully out of the envelope. I let it lie on the desk as I put the envelope aside and examined the diary's outward appearance. The cover binding of brown leather was cracked in spots and rubbed thin in others, and the spine was in similar condition. My nose twitched at the strong musty odor. I hoped the diaries hadn't suffered water damage.

"Where have they been stored?" I asked.

"My son, Beck, discovered them recently in a trunk in the attic while hunting for something else entirely. I'd never seen them before, and I don't believe my husband was aware of their existence, either."

Andrew Beckwith Long, known as Beck to most, was an aspiring politician. His father, also an Andrew, had served four terms in the state senate. Recently, however, he had announced he planned to retire when his current term expired. Everyone assumed that Beck would easily win his father's seat but there appeared to be strong opposition, in the form of Jasper Singletary, a young firebrand who served on the city council. Singletary was openly ambitious, and he had been publicly less than complimentary about the Longs and their political legacy.

"Are you and Mr. Long planning to add these to the collection of Long papers and memorabilia that we already have?"

"Yes," Mrs. Long said. "They need to be better preserved than they have been. We have no idea how long they've been up in that attic, and there could be damage. None of us looked through them much because we were afraid to cause further problems. That's why I wanted to bring them to you." She paused. "I'm sure you're aware of the terrible times that Athena faced during the Civil War and the brief occupation by Union troops. If Rachel Long recorded any of that, her information might be useful to historians."

I nodded. My knowledge of Athena during the Civil War was sketchy, but in elementary school we had heard tales of the depredations of the Union Army in the winter of 1863. Our teacher, Mrs. Bondurant, had seemed so old to us at the time, we figured she was speaking from personal experience. I discovered later, when I was older and possessed a better sense of a person's age, that Mrs. Bondurant was only thirty-eight and her grandmother, a Confederate widow, was the source of her stories.

"I'm sure there will be graduate students in the history department eager to examine them," I said. "The Southern-history students are always looking for local primary sources for their theses and dissertations."

"Excellent," Mrs. Long said. "My husband and son will be delighted to hear it. They're both avid readers of history, particularly of Southern history."

"Do you have a few minutes, while I make a quick examination of the volumes?" I asked. "I can give you a rough idea whether we will need to do any conservation work with them."

Mrs. Long consulted her watch. "I have about ten minutes before I need to be back in my office."

"Good." I opened the cover of the volume on my desk with a gentle touch. The inch-thick binding was loose enough that the cover lay open on the desk without strain. I wrinkled my nose at the smell again, but I knew I would soon become accustomed to it. The more the volumes were allowed to air out, the more the odor would dissipate.

The first page of the diary had only a few words in a small, but elegant, hand. I recognized the slightly tilted lettering as copperplate, a style of handwriting popular in the nineteenth century. The words proclaimed this as the diary of Rachel Adeline Afton, aged sixteen, with the date July 4, 1854. The paper was yellowed but still in good condition. I suspected that it was the more expensive rag paper rather than the cheaper wood pulp. The latter would have turned brown and brittle years ago and begun to disintegrate.

I turned pages carefully and skimmed the contents as I went. There were no blemishes I could see, no water stains, mold, or mildew. Overall, the diary appeared to be in remarkably good condition, other than the state of the binding and the worn cover. "If the other volumes are in similar condition," I said, "then everything should be fine. Conservation work will be minimal, though we will store them in archival folders. The paper is acid-free and won't affect the contents."

"That sounds fine." Mrs. Long smiled briefly. "We are placing no restrictions on these diaries, Mr. Harris. We want scholars to be able to use the contents for their work." She stood and passed the tote with the other volumes to me.

I took the bag and pulled out the three remaining manila envelopes, each with a diary inside. "That's excellent news. As soon as I've had the time to check each one more thoroughly, I'll let the history department know about them."

"They are already aware of the gift," Mrs. Long said. "One of my husband's good friends—and mine as well—is Professor Howell Newkirk. He was dining with us last night, and I happened to mention it to him."

"I see." That was unexpected news. I was acquainted with Dr. Newkirk. He was elderly, irascible, and pushy. He was also the most eminent historian on the Athena faculty, and he knew it. He demanded, and was usually given, what he wanted. I was surprised he wasn't already in my office asking to see the diaries.

Mrs. Long smiled. "I know Howell can be, well, rather insistent on things, but I suggested that he give you a few days with the diaries before he even thought about assigning a student to work on them. There might be others interested in them as well."

"Thank you," I said. "Then I will make sure they are ready sooner rather than later. I will add these to the list attached to your original deed of gift for the rest of the collection, if that's okay with you."

"Yes, that's fine," Mrs. Long said. She hesitated a moment before she continued. Her eyes focused like lasers on me. "You might be aware that my son, Beck, plans to run for office in the near future. And that he is facing a challenge. Rachel Afton Long was an extraordinary woman, and the more the voters know about the history of the Long family and its achievements and triumphs, the more they will want to see a member of the family in office."

With that, she nodded, gathered up her purse, and departed.

I stared at the pile of diaries on my desk. Why would the mayor think that Rachel Long's writings could affect the outcome of a twenty-first-century political race?

TWO

I continued to puzzle over the mayor's odd remarks while I worked on the four volumes of Rachel Long's diaries. Perhaps Rachel had performed some heroic act during the Civil War that the mayor thought should be better known. Even if that were the case, I wondered how it would help Beck Long politically. I eventually decided that the mind of a politician worked differently from mine and put aside the question for later.

All four volumes were in very good condition, their mustiness aside. The most obvious problem for each was its binding. On all of them the leather had dried and cracked, and for the moment the best thing I could do was construct an archival box for each. I set the boxes on a nearby shelf. Until I finished with them, they would remain in the office with me. Then I would place them in the room next door where the bulk of the archive's documents resided.

I now had less than a quarter hour left before it was time to head home. Diesel abandoned his perch and prowled around the office, a sure sign that he knew the time. He was as ready to go home as I was. The intense concentration of my task had left me with neck strain and a headache, and I quickly discovered I had no aspirin or ibuprofen in the office.

I needed to do one more job before we could leave, however. I wanted to add the diaries to the inventory of the Long family collection and update the record in the library's online catalog. Later on I would catalog the diaries separately, but for now a note on the master record would suffice.

That task completed, I shut down my computer. Diesel waited by the office door. A few minutes later we headed down the sidewalk toward home. By the time we reached the house we both had wilted from the September heat and humidity. I was ready for a cold drink, and Diesel made a beeline for the utility room the moment I opened the front door.

In the kitchen I shed my jacket and briefcase and went to the fridge for the water pitcher. Two glasses later I felt cooler and no longer parched. Diesel came chirping out of the utility room to sit at my feet. He stared up at me and meowed loudly. I knew that meow. Either his bowls needed refilling, or the cat box needed cleaning. He wouldn't stop talking to me until I took care of the problem.

Once I had accomplished these duties to the cat's satisfaction, I poured myself another glass of water and sat at the kitchen table to relax for a few minutes.

The house felt empty. My daughter, Laura, now a married woman, had moved out after her June wedding and into the house owned by her husband, Frank Salisbury. Their wedding was a beautiful occasion, full of laughter and occasional tears. Throughout the ceremony I could feel my late wife, Jackie, by my side. Both Laura and Frank taught in the theater department at Athena College, and their teaching schedules kept them fully occupied. I saw them occasionally on campus, and they came for dinner once a week. Frank was a good man, and I was happy for my daughter. I missed her presence in the house terribly, though, and I knew Diesel did as well. I think Laura was his second favorite human after me.

The ring of the kitchen phone broke the silence. I wasn't eager to answer it because family and friends usually called my cell phone. I thought about letting it go to voice mail, but in case it was important, I decided to answer.

I identified myself to the caller.

"Mr. Harris, my name is Kelly Grimes, and I'm at Athena College working on a project on the Long family. I'm looking at the library's online catalog right now, and I see that the archive has evidently acquired several volumes of a diary by Rachel Afton Long." She paused for a breath. "I believe they could be crucial to my research, and I was wondering if I could look at them this evening."

"The archive is closed for the day, Ms. Grimes." I had learned early on to stick to the stated hours. Otherwise, students would want access to the archives outside scheduled times. "The diaries were only added to the collection this afternoon, and they aren't ready for public use. I need time to examine them more thoroughly to be sure they are in good enough condition to allow any such use."

"That's really inconvenient. How long do you think it will be before I can look at them?"

I could tell by her tone that Ms. Grimes was not happy with my response to her request. I considered the matter carefully for a moment before I responded.

"The archive is generally open three days a week: Monday, Wednesday, and Thursday. I won't be there to work on them again until day after tomorrow. I'll need at least two days with them before I can make a final decision."

"So you're saying I have to wait a week, until next Monday, in fact, before I'll know if I can even *look* at them?" She didn't wait for an answer. "That really sucks. I'm on a tight deadline, and this is really screwing things up."

Her petulant tone did not advance her cause. She hadn't even known the diaries existed before today, and I couldn't understand why she was so adamant about them. I was generally sympathetic to students' needs, and I understood the pressure of academic deadlines. This woman's manner annoyed me, however, and that made me less tractable as a result. Still, I wanted to be reasonable.

"My first responsibility is to the documents," I said, trying to keep my tone even. "I have to make sure they are properly maintained, or they won't be of use to anyone. Still, I understand that you are obviously eager to see them. Why don't you call me at the archive office on Thursday, say midmorning, and I'll see if I can show them to you then."

"I guess that will have to do. Thank you, Mr. Harris. Till Thursday, then."

The phone clicked in my ear as her peevish words echoed in my head. "So much for graciousness."

Diesel warbled and tapped my thigh with a large paw. I scratched his head. He could always tell when I was annoyed by something—or someone.

"Nothing to worry about, boy," I told him. He watched me for a moment before he started grooming his right front paw, evidently satisfied that I was okay.

I rooted around in the freezer to select a casserole for dinner. My housekeeper, Azalea Berry, kept the freezer stocked for the occasions when I—or another member of the household—didn't feel up to the challenge of preparing dinner. I would be on my own tonight. My son, Sean, planned to dine with his law partner and girlfriend, Alexandra Pendergrast, and I doubted I would see him until breakfast tomorrow, if then. He spent more and more nights lately at Alexandra's house, and I expected that I would soon hear news of their engagement.

I was happy for Sean, because Alexandra was a wonderful woman, and I knew she adored my son. I had become used to having my children in the house with me, however, and I would miss the daily contact. I still had my two boarders, at least. Justin Wardlaw was a junior at Athena College now and doing exceptionally well. I was as proud of him as if he were my own son, and I wasn't looking forward to the day he graduated. He, too, would be out of the house, and I would miss him.

My other boarder, Stewart Delacorte, showed no signs of leaving anytime soon. He had become a part of the family. Not exactly a son—perhaps like the younger brother I never had. His new relationship with the taciturn Deputy Bates appeared to be a happy one, though I didn't often see them together. Stewart had said nothing so far about their sharing a home, and I suspected that was because Bates was reluctant to be open about his sexuality. That was none of my business, of course, but I hoped the two of them would be happy with each other, even if they didn't live in the same house.

Thinking of all these relationships reminded me I hadn't spoken to Helen Louise Brady, my significant other. That term felt awkward, but so did the word *girlfriend*. I was over fifty, and the thought of having a girlfriend at my age seemed a bit juvenile. Still, I loved Helen Louise with all my heart, and she loved me. We hadn't talked of marriage yet, but it was on the horizon. Sean and Laura both adored her, and somehow I knew my late wife, Jackie, would approve. She, Helen Louise, and I had grown up together here in Athena, and we had all been good friends from childhood.

I realized I was standing and staring blankly into the freezer, cold air flowing out around my head. I focused on the stacked casserole dishes on one side. I knew the oldest would be on top— Azalea had her system—so I simply pulled that one out and set it on the counter to defrost a bit.

Diesel reared on his hind legs and batted a paw at the casserole dish. When I told him not to do it, he glared at me for a moment before he stalked away, tail in the air. I didn't know whether he could detect the presence of chicken in the frozen dish, but he was always interested in what I ate. I really never should have started letting him have tidbits of human food, but it was too late to stop now.

The ringing of the doorbell startled me. I checked my watch. Who would be calling at five thirty? I wasn't expecting anyone.

I peered out the peephole, and when I saw who stood waiting I briefly contemplated ignoring the doorbell, which was ringing again. Manners prevailed, however, and I opened the door.

"Good evening, Marie," I said. "This is an unexpected pleasure." *Like finding a rattlesnake on the doorstep, that is.*

Marie Steverton was a professor in the history department at the college, and her specialty was women's history. She used her feminist beliefs as a bludgeon, and she had won few adherents with her rude tactics. I believed firmly in equality for women, but I thought Marie did more harm than good on campus.

Marie rolled her eyes as she stepped past me—uninvited—into the front hall. Typical behavior for her, and not unexpected. I shut the door behind her.

"What can I do for you, Marie?" I asked.

"For starters, you can keep that hairy behemoth away from me." Marie waved at Diesel, who had backed away the moment he recognized her. He didn't like Marie—but then, few creatures, two- or four-legged, ever did, I suspected.

"Diesel won't bother you, as I have told you before." I crossed my arms over my chest and repeated my question as I regarded her.

Marie stared up at me. "I want access to the Rachel Long diaries. Exclusive access, and I won't take *no* for an answer."

THREE

|||||||||||||||||||||||||||||||

Marie's request was so outrageous I laughed before I could stop myself. I knew she hated being laughed at, but I couldn't help it.

Her face reddened. "How *dare* you cackle at me like that. I will report you to the president of the college for your completely unprofessional and disgusting behavior."

"Go ahead and do that. I won't stop you." I glared at her. "Your request is ridiculous. I can't grant anyone exclusive access to materials in the college archives. You should know better than that."

"You could if you really wanted to." Marie scowled. "You're just like all the rest of the good ole boys at the college. You can't stand the thought of a woman achieving anything significant. With those diaries I could firmly establish my reputation."

In a way I felt sorry for her, because I knew she was desperate to get tenure. Time was running out for her because she had been an assistant professor at Athena for six years, after similar appointments at three other colleges. A significant monograph would bolster her application, but she was her own worst enemy. From what I had heard she had the same combative attitude with her students, and her evaluations evidenced it. She had no understanding of the words *tact* and *diplomacy*. Her peer in the English department was the exact opposite, one of the most highly regarded women on campus and one of the most popular teachers. She had to turn away students every semester; otherwise her classes would be too large for the college's guidelines on student-teacher ratios. Marie never had that problem. Her courses, other than the obligatory surveys, usually had the bare minimum.

"No, I could not, even if I wanted to. Only the Long family could grant access like that. You'll have to talk to Mayor Long, but I doubt she would allow it."

"We'll see about that." Marie sounded triumphant. "Mayor Long will do what I want, and I'll have the pleasure of making you eat crow." She pushed past me, jerked open the door, and left it open as she scurried down the sidewalk as fast as her stubby legs could carry her.

I closed the door and resisted the urge to utter a number of uncomplimentary—albeit well-deserved—words about my departed guest.

Diesel warbled and then commenced muttering. I had to grin. He had no such reservations about cursing Marie as only a cat could do.

"I agree with everything you're saying," I told the cat as the muttering ceased. "She is the rudest, most high-handed person I've had the misfortune to meet."

I headed back to the kitchen to put the casserole in the oven to heat up. Diesel preceded me, no doubt hopeful that tidbits of chicken would be forthcoming.

"Not for a while yet, boy," I told him as I adjusted the oven temperature. Diesel turned and walked out of the kitchen, muttering as he went.

I followed and climbed the stairs to my second-floor bedroom. Time to change out of work clothes into lounging-around duds— sweatpants, T-shirt, and bare feet. While I changed I recalled Marie Steverton's odd remark about the mayor as she stomped her way down the sidewalk.

How could she be so certain Mayor Long would grant her request so quickly? What kind of influence could a non-tenured junior professor wield? The idea sounded nuts to me. Based on my own conversation with Mrs. Long earlier today, I doubted she and her family would want access to the diaries restricted to one person. That would be counterproductive, I thought. My take on the situation was that the Longs wanted everyone to know about the diaries for their own obscure reasons.

I padded back down the stairs. Diesel stayed on my bed. He hadn't had a nap in nearly forty minutes, so he was overdue. I knew he would be downstairs right after I pulled the casserole out of the oven.

I couldn't get Marie's threat—weak as it seemed—out of my mind. What kind of connection could she have to the mayor? She had moved to Athena only six years ago. If there was any kind of dirt, though, I knew the person to ask—my old friend and coworker, Melba.

Melba Gilley and I, along with my late wife, Jackie, grew up in Athena together, and since my return home several years ago,

Melba and I had reestablished our friendship. She was executive assistant to the college library director, and I saw her at least three days a week since we worked in the same building. Melba knew practically everyone in town, and if there was anything to connect Mrs. Long and Marie Steverton, she would know—or find out as quickly as possible.

I hit speed dial on my cell phone to call Melba at home. She answered after three rings.

She listened patiently as I explained the events of the afternoon and the encounter with Marie. "What kind of connection could there be between them?"

Melba laughed. "That's easy, Charlie. They were at Sweet Briar together forty years ago. Marie may think she and Lucinda are good buddies because they went to college together, but Lucinda sure don't tolerate fools—and Marie's as big a fool as I've ever met. She always thinks she's more important than anybody else in the room. That just goes to show how stupid she really is."

Trust Melba to cut Marie down to size. I laughed. "Sounds like you know Lucinda Long pretty well."

"I sure do," Melba said. "I worked on her very first campaign as mayor, and I've supported her ever since. She's done more for this town than all the good ole boys who were in office before her."

I had to take Melba's word for that last statement, since I hadn't been here during the previous mayors' tenures. I knew better than to argue with her, anyway.

"She's not going to be paying any attention to that idiot," Melba said. "So don't even worry about it."

"Thanks," I said. "I hope the mayor's rebuff will keep Marie out of my hair. I do not want to have to deal with her having a hissy fit every five minutes because she's not getting her way."

"If Lucinda can't manage it," Melba said, "give old Dr. Newkirk a call. He can't stand the sight of Marie, and all he has to do is say, *Leap, frog*, and the head of the history department says, *How high?* He'll see to it she doesn't bug you."

"Good to hear." I knew all about Dr. Newkirk's reputation, and the fact that he was a close friend of the Long family convinced me that I could be firm with Marie and not worry about it. I didn't intend to keep her from having access to the diaries, but I certainly wasn't going to let her take them over like they were her own property.

"Enough about Marie." Melba chuckled. "When are you and Helen Louise going to set a date?"

I rolled my eyes, even though I knew she couldn't see me. There was no point in getting exasperated with Melba. She was incorrigible, and she reveled in it.

"When we do, I'm sure you'll know about it three seconds later," I said. "The CIA could learn from you and your spy network."

"How do you know they haven't already?" Melba retorted. "I notice you said *when we do*, and not *if we do*. I reckon that means you'll get around to asking her one of these days. I just hope it's before you need a gurney to get you down the aisle."

"You keep it up, and I won't let you see Diesel for a week," I said in as stern a tone as I could muster.

"That's cruel and unusual, and you know Diesel won't stand for it. Well, I guess I'd better get off the phone and see about dinner. I'll see you Wednesday."

I smiled as I set my phone on the kitchen table. Melba loved kidding me almost better than breathing, and I had come to regard her as the sister I never had.

I checked the casserole in the oven, and it wasn't quite

ready—another ten minutes ought to do it. I prepared a salad and poured a glass of iced tea. I was trying to give up diet sodas, and that meant drinking more tea. I also drank a lot of water, but I needed my caffeine.

While I ate my salad I thought more about Rachel Afton Long and her diaries. Why was there such sudden fierce interest in them? I had both a student and a professor panting to get their hands on the old volumes. I wondered whether Kelly Grimes was a student of Marie's. That could make an awkward situation even more difficult. I would do my best not to get in the middle of that, but I might not have a choice.

Diaries were an important source for women's history. Perhaps the most famous Civil War–era woman's diary was that of Mary Boykin Chesnut. Her husband, James, served as a senator from South Carolina before the war. Later he became an aide to President Jefferson Davis and a brigadier general in the Confederate Army. The Chesnuts moved in the highest social circles, and Mary's observations of life in the South before, during, and after the Civil War offered great insight into women's lives at the time.

If Rachel Long's diaries proved to be as rich in content as Mary Chesnut's, I knew Southern historians and feminist scholars would want to read them. Marie Steverton, I reckoned, wanted to prepare them for publication, and that would help her bid for tenure.

The decision regarding publication didn't fall to me. I was simply the custodian of the primary documents, and I was determined to see that they were conserved and preserved properly. No matter who worked on them.

Diesel came warbling into the kitchen the moment I set the casserole dish on a trivet on the table. The cat had impeccable timing—and an infallible nose—when it came to mealtime.

I barely had time to dish up the food when the house phone rang. I stared at it. *Not again.*

Diesel meowed, ready for a piece of chicken.

"Hold on, boy, and you can have a bite in a minute. It's too hot anyway." I kept an eye on the cat as I answered the phone. He had been known to jump up on the table in his quest for food.

"Mr. Harris, Lucinda Long here. Sorry to trouble you at home, but a situation has arisen that I need to discuss with you."

Right then I could cheerfully have consigned Marie Steverton to the farthest pit of hell. She was going to be a pain in the posterior after all.

FOUR

I struggled to keep the irritation out of my voice when I responded to Mayor Long. "That's okay, Your Honor. How can I help?" I imagined myself making a voodoo doll of Marie and sticking pins in it.

The mayor sighed into the phone. "This is all rather awkward, but I have been approached by an old friend—someone I went to Sweet Briar with many years ago. She has expressed an interest in the diaries I brought you earlier today." She paused. "I understand she has already spoken with you."

"Yes, Marie came to see me a little while ago," I said. "She was pretty insistent that she have exclusive access to the diaries, and I had to explain to her that it wasn't up to me."

"I know you were within your rights to tell her that," the mayor said. "Unfortunately Marie gets stubborn when she decides she wants something, and she doesn't always understand that the world isn't going to change its ways just for her."

I responded in a dry tone. "Yes, that was my impression."

"I'd like to help an old college friend because I know this is important to her. Frankly, she hasn't left me much choice, but that's neither here nor there." She paused for a moment. "At the same time, I'm well aware of her reputation at Athena College, and that makes me a little hesitant to grant her request."

She had probably had an earful about Marie from Professor Newkirk. According to Melba, he had little respect for Marie and her abilities as a historian.

"I see. How would you like me to handle the situation?" I wasn't going to make this any easier for the mayor. I didn't want to be in an awkward position myself, and I thought this decision was her responsibility. I would abide by it, whatever it was.

Mrs. Long still sounded uncertain when she replied. "My husband will want to see the diaries handled properly by qualified historians and students, and so do I. I would like to give Marie a chance, however, in light of her needs and interests. I must get this settled, because I have many other matters that require my attention." She paused, and I waited for her to continue. "How about this as a compromise? Marie can have exclusive access to the diaries for three weeks."

"If that is what you want, then that is what we will do," I said. "I need to make you aware of two things, however. I work at the archive only three days a week, because that is all the library budget covers. Also, I can't allow Dr. Steverton or anyone else to remove the diaries from the archive—unless you are willing to give permission and assume the risk. It's possible that they might be photocopied but I can't guarantee it."

"The most important thing to my husband and me is that the diaries be carefully conserved." Mrs. Long spoke firmly. "If you would be willing to work five days a week at the archive for the next three weeks, I'm sure my husband will arrange with the library director to cover the costs."

Frankly I was surprised the mayor was going to such lengths to accommodate Marie, even if she was an old college friend. They must have been pretty close, and still might be, for all I knew. I would have to discuss this further with Melba. In the meantime, I knew the mayor was waiting for my answer.

"I can do that," I said. "I'll also need to let Teresa Farmer know I won't be able to work my volunteer shifts on Fridays at the public library during those three weeks, but I'm sure she'll understand."

Teresa was a good friend, and I knew she wouldn't object. I looked forward to those volunteer stints, however, and I knew the staff and patrons would miss seeing Diesel as well, since he always went with me.

"I can't tell you how much I appreciate your flexibility on this." The mayor's gratitude sounded sincere—but with politicians, one never really knew.

"One final thing," I said. "If Dr. Steverton's three weeks of exclusive use could start next week, that would be most helpful. I'll need a few days to assess the condition of each volume and do conservation work."

"That sounds fair. Marie will abide by that; I'll see to it. Thank you again, Mr. Harris."

I was not in a happy frame of mind when I sat down to eat, thanks to Marie Steverton. Diesel immediately put a paw on my thigh to let me know he had waited long enough for his tidbits of chicken. I found a small piece and was about to give it to him but I noticed that the casserole included onions. They were not good for cats, so I couldn't let Diesel have any of the chicken.

"Sorry, boy, this chicken wouldn't be good for you." I pushed back from the table and went to the fridge. I found a container of sliced chicken breast and popped some in the microwave to heat. "Just a minute, boy," I said to the impatient feline now meowing piteously by my legs.

As I ate I doled out the warm chicken breast. Diesel was content, but I was not. I did not look forward to spending three weeks with Marie in my office at the archive. Her unfriendly presence would make for a tense atmosphere, and I knew Diesel would feel it and be unsettled. He would be even less happy if I left him at home those three weeks, but then I realized he could spend time with Melba instead when he needed a break from Marie. I, unfortunately, would have no such option. I would have to keep an eye on her the entire time. I didn't feel I could trust her not to do something stupid that could compromise the state of the diaries.

Then I realized there was a further complication—Kelly Grimes. She approached me first about working with the diaries. I predicted she would be mighty annoyed to find out that Marie now had dibs on them for the next three weeks. Another situation that I did not anticipate with any pleasure whatsoever.

If Ms. Grimes was that unhappy, she would simply have to make her own appeal to Mayor Long, I decided.

Before this, I hadn't had to deal with such a complicated situation regarding access to resources in the archive. I had students and professors come from time to time to consult documents, and once, I even had a visiting professor working there for a couple of months. I had never had people competing for the same resources, however.

It was only three weeks, I reminded myself.

Surely I could get through three weeks in close proximity to

Marie Steverton without throttling her or bashing her over the head.

I finished my meal and cleared the table. Diesel wanted more chicken but I told him firmly there was no more. He stared at me for a moment before he trotted off to the utility room. I heard loud crunching noises emanating from that direction as I popped my plate and salad bowl into the dishwasher.

I felt restless. For once, curling up with a good book didn't appeal to me. Helen Louise was busy at the bakery, and I would have to wait to chat with her until later in the evening when she had time to call. I had several hours to fill until then.

There was nothing to tempt me on television tonight. I could always watch a DVD of a favorite movie, but that didn't appeal, either. I finally sat down in the den with my laptop and started searching the Internet for information on Rachel Afton Long. Given all the interest in her from other parties, I figured I might as well research her life before I started working on the diaries.

I started with the online catalog at the college. I had vague knowledge of the contents of the Long family collection in the archive, and I ought to acquaint myself fully with the extent of it. The catalog record had only broad headings for the contents, but there was a finding aid created by my predecessor, Miss Eulalie Estes. It had not been digitized yet, so I would have to wait to consult it when I was back in the office. There might be letters or other documents connected to Rachel, but I wouldn't know until I delved into the collection itself.

I discovered a record in the catalog for a memoir of Rachel, however, written by her granddaughter-in-law, Angeline McCarthy Long. Privately published and part of the regular circulating collection, the memoir was only seventy-eight pages long, but it could prove helpful for background detail. Then I noticed the status of the item: *Lost.*

That annoyed me. There might be a copy in the Long collection in the archive, however. Out of curiosity I decided to log in to the back end of the catalog where I could see more detail about the item's status that wouldn't be visible to the public.

What I discovered disturbed me. The status *Lost* had been applied earlier today.

Simple coincidence? I wondered. Or was there something suspicious about the book's disappearance?

FIVE

||||||||||||||||||||

Get a grip, Charlie, I told myself. *Next thing you know, you'll be turning into a conspiracy theorist.*

The memoir could have been missing for years and its absence only discovered today when someone wanted to check it out. I speculated that either Marie Steverton or Kelly Grimes had looked for it and then reported it missing. As far as I knew no one else had been interested in Rachel Long for years, if not decades.

Still, I thought, *it* is *odd.* For a moment I fantasized a battle between Marie and Ms. Grimes over any resource connected to Rachel Long. Could one of them have stolen it to keep the other from having access to it?

My flights of fancy were becoming ever more absurd, I decided. I had yet to establish any connection whatsoever between Marie Steverton and Kelly Grimes. Let alone a link between either one of them and the missing book.

On impulse I went to the college website and entered *Kelly*

Grimes into the people directory search. I retrieved three results: *Jonathan Kelly*, *Andrea Kelly*, and *Winston Grimes, Jr.*

I was pretty sure that all students and faculty were listed in the directory. If Kelly Grimes wasn't a student or a faculty member, then who was she?

I exited the college's website and typed the name into a search engine. The first result told me what I needed to know.

Kelly Grimes was a freelance writer. She had written a couple of articles for the local paper, the *Athena Daily Register.*

Curiouser and curiouser, I thought. If a freelance journalist was interested in Rachel Long, then perhaps the mayor was right about the potential political implications of her diaries. Ms. Grimes would probably be even more irritated over the delay in access than if she had really been a student. A writer hot on the trail of a saleable story wouldn't be happy about being blocked from a source.

Loud warbling roused me from my reverie. Diesel, evidently having had his fill of cat food, butted his head against my side. He stretched out on the sofa beside me and laid his head and front paws on my thigh, nudging my laptop aside. I grabbed the computer to keep it from falling to the floor and moved it to safety on the end table. The cat moved farther onto my lap and rolled on his back. I recognized that as an invitation to scratch his chin and rub his tummy.

Happy sounds ensued for the next few minutes as Diesel received what he considered his due attention.

"How would you like to go to work tomorrow, boy?" I made a quick decision to spend the day in the archive office, despite the fact that it was Tuesday and a day I didn't normally work. My curiosity about Rachel Long had continued to grow, and I might as well get started on the diaries a day earlier than I had originally planned. The sooner I had them ready for public use, the better.

I was also burning with curiosity to discover whether the archive collection contained a copy of the missing memoir. If it did, I was going to read it right away.

I had no real plans for tomorrow except lunch with Helen Louise at the bakery. That, I could still do. Otherwise I would have spent the day at home with Diesel, not accomplishing much of anything except for staying out of Azalea's way.

Now that I had settled on a course of action for tomorrow, I decided I could relax with a book. I gently moved Diesel from my lap and told him it was time to head upstairs. He hopped off the sofa and headed out of the den ahead of me. He liked it when I stretched out on the bed to read. He always curled up next to me, his head on a pillow, and napped.

Upstairs I fluffed up my own pillows and arranged them for comfortable reading. I reclined on the bed and pulled my current read from the bedside table. I was reading the latest Maisie Dobbs novel by Jacqueline Winspear, and I looked forward to immersing myself once more in 1930s England.

While I read, Diesel slept. We spent many hours this way. By the time I surfaced from the book, having turned the last page and put it aside, I noticed it was a few minutes after ten. Helen Louise ought to be calling soon.

Seconds later my cell phone rang. "Hello, love," I said. "How are you? Exhausted as usual?"

Helen Louise laughed. "Pretty tired, sweetheart, but for once I decided to let someone else close up. I left them to it and came home. I'm going to soak in a hot tub for a while and then crawl into bed."

I couldn't let myself dwell on the image of Helen Louise

lounging in the bath, or I'd never get to sleep. I told her as much, and she laughed.

"I'd invite you over to share the tub with me," she said. "But all I'd do would be to fall asleep."

I could hear the tiredness in her voice. "Another time," I promised her. I was tempted to tell her about my day, but right now I figured she needed her rest. We could talk about it all tomorrow at lunch.

We chatted for a few more minutes, mostly about plans for the weekend and our usual Sunday dinner with the family. Then we bade each other good night. I yawned, suddenly tired myself, and turned out the light. Not long after, I drifted off to sleep with Diesel still beside me.

Next morning, eager for an early start at the office, I showered, shaved, and dressed before going down to breakfast. Diesel disappeared while I dressed, and I knew I'd find him in the kitchen. He would be watching Azalea closely, hoping for a scrap of bacon or sausage. She thought I didn't know that she occasionally slipped the cat a few tidbits, but I could usually tell from the cat's smug expression when he'd had a treat from her.

The mingled scents of fresh biscuits and sausage greeted me as I neared the kitchen. My stomach rumbled in response.

"Good morning, Azalea. How are you today?"

My housekeeper turned and nodded to acknowledge my greeting. "Tolerable, Mister Charlie, tolerable. You must be going somewhere, you all dressed up like that." She turned back to the stove. The cat sat nearby on the floor, his gaze fixed upon her every movement.

"Diesel and I are going to work at the archive today," I said. I noticed the newspaper beside my place at the table. "Thanks for bringing in the newspaper."

"Why you going in to work on your day off?" Azalea frowned as she set a plate of scrambled eggs, biscuits, and sausage in front of me. She had already poured my coffee.

"This looks wonderful, as usual," I said as I picked up my knife and fork. "I have a special project to work on that's going to take some extra time. The mayor brought me some old family diaries yesterday, and several people are anxious to look at them."

Diesel batted at my thigh with one large paw. I cut off a small piece of the link sausage and gave it to him. He grabbed it and went under the table.

"Miss Lucinda sure stays busy," Azalea said. "I was talking to her housekeeper, Ronetta, the other day. Ronetta says she's about run off her feet all the time, all the entertaining Miss Lucinda's doing because her son wants to be a senator now."

"I can just imagine." I had a bite of fluffy biscuit and tender sausage. "I guess when you're in politics, you have to entertain a lot if you're going to be asking people for money for your campaign."

"That sure is the truth." Azalea popped another biscuit on my plate.

She was determined to keep me well fed, and I gave a fleeting thought to my waistline. I really shouldn't have another one, but Azalea's biscuits were a true gastronomic delight. I'd just have to run up and down the stairs a few times to work it off.

Diesel meowed and tapped my thigh again. I gazed sternly down at him. "I'm not sure you need anything else, boy. I'll bet Azalea gave you at least a whole sausage before I made it downstairs."

The cat warbled as if to say, *Oh no, she didn't. I'm still starving.*

"That cat is shameless," Azalea said with a faint smile. "He's had him a whole sausage. You'd best not be giving him any more, or else he's going to be sick."

"You heard Azalea," I told Diesel. "If you want anything else, you'll have to go eat what's in your bowl in the utility room."

The cat stared at me for a moment before he turned and stalked away, his tail in the air.

Azalea laughed, a sound I loved to hear. She had mellowed a bit since her health scare of the previous fall. She laughed and smiled more now, and that was good.

"How's Miss Laura doing?" Azalea asked. "I sure do miss seeing her and that pretty smile of hers in the mornings."

I sighed. "I do, too. She's doing fine. I don't get to see her much, either, these days." I would have to tell Laura she really ought to drop by occasionally to see Azalea. I knew they were fond of each other, and Laura brought out all of Azalea's considerable maternal instincts.

"Well, you tell her I was asking about her." Azalea turned back to the stove for a moment. "There's more biscuits here, and a couple more sausage links." She scooped them onto a plate and set it on the table.

"I've got to get the laundry going." Azalea disappeared into the utility room.

I eyed the remaining food warily. My mouth watered but my stomach felt full. I pushed back from the table, determined to resist temptation.

"Come on, boy, let's go upstairs. I need to brush my teeth, and then we're heading to work."

Diesel reared up on his hind legs and put his paws on the table. As large as he was, he could easily see what was on the table, even if his nose hadn't already told him.

"No, boy, you have to come with me." If I wasn't firm with him, he'd be up on the table and tearing into the sausage the moment I left the kitchen. "Come on. Now."

The cat stared at the plate, then at me. He meowed again.

I sighed. This standoff could drag on indefinitely. I picked up the plate and found space for it in the fridge.

"I told you no, and I meant it."

Diesel dropped to all fours and padded toward me. I rubbed his head and praised him for minding me.

Ten minutes later we walked out the front door and were on our way to the archive. Diesel wore his harness and ambled happily beside me. He knew where we were going, and I was sure he was already looking forward to seeing his buddy Melba.

The moment we entered the old house that served both as the administrative center of the college library next door and as the archive and rare book room, I heard raised voices coming from Melba's office.

"I don't care who you are or who you know, woman." Melba's tone was heated.

Diesel and I moved closer to the open door of the office.

"You had better *start* caring, or you'll find yourself without a job. I came in here with a simple request, and all you're doing is being obstructive, and for no reason. Mayor Long is going to hear about this."

Marie Steverton barged out of Melba's office and cannoned right into me as I was about to enter.

SIX

Diesel emitted a loud yowl and scooted out of the way as Marie lost her balance and landed hard on her rump on the floor. Diesel tangled the leash around my legs, and I stumbled and almost fell right on top of Marie.

At the last moment, however, I managed to regain my balance. I unwrapped the leash from my legs, dropped it, and then bent to offer the fallen Marie a hand.

"Why don't you look where you're going?" Marie flapped my hand away and got herself up.

I turned away from the ungainly sight and did my best to hold on to my rapidly escalating temper.

"You're the one who went rushing off like a blind pig after an acorn." Melba hurried over and put herself between Marie and me. "Don't blame Charlie because you're rude and a klutz into the bargain."

Marie's face reddened. "You are going to lose your job over

this. I can't believe you're talking to a member of the faculty in this manner. You have no business working with decent people."

Melba laughed. "Well, honey, in your case, I'm not."

Marie took a moment to process Melba's last remark. Her expression promised another explosion.

"You'd better watch what you say to me," Melba continued before Marie could respond. "I'm going in my office right this minute to give my old friend Professor Newkirk a call. I was his personal secretary about fifteen years ago, and we've always been good buddies." She smirked at Marie. "I think he'd like to hear about the low-down behavior of one of his faculty members. Yes, ma'am, I do think he's going to be real interested in what I have to say."

The lightning change in Marie's demeanor was almost comical. She went from stroke-inducing fury to sickening obsequiousness in two seconds flat.

"Oh, now, there's no reason for you to disturb Dr. Newkirk." Her tone oozed sweetness. "He's *far* too busy to be bothered with such a *simple* misunderstanding. Perhaps I was a bit hasty in chastising you for doing your job. Surely you'll be willing to overlook one little lapse."

Melba and I exchanged a quick glance. What little respect I had for Marie disappeared.

"What was it you wanted, Marie?" I asked, my tone clipped. I glanced around for Diesel, but I didn't see him. He had either bolted upstairs to wait by the archive office door or had taken refuge under Melba's desk. He hated scenes like this as much as I did.

Marie eyed me warily for a moment, then offered me a tenuous smile. "Oh, I was just hoping to visit the archive and have a quick look at the Rachel Long diaries. My dear friend Lucinda Long called me last night to tell me that it would be all right."

Lucinda probably did call her, I reckoned, but I doubted the mayor told her it would be okay to try to browbeat Melba into letting her into the archive without my knowledge and approval.

I forbore to mention that when I responded. "I explained to Her Honor yesterday that I have to have time to examine the diaries more closely. I'm sure they need at least minimum conservation work before they can be handled by anyone else. I thought you understood that as well."

"Oh, I have a lot of experience handling primary documents." Marie's airy, smug tone did nothing to endear her to me. "I know how delicate they can be. Besides, I've worked in far more prestigious archives than this one."

She made as if to start listing them, but my tart response cut her off. "I don't happen to be responsible for any other archives, so I'm not that interested in your work outside Athena College. I told the mayor last night that the documents ought to be ready for you to work with the first of next week. If you're not satisfied with that, then I suggest you look for another project."

I could tell by Melba's broad grin that she was enjoying this immensely. She didn't often see me lose my temper, but she was getting closer by the second, thanks to Marie, who didn't have the sense to know when she was licked.

Marie sniffed, her expression disdainful. "You're just annoyed that Lucinda isn't letting you deny me exclusive access. I told you she would do what I want. She didn't dare refuse me, after all I've done for her."

I could have smacked her right then.

Melba saved me the trouble. "Honey, about the only thing you've done for Her Honor the mayor is be a thorn in her side from the day she was unlucky enough to meet you. Charlie said you'd have to wait until next week, and you darn well better listen to him. If I see you in this building again before next Monday morning, I'm going to get on the phone and call Professor Newkirk. If it comes down to you and the professor, who's known Lucinda all her life, I reckon I know who she's going to listen to. Now get out of my sight." She turned and walked back into her office without looking back. I spotted Diesel's head sticking out from under her desk. He would be fine there until I was done here.

Even Marie, brash and pigheaded as she could be, wasn't foolhardy enough to talk back to Melba after that set-down. Instead she shot me a glance of utter loathing, picked up the briefcase she had dropped earlier, and stomped her way to the front door.

Where she promptly ran into another person, this time a tall, rangy young woman who looked like she would be comfortable on a tennis court or golf course.

"Out of my way." Marie snapped out the words and made as if to push by the stranger.

"Hold on there, Professor," the young woman said, her tone firm. "I've got a bone to pick with you." She refused to budge from the doorway, and Marie had to step back.

The stranger's voice sounded oddly familiar, and it took me a moment to place it. This must be Kelly Grimes, the writer who also wanted access to the diaries. Evidently she did know Marie after all.

"What's going on?" Melba whispered. I hadn't heard her approach.

"Let's see," I said in an undertone.

"What could you possibly have to say to me? I have no idea who you are. Kindly get out of my way." Marie stepped forward, but Kelly Grimes stood firm.

"You surely ought to remember me, Dr. Steverton." Ms. Grimes laughed as she stared down at the shorter, squatter woman. "I was one of the few students who actually made it through your so-called seminar on the role of women in the Civil War five years ago. You don't have that many upper-level students, so I find it hard to believe you really don't know who I am."

Marie's gaze flicked toward Melba and me. We stared back with obvious interest. Marie turned toward her former student again.

"Oh, yes, of course," she said. "Ms. Grimes, isn't it? I didn't really get a good look at your face before. It's always a pleasure to see former students, but I'm afraid I have no time to talk right now, so you'll have to excuse me."

She tried once again to push past the writer, but Kelly Grimes simply laughed again.

"I do have time, Dr. Steverton, and you're going to listen to me now. I found out you're trying to hog something for yourself that I need, and that's really unfortunate. You're going to have to share, or there will be sad consequences."

Melba nudged me in the side. "Who is she? She looks familiar, but I can't place her."

"Freelance writer," I said. "She wants to look at those diaries pretty badly, too."

"They must be pretty hot stuff," Melba said. "How old are they?"

"From the Civil War," I said.

Marie had been talking during our little exchange, and I tuned back in.

". . . needs of scholarship far outweigh any claim from the press; surely you must see that." She glared at the young writer.

39

Kelly Grimes snickered in her face. "Scholarship, my aunt Fanny. You'd do anything to get tenure. Short of sleeping with old Newkirk, that is, but even he has standards."

"Get out of my way before I slap the living daylights out of your stupid face," Marie bellowed. She grabbed at Kelly Grimes and managed at last to shove her out of the way. Grimes stumbled sideways and almost slipped on the marble floor of the entryway but righted herself in time.

Marie charged out the door and disappeared.

Kelly Grimes glanced over at Melba and me. "Seen enough?" Her tone was cool. She straightened the jacket of her tailored suit and then stepped forward.

"In case you hadn't figured it out already, I'm Kelly Grimes." She thrust out her hand toward Melba.

They shook hands, and Melba introduced herself.

"This is Charlie Harris," Melba said. "I expect you're here looking for him."

The writer offered me a wry smile as we shook hands. "Yes, I am, though I didn't expect to have to deal with a lunatic."

I ignored that little sally when I replied. "I am a bit surprised by your visit, Ms. Grimes. When we spoke on the phone last night, I asked you to call me on Thursday. Why did you drop by this morning, on a day when I don't usually work at the college?"

Her smile faltered at my not-so-welcoming words. "I was on campus already, on my way to the library, and I thought I'd drop by on the off chance that you'd be here."

Thanks to Marie, and now this unexpected visit from the tenacious writer, I felt beleaguered. I didn't like feeling beleaguered, and no doubt my tone betrayed that when I replied. "I suppose you had better come upstairs to the office for a moment."

I turned to Melba. "Do you mind keeping Diesel down here for a while?"

Melba grinned. "Of course not. Let me know when you're free, and I'll bring him up." She nodded a good-bye to Kelly Grimes.

I turned to the stairs and started up without waiting to see whether the writer followed me.

She caught up with me after five steps. "Diesel is your cat, right? Ray Appleby mentioned him to me once when I turned in a story he bought. He's a Maine Coon, I believe."

Ray Appleby was a member of the staff of the local paper. We had become acquainted the past couple of years, thanks to my involvement in several murder cases.

"Yes, Diesel is a Maine Coon," I replied tersely. Her attempt to be pleasant and chatty wasn't improving my mood. She evidently took the hint and kept quiet until I unlocked the office door and motioned for her to enter.

"Have a seat," I told her and pointed toward one of the chairs in front of my desk. I went to my chair, sat, and switched on the computer. I turned to face the writer.

Kelly Grimes cocked her head to one side and gazed at me. "We've gotten off on the wrong foot, and it's totally my fault. I'm really sorry about that, Mr. Harris. I forget how brusque I can sound on the phone, and of course my little encounter with Dr. Steverton didn't improve matters." She grinned. "I couldn't help it. That woman irritates the heck out of me just by breathing."

I felt myself thawing toward the writer. Her apology was gracious enough, and I certainly couldn't blame her for her antipathy toward Marie.

"You were a student here at Athena?" I asked.

Ms. Grimes nodded. "Yes, I majored in history. Didn't want to teach school, and I wasn't ready for a graduate program. So I got myself hired as a writer on the daily paper." She shrugged. "It's not much of a living, but it sure beats ditch-digging."

"I'm sure it does," I said. "What's your interest in Rachel Long's diaries? Are you planning some kind of feature article on them for the paper?"

"You might say that." Ms. Grimes glanced away for a moment. When she looked back at me, her expression was the epitome of sincerity. "I'm going to level with you. I do have an important reason to look at those diaries, and it has to do with politics."

I figured as much as soon as I found out she was a writer, but I didn't tell her that. "How so?"

She took a deep breath, held it for a moment, then released it. "I'm hoping I'll find something in those diaries that will help my boyfriend. Well, fiancé, really. And the sooner I can do it, the better. He's got a long, hard slog ahead of him if he's going to win his election. He's losing ground in the most recent polls."

"Who is your fiancé?"

The writer frowned. "This is a delicate situation. You have to understand that. His family doesn't know about our relationship, and they won't be happy when they do find out." She paused. "I'm in the process of divorcing my husband, you see. Also, I grew up poor, and nobody in my family has any kind of political pull. They aren't going to look kindly on their son being involved with me, not at a time like this. Maybe not ever."

I thought she was probably right about that, because I was pretty sure I knew the name of her fiancé: Andrew Beckwith Long, scion of a proud and wealthy family, with political connections—and ambitions—enough to make a poor girl from the wrong side of the tracks a liability.

SEVEN

Ms. Grimes seemed hesitant to speak the man's name. I was tired of this shilly-shallying around, so I did it for her.

"Andrew Beckwith Long," I said.

She nodded. "There's one other thing, though." She paused. "He doesn't know I'm doing this. He wants me to stay on the sidelines for now, but it's driving me crazy, not being able to help him. At least publicly, that is. I've been researching his family, and the minute I saw those diaries listed, I thought they might be useful. Plus I could do it without anyone in the family catching on."

I could follow her trail of reasoning. "Then if you discovered anything truly useful that could help boost his chances, his family would look more kindly on you as a potential daughter-in-law."

"Yes, that's pretty much it." She laughed. "I guess I can't fool you."

I didn't respond to that comment. For one thing, I didn't fully trust her. I couldn't put my finger on it, but there was something about her that didn't ring quite true.

She must have picked up on my doubts somehow. She leaned forward in her chair and stared hard at me. "Look, I know this must sound crazy to you, but this is politics after all. You know how weird they can get in this state. Old Southern families and their precious images are golden. The Beckwiths and the Longs have been Athena royalty since before the Civil War, and the Grimes family were poor tenant farmers back then and pretty much still are." Her gaze turned somber. "I'm proud of who I am. I worked hard to get an education, and I'm doing my darnedest to make the best of it, and of myself."

I understood her sentiments, and I sympathized with her to a certain extent. I simply couldn't shake the feeling that there was something she wasn't telling me.

"Are you going to let me look at those diaries or not?"

"I am," I said, "but not today." I held up a hand to forestall the protest I could see forming on her lips. "The mayor asked me to give Dr. Steverton exclusive access to them for three weeks. I have to abide by her wishes on this."

Kelly Grimes's shoulders slumped in defeat. "That sucks, you know. That really and truly sucks big-time."

"I understand that," I said. "But I haven't finished. I will talk to the mayor again about letting another person have access, without giving anything away about your purpose or your connection to her son."

"Fair enough." The writer bounced out of her seat and stuck her hand across my desk. "Mr. Harris, I can't tell you how much I appreciate that. And in the long run, Andrew will appreciate it, too."

I shook her hand. "I hope the diaries will prove to be worth all this trouble. Now, if you'll excuse me, I really need to get to work."

"I know my exit cue when I hear it." Ms. Grimes offered me a broad smile before she turned and loped out of the office with her long-legged stride.

If I were a drinking man, I would have a bottle of bourbon in the desk drawer. Right about now, I'd pull it out and pour myself a shot and knock it back. Then do it again.

I wasn't a drinking man, however. Instead I settled for getting a cup of water from the cooler and downing a couple of the aspirin I'd brought with me. Thanks to the combined efforts of Marie Steverton and Kelly Grimes, I discovered, I had a raging headache from all the morning's tension.

I leaned back in my chair and closed my eyes for a couple of minutes. My attempt at relaxation helped ease the throbbing in my forehead.

During my talk with Kelly Grimes my mind had not been completely focused on the conversation. I was thinking of some way to make access to the diaries simpler for everyone concerned. From my cursory perusal of them yesterday I didn't think they were good candidates for photocopying. The paper wasn't brittle, thankfully, but the bindings wouldn't hold up being flattened on the bed of a photocopier.

The archive did possess an overhead scanner to capture images of the pages, and a researcher could also use a digital camera for the same purpose. Both were tedious and time-consuming processes, but in the long run this might be the best option for both Marie Steverton and Kelly Grimes. My half-formed thought was to discuss this with Mayor Long and see whether she would allow it. It was a reasonable request, I figured, and I didn't think she would have any serious objections.

Before I could reach for the phone, Melba appeared in the doorway with Diesel. "Here we are," she said. She hung Diesel's harness and leash on a coat hook near the door.

Diesel ambled forward and around my desk to jump into the broad window ledge behind my chair. This was his favorite spot while I worked, and he had an ongoing feud with the squirrels and birds who appeared in the large oak right outside the window.

Melba made herself comfortable in the chair recently vacated by Kelly Grimes. "I really will call Dr. Newkirk about the Steverton witch if you want me to. He owes me a favor from years ago. I hate to think of you being stuck with that lump of misery in your office while she does whatever it is she thinks she's doing."

One thing I loved about Melba: Her loyalty was absolute. I knew all I had to do was say the word, and she would do whatever she could to get Marie banned from the archive. I didn't dare imagine what Dr. Newkirk had done in order to incur a debt to Melba, and I knew better than to ask. Melba loved gossip, but she understood the importance of discretion when it came to her friends.

"I appreciate the offer," I said. Behind me, Diesel warbled loudly. He wouldn't be happy with Marie in the office, either, but we would both have to live with it. "Although I don't think we need resort to such a drastic measure just yet."

"I get why Dr. Steverton wants to poke around those diaries, but what's in it for the writer?" Melba asked.

I couldn't divulge the complete story, but I could share part of it, I reckoned, without violating Kelly Grimes's trust. "Background for the state senate race between Beck Long and Jasper Singletary."

"That's reaching pretty far back." Melba frowned. "I don't see the point, because frankly I don't think Jasper Singletary stands a chance. Not against Beck Long. Jasper's basically a nobody, even though his family's been here in Athena since before the Civil War."

"Maybe delving into the glorious past of the Long clan will help Beck Long keep his lock on the race," I said. "Between you and me and the cat, I don't see much point in it, either, but it's not my decision."

"Guess not," Melba said after a moment. "I'd better get back downstairs before Peter realizes I'm not there. See y'all later."

Peter Vanderkeller, the director of the library, leaned heavily on Melba, and he tended to get antsy if she wasn't nearby the moment he needed her.

"Later," I called to her retreating back. Diesel added a loud meow, and Melba turned to flash a grin at us before she disappeared into the hallway.

I thought again about calling the mayor to propose my compromise, but after further consideration I decided I ought to spend more time examining the four volumes of the diary first.

Diesel watched with sleepy-eyed interest as I pulled the archival boxes from the shelf and set them on my desk. He yawned, then put his head down on his front paws and appeared to go to sleep.

Smiling, I put on some cotton gloves before I opened the first box and extracted the initial volume of Rachel Long's diary.

As I had noted yesterday, the paper appeared to be the usual linen-and-cotton rag, typical of writing paper from the first part of the nineteenth century. I recalled that I had not spotted significant blemishes or other problems on the pages from my hasty skimming. Now that I had time for a closer, more thorough examination, I realized there were issues with the condition.

These problems stemmed largely from the ink. The standard ink used at the time was iron gall, or oak gall, ink, made from a combination of iron salts, tannic acids, and vegetable matter. The latter tended to be the galls, formed by wasps that infested oak trees and caused the plant tissue to swell. The resulting ink is acidic and sometimes caused so-called ghost writing on the obverse side of the writing surface, usually vellum or paper.

Iron gall ink, due to the ease of its composition and its durability, had been in use since at least the early fourth century A.D. One of the earliest—and vaguest—recipes, I recalled, came from Pliny the Elder, who lived during the first century A.D. I had seen medieval English manuscripts written in this ink, and the clarity of the writing, even after several centuries, amazed me.

In addition to some of the ghost writing, I saw the occasional hole in the paper where the ink had eaten through. Overall, I concluded, the paper was in remarkably good condition, despite the fact that the diaries had been stored in an attic without significant temperature control. The ravages of unchecked humidity could be extensive, but somehow this volume had escaped them.

As long as the other three volumes were in similar condition to this one, there should be no problem with scanning or photographing the pages. Having them digitized would cut down on the necessity of handling the originals and thereby would help conserve them.

For the next two hours I pored over all four volumes to check the condition of each. I had to resist the lure of reading the diaries, though I did indulge myself and read the occasional brief passage. The first volume was filled with details about parties and the social whirl in 1850s Athena. Evidently Rachel Afton found herself in demand for various events, with a handful of young suitors vying for her companionship. In the bits I read she came across as modest, noting once with sharp wit that "no doubt Father's extensive holdings in the Delta enhance my appearance and charm" for the less well-heeled young men chasing her.

By the time I finished the final volume I discovered I was hungry, Azalea's big breakfast notwithstanding. Diesel slept throughout the time I worked, but when I stood up his eyes opened. He yawned and stretched on the windowsill.

"I'm ready for lunch, boy. How about you?" I stretched my back in imitation of the cat. I felt stiff and cramped. I should have taken a break or two to stretch earlier, but I was so engrossed in my work I didn't stop.

"Let's go see Helen Louise." I retrieved the harness and leash, and Diesel jumped down from window and trotted over to me. "We'll have to go home and get the car because I don't feel like walking to the bakery in the midday heat."

Diesel warbled, as if he understood and agreed. After a brisk walk home to retrieve the car, we headed for the center of Athena and the town square.

I found a parking place near the bakery, and Diesel and I headed down the sidewalk. Diesel loved Helen Louise, and he knew there would be chicken to eat. He walked fast and tugged on the leash, eager to get inside.

Newcomers to Helen Louise's bakery sometimes looked askance at a large cat walking in as if he owned the place, but Diesel knew his corner and went straight toward it. Helen Louise had had a lengthy chat with the health inspector, who, ever since, had turned a deaf ear to protests. This was the kind of thing that could happen in a small town like Athena, and Diesel was so popular with most people, anyone offended by his presence took his or her business elsewhere.

As I followed Diesel to our corner I noticed a cluster of several people at the cash register. The tallest, a young man, chatted with Helen Louise. She had not yet spotted Diesel and me because she appeared to be engrossed in the conversation. When I sat, at a right angle to the register, I had a better look at the young man and what seemed to be his entourage. I recognized the handsome features of Beck Long.

Was this a campaign stop? I wondered. Or was he here simply to have lunch?

I scanned the room. As expected, at lunchtime, the bakery was nearly full. To my surprise, I spotted Kelly Grimes in the far corner. Her gaze seemed riveted on the cash register area. I glanced at Beck Long again and saw that he now had one arm draped around the shoulder of a beautiful blonde. He looked down at her and smiled.

When I turned back toward Kelly Grimes, I could see she did not appear at all happy with her secret fiancé and his closeness to another woman.

EIGHT

The writer's gaze shifted for a moment in my direction, and I caught a slight start as she recognized me. She inclined her head to acknowledge me, but her attention moved right back to Beck Long and the young woman beside him.

There was enough bustle and buzz of conversation in the bakery that I couldn't make out what Beck Long and Helen Louise were talking about. He didn't appear to be ordering anything, so I wondered whether this was a stop on his campaign trail after all.

I hated the last couple of months before an election. The media bombarded us with political ads, almost all of which consisted of mud being flung in every direction. The choice often came down to voting for the least objectionable candidate, rather than for the truly outstanding one. I hadn't yet made up my mind about Beck Long or his opponent, Jasper Singletary, but I had to admit their campaigns seemed to be running cleaner than most. A little dignity in politics went a long way these days, sad to say.

I heard the bell on the door jingle to signal a new arrival, and at the same time, the buzz of conversation grew louder. I turned to see who had entered and spotted a group of five men making their way toward the counter. After a moment I recognized the tallest among them, Jasper Singletary.

This ought to prove interesting, I thought. *The two candidates—both hometown boys—crossing paths in a local business.*

Diesel tapped my thigh with one paw, and I looked down at him. He chirped a couple of times, and I interpreted the sounds as a question: *Where's my chicken that Helen Louise always gives me?*

"In a minute, boy," I said in an undertone. "She's busy right now. We'll both have to wait."

The cat stared at me for a long moment before he resumed his position at my feet beneath the table. I found it uncanny sometimes the way he seemed to understand what I told him.

When I focused my attention again on the two politicos and their opposing camps, I saw Singletary making his way toward Beck Long. Beck didn't appear to have noticed Singletary yet, but then the latter spoke.

"Good morning, Beck. Glad-handing the voters, I see." Singletary's tone was jocular, yet I thought I heard a sharp edge to it.

The noise of conversation in the bakery suddenly dropped to a low hum as most people tuned in to the chat between the two young men.

I regarded the pair for a moment. They definitely formed a study in contrast. Beck Long was the proverbial golden boy—tall, blond, blue-eyed, with the body of a trained athlete. Top of his class in law school, partner in a successful practice in Athena, he seemed to achieve anything he wanted with ease. Jasper Singletary had the dark good looks of the Black Irish, as my late aunt would have said. Not quite as tall, chunkier like a heavyweight boxer, he also had a pugnacious attitude—or so I had gathered from reading about some of his encounters with the press.

"Hey, Jasper." Long turned with a smile and an outstretched hand. "Yeah, you know the drill. Have to get out into the community and talk to everyone." The two shook hands. "Have you met the owner of this fine bakery, Helen Louise Brady?"

Singletary inclined his head at Helen Louise, who smiled warmly at him. "I have indeed. She makes some of the best chocolate cake I've ever eaten."

Beck laughed. "Amen to that." He patted his trim waistline. "I've spent many an hour in the gym to compensate for it, let me tell you."

"I'd love to work out in a gym," Singletary said with a slight smile. "I have bigger priorities for my budget, however, so I have to settle for jogging around the neighborhood."

Singletary's reference to his budget was a subtle nod to the fact that, unlike Beck Long, he hadn't grown up in a privileged, wealthy family. The son of an impoverished local farmer with only a small holding, he had worked two jobs to put himself through college and law school. His ambition and hard work paid off as he became a successful lawyer in Memphis, but in the past year he'd moved back to Athena, evidently to enter politics in his home state.

Long gave little outward sign that he registered Singletary's jab. "You're lucky you've got the knees for it. I guess I played too much tennis, because my knees give me heck these days."

I remembered reading that Long had been a tennis champion all through high school and college and had even flirted with the idea of turning professional, but decided instead to stick with family tradition.

"That's too bad," Singletary said in a patently insincere tone. "My advisors and I are planning to have lunch in this excellent establishment, and our schedule is tight. Have you finished here?" He waved a hand toward the cash register.

"Yes, I'm afraid we have to push on. No time for lunch today. So many folks to see. We just stopped by to say hello to Ms. Brady."

Long's entourage of five evidently took that as their cue, because they started moving away from the counter and toward the door. Long turned back to Helen Louise and nodded. "Always good to see you, Helen Louise. Let me say again how much my parents and I enjoyed your food the other night."

"My pleasure, Beck," Helen Louise said.

I watched as Long paused on his way toward the door to shake a few hands. My attention switched back to the counter, however, when I heard Helen Louise greet Singletary.

"Nice to see you again, Jasper," she said. "We have that chicken salad you like so much today. How about that?"

Singletary grinned. "You know my weakness, so how can I say no?" He motioned for his companions to join him at the register.

I listened for a few moments but when I realized all they were talking about was food, I lost interest. I hoped they would finish soon because I was getting hungrier by the minute, I realized. Diesel chose that second to reappear from under the table and tap my thigh again. "I know," I told him. "I'm hungry, too. Won't be long, though, I'm sure."

The cat appeared to understand, though the look he gave me was far from happy. He meowed twice and slunk under the table as if disgusted.

When I focused on the register area again, there was no line. I surveyed the room and spotted Singletary and his companions sitting on the far side of the bakery from me. They occupied a table next to the small one where Kelly Grimes sat. I was surprised to see her still here, because I thought she might be following Beck Long discreetly for either personal or professional reasons.

Instead I noticed her shooting covert sideways glances at Singletary—or so I thought. He sat at about a forty-five-degree angle from her spot in the bakery. From what I could tell, though, he didn't appear to notice her. Perhaps she was hanging around to get a chance to talk to him. A good writer wouldn't turn down an opportunity like this, I reckoned.

She did nothing but continue to sit there, however, as I watched. I became fascinated by the way she glanced his way, then back down at her plate, at regular intervals. What was going on here? She wasn't shy; I knew that. So why didn't she get up and go to his table?

"Are you sitting there ogling another woman, Charlie Harris?"

Helen Louise startled me. I had been so engrossed in watching Kelly Grimes, I hadn't noticed her leaving the cash register and walking over to my table.

She grinned at me as she leaned down to give me a quick kiss. Diesel warbled at her, determined to be noticed. She laughed. "I'd never forget you, honey." She rubbed his head, and he purred contentedly. I knew it wouldn't be long, though, before he would be hunting for his usual treats from her.

"How could I ogle any other woman when you're around?" I asked.

Helen Louise grinned impishly. "Do I take that to mean that you do ogle other women when I'm *not* around?"

"Oh, yes, I roam the streets of Athena just looking for women to leer at," I said as I rolled my eyes at her.

"You cad, you. I didn't realize you were such a roué," she said in a mock-horrified tone, "or I never would have gotten involved with you."

"You're just feeling giddy because you've had two young, attractive men fawning over you." I frowned. "I had no idea your affections were so easily shifted, and all for a pretty face." I shook my head, my expression doleful.

Her peal of laughter made me smile. "I do love you so," she whispered as she bent to graze my cheek with a kiss.

I grinned at her. "Ditto. Now, how about some food, woman? The cat and I are practically malnourished, we've waited so long for you to stop flirting and take care of us."

Diesel warbled loudly, and Helen Louise and I exchanged a smile.

"Guess I'd better feed you right away," she said. "I can't have you fading away to nothing in my bakery. I'll be right back." She scratched Diesel's head before she headed to the kitchen.

I was a lucky man, and I knew it. Helen Louise was not only smart, beautiful, and talented, she also shared my goofy sense of humor. We laughed a lot together, and I relished every moment spent with her.

Helen Louise's teasing about my ogling other women notwith-standing, I couldn't help glancing over at Kelly Grimes again. I was curious to see whether she would approach Jasper Singletary.

While I watched, she gazed back and forth between him and her plate. Then she paused as she seemed finally to catch his glance. She started to push her chair back, and I looked at Singletary.

He frowned and shook his head so slightly that I thought for a moment I imagined it.

Kelly Grimes, half standing by now, sat down again. She looked annoyed.

That little interchange was decidedly odd. What was going on here?

NINE

IIIIIIIIIIIIIIIIIIIIIIIIIII

I wouldn't admit it to many people, but I was a bit on the nosy side. People fascinated me, particularly when I observed what I considered odd behavior. I detected an undercurrent between Jasper Singletary and Kelly Grimes, mainly due to the latter's focus on the former. She might think she was being discreet—and perhaps most people wouldn't have noticed—but I was sure all her attention was squarely centered on the young politician.

"I thought you might like something different today." Helen Louise once again startled me, and I hastily turned my attention to her.

"Smells wonderful," I said as I took a second deep breath of the rich aroma. "What is it?"

"Chicken chasseur," she said. "Chicken cooked in a sauce of butter, mushrooms, cognac, white wine, and shallots. Plus a few other things. Served with rice and fresh bread." She set a small plate of plain cooked chicken on the table as well—treats for the cat.

Diesel put both front paws on my thighs and raised his head to stare at the food on the table. He meowed and looked back and forth from me to Helen Louise.

"Poor starving kitty," Helen Louise said. "Things are a bit busy at the moment, so you'll have to get Charlie to feed you, boy. See you soon." She hurried back to the register.

I knew better than to taste my own food before giving the cat a bit of his own. While he was occupied with a chunky morsel, I tried the chicken chasseur. I would have to ask Helen Louise later what *chasseur* meant. In the meantime, I decided after one savory mouthful, I would tuck in and enjoy myself.

For the first few minutes I was busy stuffing my face and keeping Diesel happy with his lunch, and I didn't pay any attention to Kelly Grimes and Jasper Singletary. When I did look over in their direction, I saw that the politician seemed engrossed in food and conversation with his companions. The writer, her plate empty now, was scribbling furiously on a notepad.

The bell jangled again to signal fresh arrivals, and I of course had to see who it was. To my surprise, I saw Lucinda Long headed for the register.

Helen Louise had finished with the previous customer, and she greeted our mayor with a smile. "Good afternoon, Lucinda. Nice to see you. What can I get for you today?"

The mayor smiled briefly. "I'm sorry, Helen Louise, no time for food today. I was hoping to find my son here. I checked with one of his aides, and she told me he would be stopping in here right about now."

"You just missed him," Helen Louise said. "He and his group

left about five minutes ago. I don't believe I heard anyone say where they were heading next."

The mayor sighed. "How aggravating. I barely get to talk to him these days, he's so busy with his campaign. I was hoping to snatch a few minutes of his time."

"Campaigning is hard work, and it must take a toll on family life." Helen Louise offered Mrs. Long a sympathetic smile.

"That it does," the mayor said. She stood at the register, her shoulders slumped.

"Are you sure I can't get you something to take back to the office with you?" Helen Louise waved a hand toward the dessert case. "Maybe a piece of your favorite chocolate cake?"

Mrs. Long said, "I really shouldn't. I had a big lunch." She paused. "But it's going to be a long afternoon. Why not? Yes, that would be lovely."

"I'll be right back," Helen Louise said.

As I chewed another bite of my delicious meal, I saw Kelly Grimes leave her table and approach the mayor. Mrs. Long had her back to the writer, and she started slightly when Kelly Grimes touched her shoulder.

"Pardon me, Your Honor," Ms. Grimes said. She identified herself. "I'd like to ask you a couple questions about your son's campaign if you have a few minutes."

Mrs. Long shook her head. "Now is not the time. You need to call my office and arrange an appointment with my secretary. I'm swamped this afternoon, and I have to get back to the court-house."

The writer shrugged. "Very well. I'll do that, but I really want to talk to you as soon as possible."

"Just call my office and make an appointment." Mrs. Long

sounded impatient. "Now, please, let me get on with what I'm doing."

Ms. Grimes stared at her for a moment before she nodded and headed back to her table.

Helen Louise came back to the register with a small to-go container. "Here you are, Lucinda. I think this will help perk up your afternoon."

The mayor frowned. "Oh, dear, Helen Louise, I came away from the office without my purse or even any money in my pocket. I'd better pass on the cake for now."

"Nonsense." Helen Louise laughed. "I know you're good for it. Or we could simply call it a frequent-customer perk. Take this with you and enjoy it."

"I can't resist an offer like that." Mrs. Long gave a grateful smile as she accepted her cake. "The afternoon looks better already." She thanked Helen Louise and then bade her good-bye.

As she turned away she spotted me. Naturally I had a mouthful of chicken chasseur when she came over to me, and I swallowed hastily. "Good afternoon, Your Honor."

"Good afternoon, Mr. Harris." She smiled when she spotted Diesel's head suddenly poking up above the table. "And your beautiful boy as well. How are things going with the diaries?" Her expression turned grave. "I hope you haven't had too much trouble over them."

I figured that was an oblique way of referring to Marie Steverton. I didn't intend to burden her with the details of the morning's nasty scene. I decided, however, to take this opportunity to broach my idea about a digital copy of the diary.

"No, everything's fine," I said. "I know you're in a hurry, but

I would like to suggest something to you that I think will make access to the diaries easier for everyone interested in them."

The mayor glanced at her watch. "Certainly, do tell me." She remained standing, and I knew this was my cue to be succinct.

"The diaries are in good condition, but I think scanning them and making a digital copy is the best way to proceed. That cuts down on the actual number of people handling them and will preserve them better in the long run. I have the necessary equipment in the archive office, and I can do it myself, or I can get help from other library staff. What do you think?"

Diesel chirped a couple of times, as if he liked my idea. Mrs. Long laughed. "Your assistant seems to think it's a good idea. I do, too. That would probably make all our lives easier. How long would it take, do you think?"

I considered that for a moment. The scanning process wasn't fast—not if you wanted the best-quality results—and it was tedious. Even so, I could get a significant amount of it done this week, if I had help.

I told the mayor that, and she nodded. "Sounds good. Go ahead, and if you need funds for additional help, let me know. I'm sure my husband will be happy to discuss arrangements with the library director." She glanced at her watch again. "Now I really have to get going. Good-bye for now."

"Thanks, and have a good afternoon," I called after her as she headed for the door.

Helen Louise came over to the table. "What's all this about diaries?"

"Do you have a few minutes to sit with me? I can tell you all about it."

She surveyed the room. Her two staff members were behind the counter and were not busy at the moment. "Looks like things have slowed a bit, and I'm more than ready to sit for a while." She pulled out a chair.

"First, fabulous lunch. Thank you."

Diesel, who had finished his chicken, chimed in with chirps and a meow or two. Helen Louise grinned. "Have to keep my men well fed and happy. I'm glad you both enjoyed it. Now, about these diaries."

"They belonged to a relative of Andrew Long—Rachel Afton Long. Great-great-grandmother, I think. Can't remember exactly how many *greats* at the moment." I went on to tell her about the interest in the diaries from Marie Steverton—at whose name she grimaced—and Kelly Grimes. "And there's the latter over in the corner, next to Jasper Singletary's table."

Helen Louise turned her head to see where I indicated. She turned back to me with a frown. "That's interesting," she said. "I've seen her in here several times recently, but I had no idea who she was. She's never introduced herself. The truly odd thing is, though, every time she's been in here, so has Jasper."

TEN

||||||||||||||||||

"Too many times to be mere coincidence, would you say?" I asked.

Helen Louise nodded. "Yes, but I wouldn't have remarked on it, probably, until you explained who she is."

"Maybe she's following him around, trying to catch him out on something." That seemed possible, given she was secretly engaged to Singletary's opponent. I couldn't tell Helen Louise that, however.

"She's being rather obvious about it, wouldn't you say?" Helen Louise glanced back in the direction of Kelly Grimes. "Surely he, or one of his aides, would have picked up on it by now."

"True," I said. "They can't all be oblivious." I watched the writer for a moment.

At the table next to her, the men pushed back their chairs and stood. Jasper Singletary motioned with his hand, and the other men began to file toward the door. He turned in the direction of the restroom. He didn't appear to notice Kelly Grimes when he passed her.

She stared after him until he disappeared into the hallway where the restrooms were located. Then she gathered her things and made her way out of the bakery. Was she going to follow Singletary to his next stop? I wondered.

Helen Louise turned to me and shrugged. "Guess that's over for now." She stood and picked up the two empty plates. "How about dessert?"

I shook my head. "No, after that wonderful meal and the big breakfast Azalea cooked, I'd better not. Otherwise I'll have to run to Memphis and back to work it all off."

We shared a laugh, and Helen Louise said, "I'll be back in a minute," before she walked away with the plates.

"We're going to have to get back to work," I told Diesel, who stared longingly after Helen Louise. He wanted more chicken, but he'd had more than enough already. He turned to me and meowed. "I want to stop by the bookstore first, though. We haven't been in there lately, and I want to see what's new."

The cat meowed again. I thought he recognized the word *bookstore*. He liked going to the Athenaeum, the town's only independent bookstore. The owner, Jordan Thompson, always made a fuss over him. Today, however, I would have to tell her not to give him any cat treats. Otherwise, he might have to join me on that jog to Memphis and back.

While I waited for Helen Louise to return, I decided I might as well make a restroom stop before we left. "Come on, boy," I told Diesel and picked up his leash.

I had taken only a couple of steps when I saw Jasper Singletary return to the dining room. As I moved closer, I saw him pause right by Kelly Grimes's vacated table and pull out a cell phone. He stared down at it, and if I hadn't been watching closely, I would have missed what happened next.

With his free hand he picked up something from the table and thrust it into his pocket. He stared at the cell phone a moment longer, and then he tucked it back into its holster on his belt. He strode toward the door and nodded at me as we passed each other.

More strange behavior. There was definitely something afoot. What had he scooped up from the table? I pondered that as I completed my business in the restroom. Diesel waited patiently near me.

I couldn't really see what Jasper had picked up, but it had to be something small. The writer had been scribbling in a notebook earlier, so perhaps it was a piece of paper. A note of some kind?

That sounded probable. But why the secret communication, if it was indeed a note?

Back at the table, where Helen Louise waited, I told her what I'd seen. She grimaced. "*Incroyable!* Sounds almost like CIA stuff, and that's just plain silly."

I shrugged. "It's politics, so who knows? If I run into Maxwell Smart or Ninety-nine, I'll ask them to look into it."

Helen Louise laughed at my reference to the old sixties television show. "It had better be Maxwell. Ninety-nine is far too attractive."

I gave her a quick kiss, and we said good-bye. "Come on, Diesel. Time for the bookstore."

The bookstore was only a short walk from the bakery. The early afternoon sun was hot, but most of the storefronts had awnings. Diesel and I kept in the shade on the way, but I was feeling sweaty by the time we opened the door at the Athenaeum and stepped inside.

As I let the door swing shut behind Diesel and me, I paused to drink in the smells and the atmosphere of the bookstore. There was no place I liked better, except a library. To be surrounded by so many books made me happy. The large space—around four thousand square feet—contained many freestanding shelves, and all the walls were lined with them as well. Comfortable chairs were scattered about, creating small nooks where a customer could relax and check out a few pages of possible purchases.

Soft classical music wafted through the space, and I recognized a Telemann oboe sonata. Perfect mood music for browsing. I didn't see the owner, Jordan Thompson, anywhere, but the tall redhead would be easy to spot. Diesel meowed, and I knew he was urging me to go in search of Jordan.

"No treats," I told him as we moved farther into the store. I saw only four customers in the front area. I headed toward the back, where the mysteries were shelved. Jordan had a shelf there for the latest arrivals, and I wanted to see what new titles might tempt me.

I heard the murmur of voices in the back corner of the section as I approached. I paused by the new arrivals shelf to scan the titles, and I picked up one hardcover with an intriguing cover illustration. An old house on the cover always snagged my interest, and this one looked promising. When I realized it was a ghost story, though, I put it back. I liked ghost stories occasionally, but I wasn't in the mood for one now.

Diesel muttered, but I ignored him. He wanted to find Jordan, but I wasn't going to let him loose in here. He would have to wait. Besides, I realized, she might not even be here. One of her assistants could be running the store instead.

I moved toward the back of the section against the wall and the beginning of the alphabet. A tall, freestanding set of shelves separated me from the continuation of the section around the corner. The sound of voices grew louder the closer I came to the back wall.

With a start, I recognized the voices and halted.

"How long before you find out anything worthwhile?" Jasper Singletary sounded impatient. "The evidence ought to be there somewhere; you just have to find it. My grandmother swears to it."

"I'm doing my best," Kelly Grimes responded, sounding exasperated. "I told you, I have to have access if I'm going to look, and I haven't been able to get access. If someone would just push Marie Steverton over a cliff, that would help."

Diesel chose that moment to start chirping—loudly—and the conversation on the other side of the shelf ceased. I turned to see Jordan Thompson headed our way, and Diesel strained at the leash to go to her. I let him go and turned back to listen, hoping to hear more.

I heard the sound of stealthy footsteps. I stepped around the shelf to the other side, but all I saw were the backs of the rapidly retreating pair.

"Hey, there, Charlie." Jordan Thompson claimed my attention, and I walked around the shelf to see her squatting down so that her head was level with the cat's. They rubbed noses, and Jordan laughed, her short, curly red hair bouncing around her head.

"Afternoon, Jordan," I said. "Diesel and I thought we'd drop by, since we haven't been here in at least a week." Even though I knew it was wrong to eavesdrop, I was sorry Diesel and Jordan had interrupted whatever was going on between Jasper Singletary and Kelly Grimes. I had a fleeting thought about the note—if that was what it was—Singletary picked up from the table in the bakery. Perhaps it set up this little assignation.

"I know," Jordan said, "and my cash register is feeling it." She grinned. "Seriously, it's always good to see you two. How about a T-R-E-A-T for my buddy here?"

I shook my head. "No, your buddy has a tummy full of Helen Louise's chicken, and he doesn't need another bite."

Jordan looked down at the cat. Diesel gazed expectantly up at her, thinking his treat would soon be forthcoming. "Sorry, boy," she said. "Next time make sure you drag Charlie in here *before* lunch, okay?"

The cat meowed, and Jordan and I shared a grin. All he probably understood was that he wasn't getting a treat. He continued to stare up at Jordan, however. He was an optimistic cat.

"I'll try to remember," I promised.

"Why don't y'all come back up by the register?" Jordan cocked her head in that direction. "I've got a few things set aside for you that I think you might like."

That was all I needed to hear. Service like this was the reason I loved shopping at the bookstore, rather than online.

From the shelves behind the main counter Jordan retrieved a stack of five paperback books, each of them the latest entry in series I enjoyed.

"They showed up just this morning," Jordan said. "I was going to call you earlier but I got busy."

"Guess I must have sensed somehow that I needed to stop by." I smiled to show my appreciation. "I'll take them all."

While Jordan was ringing up my purchases, I decided to do a little fishing. "You certainly have a wide range of customers. Right before you came back to say hello, I thought I spotted one of the writers from the paper and one of our political hopefuls chatting together."

Jordan frowned. "Really? Which ones? I haven't seen Ray Appleby in a couple of weeks. He usually takes time to talk when he comes in."

"Not Ray Appleby. A young woman named Kelly Grimes. I thought I saw her talking to Jasper Singletary."

"I don't know her. I think I've seen her name in the paper, though," Jordan said. "I went to school with Jasper." She paused. "In fact, we dated in high school, but he was a little too intense for me. Too driven."

"Is that so?" I said, realizing how inane a remark it was even as it left my lips.

Jordan didn't appear to notice. "I heard he had a girlfriend, but I don't know what her name is. The friend who told me didn't know, either, only that Jasper was finally involved with someone." She giggled. "Frankly, we were all starting to think he was gay, because nobody ever saw him with anyone but all those guys who seem to follow him around everywhere."

"He seems to be working pretty hard to get himself elected," I said as I handed over my credit card. "If he's still as driven as he was in high school, then I'd say he probably doesn't have much time for a personal life."

"True." Jordan swiped the card in her machine and then handed it back to me. I signed the receipt, and she bagged up the books. "He was always pretty single-minded. Wouldn't let anything—or anyone—get in the way of his goals." She giggled again. "Evidently I wasn't one of his goals, though back then I sure wanted to be. He's a hunk and a half."

"If you say so," I murmured. Jordan had the reputation of going through men like some women go through shoes, but I didn't know whether there was any truth to the stories I'd heard.

Melba had never said a word against her, and I took that as a sign that the rumors were simply that: rumors.

Jordan frowned suddenly. "Kelly Grimes, you said?"

I nodded.

"I heard that name somewhere recently," she said slowly. "In the paper, like I said, but I heard someone talking about her not that long ago." She leaned against the counter and crossed her arms over her chest. "This is going to bug me until I remember."

"I know. It's irritating when you're trying to dredge something up." I thought my fishing expedition might reel in a bit of information after all. I hoped she could recall what it was she'd heard.

Diesel meowed loudly to remind me that he was there and in desperate need of attention. Jordan laughed as I scratched the cat's head.

"I've got it," she said suddenly. "I know where I heard her name." She glanced around us, perhaps to see whether anyone else was in earshot. Evidently satisfied we couldn't be overheard, she leaned toward me.

"It was the other day at the Chamber of Commerce breakfast," she said. "I overheard the mayor's secretary gossiping about her to one of the other business owners. *That Grimes girl is stalking him like a cat in heat looking for a tom.*" She shrugged. "That was it. I never did hear who the *him* is."

ELEVEN

I could have satisfied her curiosity on that point, I thought. Then I realized I couldn't be sure.

At first I would have assumed the mayor's secretary was talking about Beck Long, given that Kelly Grimes told me they were secretly engaged. When I considered what happened at the bakery a little while ago and here in the bookstore only a few minutes ago, however, I had to reexamine the situation.

Jasper Singletary and Kelly Grimes had more than a passing acquaintance with each other. That much was obvious. I recalled Helen Louise's remark about the CIA and the silliness of what we observed. Perhaps espionage wasn't so far off the mark after all.

I had only Kelly Grimes's word for it that she was engaged to Beck Long. Had she insisted on utter secrecy because the whole thing was fabricated? I was beginning to realize that could well be the case. The conversation I overheard between Ms. Grimes and

Singletary told me the two had to know each other intimately—and were involved in some kind of plot together.

Moreover, the plot centered around the Rachel Long diaries. Kelly Grimes's remark about trying to get access had to refer to them. Singletary wanted her to find evidence of something in them, something his grandmother had allegedly told him about.

All too vague, I thought.

"Charlie, did you hear me?" Jordan poked my arm with a light touch.

"Sorry," I said. "Woolgathering, as usual. Did I hear you about what?"

Jordan shook her head. "Professors are supposed to be the absentminded ones, not librarians. Did you hear what I told you about the mayor's secretary and what she said?"

"I did." I nodded. "It's all very curious, isn't it? I'd love to know who the man is."

"Me, too." Jordan laughed. "Why don't you ask your friend Miss Melba? She always seems to know everybody's business."

"I might just do that," I said.

"If you find out, let me know. I'm beginning to think it could be this Kelly Grimes. Like I told you, one of my friends says Jasper has a new girlfriend. Could be her."

"You might be right," I said. I knew one thing for sure. The next time I saw Ms. Kelly Grimes, I was going to sit her down and grill her for all she was worth. I didn't like being lied to, and I would tell her so.

"Are you sure I can't give him just one little T-R-E-A-T?" Jordan pointed to Diesel, now lolling on his back, his head to one side, in his most winsome pose.

I sighed. "Okay. One, and only one. Then we have to get going. I've got a big project to work on."

Jordan grinned as she reached beneath the counter for a bag of Diesel's favorite treats. The minute he heard the crinkling of the plastic, he was on his feet. He put his front paws on the edge of the counter and watched her closely. She picked one morsel out and gave it to him. He grabbed it and dropped to the floor. A moment later he stood on his hind legs again. Clearly he expected another one.

"No," I said. "No more."

Jordan put the bag away and then waved her hands to indicate they were empty. Diesel meowed before he dropped to all fours and turned to sit with his back to us. Jordan and I shared a laugh.

"See you later," I said as I strolled toward the door. Diesel meowed in a mournful tone as Jordan bade us good-bye.

We walked back to the car. I cranked it to get the air conditioner going before I settled Diesel in the backseat. I decided to go to the college and park rather than go home and walk back. I was eager to resume work on the diaries.

I parked in the small lot between the old antebellum home that housed the archive and the more modern structure that was the actual college library. Diesel and I went in the back way. When we reached the front hallway and the stairs, I saw Melba enter the front door.

"You just getting back, too?" she said. "I had a nice lunch at the faculty club." She shot me an arch smile. "Want to guess who I ate with?"

There really was no telling, I thought. Melba had friends all over campus. "You have way too many beaus around here for me to single out only one."

"Can't help it if I'm popular." She motioned for Diesel and me to follow her into her office. "Come on in a minute. I have got to tell you about lunch."

I suppressed a sigh. I really wanted to get to work on the diaries, but I knew Melba would follow me right up the stairs if I didn't listen to her now.

The cat and I walked into her office. I didn't sit, however, and I hoped she would understand that meant I had things to do.

Melba looked pointedly at the empty chair beside her desk, then at me. She cocked her head to one side and stared hard at me.

I gave in and sat down. Diesel stretched out on the floor between us, his head right by Melba's chair. She reached down to pet him, as he intended her to.

"Okay, who was your lunch companion?" I asked. I could take the silence only so long.

Melba grinned. "Dr. Newkirk. I happened to run into him on my way out to lunch, and we ended up eating at the faculty club. I was his guest." She preened a little.

"Let me try to guess what you talked about over lunch," I said in a mock-puzzled tone. "I don't have a clue. You'll have to enlighten me."

"If I had something heavy enough, I'd throw it at you right now and knock that silly smile off your face." There was no rancor in Melba's tone. "You know dang well I talked to him about Marie Steverton and those diaries she's got the hots for."

"Did you tell him about the scene between Marie and the writer this morning?"

Melba continued to scratch the cat's head as she replied. "I thought about it. That witch deserves trouble on account of the way she behaves, but I decided not to. Instead I asked him about your diaries and why they might be important."

"What did he have to say on that subject?" I asked.

"He talked a lot about daily life back in the old days around the Civil War and how bad things were here while the war was going on." Melba paused for a moment, her expression thoughtful. "I'm sure glad I wasn't around then. Women had it pretty rough while the men were off fighting the war."

"Yes, they did," I said. "Everyone in the South went through a lot of privation and violence during the war. It was a nasty business for everyone concerned. War always is."

I was not one of those Southerners who had a romanticized view of the War Between the States, the Late Unpleasantness, or the War of Northern Aggression. Nearly three hundred thousand Southern men and boys died in the war—in battle, from disease, or as prisoners of war. Close to another two hundred thousand were wounded in action. Many came home permanently maimed, missing limbs or otherwise horribly scarred both physically and mentally. There was nothing romantic about it.

"I know." Melba shuddered. "I remember my great-granny talking about how her daddy came back from the war with one leg shot off and part of an arm. She lived to be almost a hundred, and I still remember what she told me, even though I was an itty-bitty girl at the time. She had a picture of him, and it scared me, he looked so terrible."

Diesel warbled, evidently sensing her momentary distress. Melba rubbed his head, and I could see her relax as she did.

"It sure made a powerful impression on you," I said. "Did you and Dr. Newkirk talk about anything else?"

"We talked about Marie. I didn't bring her up, though. He did, talking about the diaries. He sure doesn't think much of her," Melba said. "In fact, she got hired here over his objections. He said she's intelligent enough, but that her work is limited by her prejudices." She frowned. "I think that's the way he put it."

Dr. Newkirk's reaction to Marie Steverton's feminist rhetoric didn't surprise me. He was definitely of the old school, the one that looked on women in academia with intense suspicion.

"Was that all?" I said.

Melba's expression turned grave. "No, he let on to something he really shouldn't have told me, and I'm not sure he realized he had. He was knocking back the wine pretty good over lunch." She paused. "He confirmed what I told you the other day. Said Marie won't get tenure unless she comes up with a real knockout book. Her last hope is these diaries."

I had pretty much figured that already. I felt sorry for Marie. Life for non-tenured faculty could be rough. Lower salaries, moving from job to job trying to find the one where tenure might actually be possible. Desperation, however, did not excuse the way Marie behaved.

"I hope for her sake the diaries prove to be worth all the effort she's going to put into studying them." I rose. "And speaking of the diaries, I really have to get to work on them. Diesel, do you want to stay with Melba for a while?"

The cat looked at me and warbled, and I took that for a *yes*. "I'm assuming that's okay with you," I said.

"Of course. We'll be up later to check on you."

I left the two of them happily in each other's company and trudged up the stairs. When I reached the office door, I inserted my key in the lock. Then I realized it was already unlocked.

That was odd. I always locked the door when I left the office, even for a few minutes. I could have forgotten it today—it did happen occasionally—but I was pretty sure I remembered locking it when Diesel and I left for lunch.

I turned on the lights and walked over to my desk.

My heart hit the bottoms of my shoes and kept on going.

The Rachel Long diaries were gone.

TWELVE

IIIIIIIIIIIIIIIIIIIIIIIIIIIIIIIIIII

I called myself all kinds of idiot while I waited for the college police to respond to my call. How could I have been so stupid? Leaving the door unlocked, as I must have done, was inexcusable, and thanks to my forgetfulness, someone had been able to walk in and take the diaries.

After a cursory examination I thought nothing else was missing, but I wouldn't know for sure until I could do a more thorough search. I didn't want to touch anything until after the police finished investigating.

At least I could give the police a short list of suspects: Marie Steverton and Kelly Grimes. I thought about adding Jasper Singletary's name, based on what I'd overheard earlier, but I realized that was only hearsay. Both the professor and the writer had made determined efforts to get their hands on the diaries, and I was willing to bet one of them had walked into the office and out again with the four volumes.

But why? What was the urgency?

I couldn't figure out what could be so important about those diaries that a person had to have access to them today rather than wait just a few days more.

Perhaps I was looking at this from the wrong way round. What if the thief already *knew* what was in the diaries and didn't want something in them made public?

The whole thing didn't make much sense to me. Those diaries recorded events that happened a century and a half ago. I understood, like any reasonably intelligent person, that the past did affect the present. But in this case I was stumped. Until I could read those diaries for myself, I wouldn't be able to figure this out.

I didn't want to consider the possibility that the thief took the diaries in order to destroy them, but I couldn't ignore it. They could already have been destroyed, consigned to a fire, or hacked apart and shredded.

That made me feel sick to my stomach.

"Mr. Harris? You called and reported a theft?"

The deep, authoritative voice brought me out of my self-absorption. I turned to see the college's chief of police in the doorway.

"Yes, I did, Chief. Thanks for responding so quickly," I said.

Martin Ford, a grizzled veteran Marine Corps retiree, had been at the helm of the campus police for about six months, I recalled. He had a distinguished record in the Corps, based on what I'd read about him. This was only the third time I'd met him, but I'd found him businesslike and professional in our previous encounters.

"Tell me again what's missing. Something connected with the Long family, I believe."

I nodded. "Yes, I think I mentioned that to the dispatcher. Sorry, but I'm still a bit in shock." I paused for a deep, steadying breath. "Right. Yesterday the mayor brought four volumes of a diary written by one of her husband's ancestors, Rachel Afton Long. She donated them to the archive to add to the Long family's already extensive collection. I was in the process of preparing them for use by the public. I hadn't made much progress, and now they've disappeared."

"When was the last time you saw them?" Chief Ford's laser-like gaze made me feel like a bug pinned to a board.

"Right before I left for lunch. I was pretty sure I locked the door behind me—I am usually very careful about that—but the door wasn't locked when I returned from lunch a few minutes ago and found the diaries gone."

"How long were you out of the office?"

I checked my watch for the current time. "Close to two hours."

"Plenty of time for the thief to come in here and walk out with the diaries." The chief nodded. "They had to risk being seen, but I guess y'all don't get a lot of people in the building most days."

"No, but Melba Gilley, the library director's executive assistant, has a pretty good view of the door. She usually sees who comes in and out. But I met her coming back from lunch when I got back, so she was probably out of the building, too, for an hour or so."

"I'll check with her on that shortly," the chief said. "I want to have a look at the lock first."

"Sure." I watched as he pulled a small flashlight off his belt and crouched by the door. My nerves tautened while I waited, wondering whether he would find any signs that the lock had been picked or forced. I wouldn't feel so stupid if the thief had broken in, instead of waltzing in through a door I forgot to lock.

Chief Ford grunted as he stood and put away his flashlight. "That lock should have been replaced twenty years ago." He shook his head. "Way too easy to pick or force. Looks to me like it was picked recently. Maybe you're off the hook for leaving it unlocked."

"I'm glad of that," I said, "though it disturbs the heck out of me that someone could pick the lock so easily. I'll talk to the library director right away about installing a new lock. They put in a new one on the door to the storage area about four years ago. I don't know why they didn't upgrade this one at the same time."

I realized I was babbling, so I shut up. The chief's stern countenance and steely gaze made me feel guilty even if I hadn't goofed and left the door unlocked.

"Any idea who might've done this?" The chief pulled out a notebook and pen.

"Yes, I do. There are two people who have been pretty determined to get access to the diaries. The first is a professor, Marie Steverton. Member of the history department. The other is a writer for the *Register* named Kelly Grimes. Ms. Grimes," I added.

"Other than being real interested in these books, why would one of them break in here and steal them?" Again the intense stare.

I shrugged. "The whole thing sounds nuts to me, frankly. The mayor, who's an old college friend of Dr. Steverton, arranged for her to have exclusive access to the diaries for three weeks. Once I had them ready for use, that is. Ms. Grimes was the first to approach me about them." I gave the chief a quick summary of the writer's initial phone call. "Then she showed up here this morning, and she and Dr. Steverton had a bit of an altercation."

The chief shook his head as if in amazement at such behavior. "And how old are these books?"

"They date back to before the Civil War," I said. "I couldn't put a monetary value on them, but they could be valuable as historical documents."

"I'll be talking to both those ladies about this," the chief said. "Anybody else you can think of might want to get hold of the diaries?"

I hesitated. Should I tell Chief Ford what I suspected about the connection between Kelly Grimes and Jasper Singletary?

My poker face evidently failed me.

"You've thought of something," the chief stated flatly.

"It's hearsay, probably. Something I saw today and then a short snatch of conversation I overheard."

"I'm listening," the chief said.

I wondered briefly whether Chief Ford had heard about my previous experiences with the murder cases I'd been involved in, and what he might think about me as a result. With Kanesha Berry, chief deputy in the sheriff's department, I was on a surer footing. She knew me pretty well, but Chief Ford and I were barely acquainted. I decided that, if necessary, I'd refer him to Kanesha to check my bona fides.

"Okay, here's what happened." I launched into a description of the events at the bakery and the epilogue at the bookstore.

"Sounds like you have a knack for being in the right place at just the right time," the chief commented when I finished. His expression gave me no clue as to whether he was making a joke.

He didn't wait for a response. "Does sound to me like there's a connection to the diaries. Pretty logical, based on everything you've told me. Looks like I'm going to need to work with either Athena PD or the sheriff's department on this, though."

Here was my chance. "If you work with the sheriff's department, I'm sure Chief Deputy Berry will vouch for me, in case you need any reassurance."

The chief nodded. "Anything else missing?"

"I haven't really looked yet," I said. "I figured I should wait until you arrived. Shall I go ahead now?"

"Yes," the chief said. "Touch as little as possible, because we're probably going to check your desk for fingerprints and trace evidence. The diaries were on your desk, right, when you left for lunch?"

I confirmed that they were before I checked around my desk. Without inventorying the shelves in my office I couldn't say for sure whether anything else had been taken, but I didn't get the feeling that anything was missing from the shelves. Everything looked as it should.

"I don't think the thief took anything else," I said finally.

"Okay," the chief said. "How about you go wait downstairs in Ms. Gilley's office? I'll be down soon to talk to her. Meantime, I'm going to get a couple of my officers over here, and I'm going to contact the locals and see how they want to proceed. I can question Dr. Steverton, but they'll probably have to track down Ms. Grimes." He whipped out a cell phone without waiting for a response.

"I'll be down there if you need me," I said. I didn't think he heard me, so I headed downstairs. Melba would be bouncing with excitement when I told her what happened.

Mayor Long, on the other hand, would probably be angry, and I wasn't looking forward to that conversation.

THIRTEEN

||||||||||||||||||||||||||||||||||||||||||||||||

By the time I got home that evening, I felt like I'd been dragged backward through the briar patch. That's what my late mother used to say anytime she was exhausted. Occasionally she'd say she was "plumb wore out." No matter how I described it, I was beat.

Poor Diesel was fatigued, too. All the noise, with law enforcement personnel going up and down the stairs outside Melba's office, and the tension he picked up from me, wore him plumb out. We were both glad to get home to the quiet and peace of an empty house.

Or so I thought. Sean came noisily down the stairs about five minutes after Diesel and I walked into the kitchen. I was seated at the table, and the cat was stretched out beneath it after a visit to the utility room.

"Hey, Dad," he said as he headed for the fridge. "How was your day?" He pulled out a beer and popped the cap off with his thumb. The cap hit the floor, but Diesel couldn't be bothered.

Usually he would bat it around until I took it away from him to stop the noise.

"I've had better." I leaned back in my chair.

Sean put his beer on the table and sat across from me. "You look out of it," he said. "And when Diesel doesn't want to play with a bottle cap, I know he's out of it as well. What happened?"

I realized I hadn't seen my son for at least a couple of days; thus I had a lot to tell him. "Tell you what. Pour your poor exhausted old dad a glass of iced tea, and I'll fill you in."

"Deal." Sean got up and went to the cabinet for a glass. "I'm not buying the poor old dad bit, though. You're not quite ready for the old folks' home. Next year maybe, but not now." He grinned broadly as he set the full glass in front of me.

I clinked my glass with his bottle once he resumed his seat. I drained half the tea before I started talking. "This will take a few minutes."

"I've got the time." Sean leaned back in his chair and sipped his beer.

The cold tea and the caffeine revived me a bit, though by the time I finished my recital of the events of the past two days, I was ready to go up to bed and forget about dinner.

Sean's first question surprised me.

"What did the mayor say when she found out about the theft?"

I shrugged. "Luckily for me, the college police chief called her. I didn't talk to her until after she'd had time to cool down. She wasn't happy, but she did say at least twice she didn't hold me responsible."

"You took reasonable precautions for the safety of the diaries." Sean sounded like the lawyer he was now, rather than just my son.

"I locked the door to the office when I left for lunch," I said.

"It's such a habit with me, I can't believe I didn't do it today. So, yes, I took reasonable precautions. I don't have a safe to put things in." I paused for a moment. "I suppose I could have put them in the storage room next door. It has a much better lock, one that's not easily compromised."

"You could have," Sean said. "But did you have any reason to suspect that the diaries were vulnerable to theft?"

I shook my head. "No, but I knew there were two parties anxious to get hold of them."

"Do you think the professor or the writer stole them?"

"Surely it must be one of them," I said. "At least, I *hope* it was one of them, because I don't think either of them would destroy the diaries. My biggest fear is that the thief might do that for some unknown reason."

"Let's hope the cops find them before the thief has a chance to do anything drastic to them," Sean said. "Right now I'd give a lot to know what's in those diaries to stir up this kind of kerfuffle." He shook his head. "By now I'm pretty much used to weird things happening around you, but this is even more bizarre than usual."

"Thanks for that," I said sourly. "Are you sure you weren't serious about putting me in a home?"

Sean laughed. "I wouldn't dare. For one thing, Helen Louise would extract my liver and then feed it to me. As would Laura, and probably Azalea as well." He got up for another beer, and I motioned that he should refill my glass, too.

"Seriously, Dad, how do you keep getting involved in these things?" Sean frowned as he set my refilled glass in front of me.

"Must be karma," I said, half joking. "Maybe in my last existence I went around whining about being bored all the time, and this is the payback."

Sean rolled his eyes. "People are going to stop letting you come near them at this rate."

"It's not my fault," I protested. I was beginning to get a little annoyed with my son. "I don't go out of my way to find dead bodies or get involved in thefts. They just happen, and there I am."

My son burst out laughing. "You are *way* too easy, Dad."

For a moment I contemplated throwing the contents of my glass across the table at him, but then I started laughing, too. I could feel the tension drain away. Diesel joined in with a few chirps. Even if he didn't understand the words, he understood the mood.

Time for a change of subject, I decided. "How is Alexandra?"

"Fine," Sean said. "And before you ask, no, I haven't asked her to marry me yet."

"I wasn't going to ask," I said. I knew better. Sean had never liked being hounded—as he called it—about anything. "The last time I saw her she was having trouble with her allergies. I hope she's feeling better."

Sean looked mollified. "She is. Whatever was blooming seems to have stopped, so she's not sneezing and getting watery eyes like she was a few days ago."

"Staying busy at the office?" I asked. Sean had recently become a partner in the law firm established by Alexandra's father, the legendary Q. C. Pendergrast.

"Plenty of work," Sean said. "Q. C.'s starting to take it easier, so Alex and I are taking on more of his work."

"That's good." A few months ago Sean and his prospective father-in-law were locked in a battle of wills. Q. C. wanted to make Sean a partner as a wedding gift, but my stubborn son wanted to pay his own way and buy into the firm. They finally came to an agreement over the summer. I kept out of it.

"Are you in for dinner?" I asked.

Sean shook his head. "No, sorry. I'm about to head upstairs for a shower and a change of clothes. Alex and I are going to a Chamber of Commerce dinner tonight. Three hours of rubber chicken and listening to speeches. The mayor has some new plan for attracting more tourists to Athena."

I loved my hometown, but I would be hard-pressed to name enough local sights or activities that would interest many tourists. We did have a number of historic homes from the antebellum era, and a few were open to the public. Nothing like the spring pilgrimages, as they were called, held every year in Natchez and Holly Springs, though.

"I'm sure local business owners would love that," I said. "I'll be curious to hear about the mayor's plan."

"I'll tell you all about it tomorrow." Sean got up to drop his two beer bottles in the recycling bin. "Gotta get a move on, Dad. See you later." As he walked past, he gave my shoulder a quick squeeze.

As the sound of my son's footsteps faded away, I let the quiet of the kitchen settle around me. I could hear Diesel purring and the ticking of the wall clock, but otherwise there was blessed calm. I sat and enjoyed the peace for several minutes. Then I decided it was time to eat.

I still had half the casserole from last night and a bit of salad that would be fine for my dinner. There was some more of the boiled chicken for Diesel. While the two of us enjoyed our meal, Sean popped back through the kitchen on his way to meet Alexandra. He looked distinguished and handsome in his black suit, white shirt, and dark red tie, I thought. Every inch the successful young professional. I was proud of my accomplished son, but I didn't tell him. I knew he would only squirm with embarrassment, so I simply smiled and bade him good night.

Diesel and I were halfway up the stairs when the doorbell rang. I had an uneasy feeling that if I went down and opened the door, it wouldn't be to good news. I was tempted to ignore it and take refuge in my bedroom, but the adult in me prevailed.

I turned and clumped back down the stairs. I peered out the peephole. There was still enough daylight left that I could see who stood on the doorstep.

I felt my blood pressure start to rise as I opened the door.

FOURTEEN

"Evening, Marie." I stood in the doorway and glared down at her upturned face. "What do you want?"

From the wild gleam in the woman's eyes, I knew I was in trouble. She put her head down and butted me in the stomach. Hard.

I stumbled back and almost tripped over Diesel. I managed to step around him. He darted up the stairs while I turned to face my attacker.

"Why did you do that, woman? Are you insane?" I rubbed the spot where her head had connected with my midriff. "I have a good mind to call the police and charge you with assault."

"You already set the police on me." Her pitch rose with every syllable. "I could kill you for what you've done to me. Why do you hate me? What have I ever done to *you*?"

To my dismay she broke into wild sobs. Tears rolled down her face. She stood there, arms hanging down listlessly, and continued to cry. Despite my anger at her attack, I felt a sneaking sympathy for her distress. I stepped around her to close the door, then came back to where she could see me.

"What happened?" I asked in a gentle tone.

Her chest heaved as she struggled to regain enough composure to respond to me. "The police showed up at my house this afternoon and accused me of theft. That's what happened. Then they tore my house apart looking for the diaries. You were responsible for it—I know you were—so don't try to deny it." Suddenly she collapsed in a seated heap on the floor and started sobbing again.

I knelt by her. I was afraid to touch her because the good Lord only knew how she would react.

"Marie, I'm sorry for your distress," I said. "I did report the theft of the diaries, and naturally I had to give the authorities the names of anyone I knew who had expressed interest in them. I didn't do it out of malice, I swear to you. It was simply the truth."

"It was humiliating." Her voice was so low I barely made out the words. The volume grew as she continued to speak. "Never in my life have I been so embarrassed. I'll be a laughingstock on campus because of this. And on top of everything else, the diaries have disappeared. Now I'll never get to work on them, and I won't get tenure."

"Did you steal the diaries?" I asked her. Time for a tougher approach, I thought. Maybe that would force her to see sense, if anything would.

She glared at me, her expression full of loathing. "No, I did not. I've never stolen anything in my life."

"Then stop acting like a drama queen trying to hide her guilt." I stood and extended a hand. "Get up off the floor and come into the kitchen with me. I'll give you coffee or something stronger, and we'll talk about this."

Her eyes narrowed as she stared at me, then at my hand. After a long moment, she grasped my hand, and I helped her get to her feet.

"How about brandy?" She sounded hoarse now from the crying and carrying on.

"I have some," I said. Might as well have some myself, I decided. I glanced up at the stairs, but there was no sign of the cat. Diesel was probably under my bed. He would be okay until I had Marie calmed down completely and out of the house.

Marie pulled out a chair and plopped down. Her short legs barely touched the floor. I found the brandy in the cabinet and poured some for both of us.

"Thanks," she said in a less than gracious tone before she knocked it back in one go.

I held up the bottle, and she nodded. This time she had a sip and set the glass down. "I'm waiting," she said. "Talk. I want you to explain to me how you were careless enough to let someone walk in and steal those diaries."

I set the brandy bottle down before I was tempted to slug her with it.

"Chief Ford examined the lock on the office door," I said as evenly as I could. "He believes the thief picked it. I always lock the door whenever I leave the office, even for a few minutes. I'm sure I did that today when I left for lunch."

Marie looked skeptical. "Why didn't you have them somewhere more secure, like a safe?"

"For one thing," I said, "I don't have a safe in the archive. I could have put them in the storage room next door. It has a better lock on it, one that's difficult to get into." I shrugged. "But there was no reason to. I had no reason to think someone would steal the diaries. They aren't that valuable."

"I guess you're right," Marie said. "At least about locking them up. They *are* valuable, though, extremely valuable. Not in terms of money, of course. To me they're priceless."

"I can understand that they *could* be valuable to your research," I said. "What I don't get is why you're so convinced they *will* be. You don't know there's anything interesting or worthwhile to a historian in them."

Marie looked down at her hands. "No, I don't know for sure, but those diaries are still the best shot I have at finally getting tenure." Her shoulders sagged. "And now they're gone. It isn't fair."

She didn't look at me once while she spoke. Even now she appeared to be absorbed by her hands. I figured that meant she was lying about something. But what? I suspected that she had knowledge—just how, I didn't know—of the contents of the diaries. Either that or she was gambling against less than convincing odds.

"What is it you're not telling me?" I asked.

Her head shot up, her expression indignant. She opened her mouth to speak, then clamped it shut while I stared hard at her.

"Come on, you do know something," I said. "Tell me."

She took a deep breath. "You might as well know." Her tone was grudging. "I can't say specifically what is in those diaries, but I do have a source that gives some indication. According to the source, Rachel Afton Long had a lot to say about everything happening around her. Including less than savory things about the great families of Athena."

Family scandals. That could explain a few things, I thought.

93

"What is the source?" I asked, though I had an inkling of the answer.

When Marie didn't respond right away, I continued. "Your source wouldn't be Angeline McCarthy Long's memoir of her grandmother-in-law, would it?"

"You think you know everything, don't you?" The venom in her tone didn't surprise me. "Yes, that is my source. Angeline is pretty vague about some of the details, but she hints at an awful lot. Particularly about the juicy stuff. I figure she's talking about things that happened during the war. Things that some of the families around here would just as soon not have come to light."

This could explain why the copy of the memoir in the library went missing, I thought. Tomorrow one of my priorities would be searching the Long collection in the archive for a copy of that little book.

"I ran across the memoir in the online catalog," I said. "I also found out that it has been declared lost, as of yesterday. You wouldn't know anything about that, would you?"

"Why should I know anything about it?" Marie practically spit the words at me. "I told you I am not a thief. I would never steal a book from the library, and if you try to tell anyone that I did, I'll sue you for everything you have."

I held up my hands in a placatory gesture. "I didn't say you stole the book. I simply asked whether you knew anything about its disappearance. For example, when was the last time you used it?"

Marie didn't appear mollified by my words, but she answered my question. "Four or five years ago. I had mostly forgotten about it until I overheard that dinosaur Newkirk talking about the diaries with the departmental secretary a couple days ago."

"Do you know of any other copies of the memoir? Do the Longs have one?"

Marie shook her head. "I don't think so. Not that many were printed to begin with, and who knows what happened to them over the years. You're the librarian. Why are you asking me? Don't you have some database you can check?"

"Of course," I said. "And I will check. I'm also going to talk to the mayor, because I'm beginning to think that little book might be an important clue as to what the heck is going on with the missing diaries. The sooner we can find another copy and analyze what the granddaughter-in-law wrote, the better."

"If the diaries are destroyed, there won't be much point." Marie sighed. "I'm afraid we'll never see them again."

"That's possible," I replied. "Try to remain positive, though. The authorities will find them, and you'll be able to complete your research and write your book."

Marie didn't appear convinced. "As long as you were giving names to the police, did you tell them about that horrible writer?"

"If you're referring to Kelly Grimes, yes, I did. What is the beef between you two, anyway?"

"I can't stand her. She lied to me and used me. She has no ethics at all." Marie grew red in the face. "If she ever steps in front of my car, I'll flatten her."

"What did she do?"

"If you must know," Marie said, "she interviewed me a couple of years ago for a feature article she was writing on feminist studies at the college. She'd been a student of mine for a semester before that. I gave her several hours of my time near the end of the semester when I already had more than enough to do, and then she ended up barely mentioning my name. Instead she wrote about that arrogant Geraldine Comstock in the English department."

"That wasn't fair," I said. "I don't blame you for being angry with her." I did have to wonder, though, how much Marie's unpleasant personality and self-absorption influenced the outcome of the article.

"If anybody stole the diaries," Marie said, "it was her." She called Grimes a pretty nasty name. "I've got a good mind to track her down and beat the truth out of her."

"I wouldn't advise that," I said, a little alarmed. Marie was crazy enough to do it, but I didn't know how I could stop her, other than by calling the police.

She stood. "Thanks for the brandy. I've got work to do." She stalked off in the direction of the front door. Before I made it out of the kitchen I heard the door slam behind her.

That was the last time I saw her. Early the next morning Kanesha Berry called to tell me that Marie had been run down and killed by a car in the street in front of her house.

FIFTEEN

IIIIIIIIIIIIIIIIIIIIIIIIIIIIIIIIIIII

I was only half-done with my breakfast when my cell phone rang that morning. I saw Kanesha Berry's name and number flash on the screen. Kanesha almost never called me with good news. When she told me Marie Steverton was dead, I couldn't take it in at first.

"What happened?" I asked. I stared at my plate, my appetite gone. Diesel warbled anxiously because he could still smell bacon. I patted his head absentmindedly as I listened to Kanesha's reply.

"Neighbor across the street heard a crash outside around two this morning. Ran downstairs and out onto the front porch. He saw the body in the street and taillights disappearing way down at the end of the street. He immediately checked on Ms. Steverton, but there was nothing he could do."

"What was she doing out in the street at that time of the morning?" I couldn't understand any of this. Why would someone want to kill Marie? Despite her enormously irritating personality, and my own jokes about batting her over the head, I couldn't fathom her murder. I couldn't believe it was an accident, either.

"We have no idea yet," Kanesha said. "How well did you know her?"

"We weren't friends," I said. "I knew her, of course, from activities on campus, and a couple of years ago she did a few days' research in the archive." I paused for a sip of coffee—my throat went suddenly dry and tight. "The past few days, however, I had several encounters with her over those diaries that are missing."

"The ones Mayor Long gave you," Kanesha said. "Still no sign of them, by the way."

"That's so frustrating," I said. I wanted to ask whether anyone had searched Kelly Grimes's home—or Jasper Singletary's, for that matter—but I didn't want to poke the bear too much. Kanesha could definitely resemble a grumpy bear on occasion. She would tell me only as much as she deemed necessary.

"I'll need to talk to you in-depth about the events of the past few days," Kanesha said. "There has to be some connection between Dr. Steverton's murder and the theft of the diaries. Will you be in your office at the archive today?"

"Yes, from about eight thirty on. Come anytime you want."

"I'll see you about nine." Kanesha rang off.

"That my daughter on the phone?" Azalea asked when she walked back into the room with a load of freshly washed and dried dish towels. "Reason I ask is you got that look on your face you usually get when she calls you and reads the riot act."

I had to suppress a smile. My relationship with Kanesha had been one fraught with conflict, though recently Kanesha tended to be more at ease with me.

"Yes, that was Kanesha," I said. "Calling to share some terrible news." I told my housekeeper about the hit-and-run murder of Marie Steverton.

Azalea set the dish towels on the counter, closed her eyes, and said a short prayer under her breath for Marie. "That poor lady," she said aloud to me when she finished. The simple dignity of her action touched me deeply.

"Yes, it's horrible," I said after a moment. "She was one of the most irritating women I have ever met, but I wouldn't have wished that on her." I shook my head. "I pray her soul can find peace."

"She's in the Lord's hands now," Azalea said. She picked up the dish towels and placed them in the drawer where they resided.

Diesel, not pleased at being ignored while I talked on the phone and then with Azalea, stood on his hind legs beside me and reached onto my plate with one paw to steal a piece of bacon.

I caught his paw a second before he got hold of the bacon. "No, bad kitty," I told him in a firm tone, one I knew he would recognize. "You do not take food off my plate. Bad kitty."

I released his paw, and he stared at me for a moment. He warbled sadly, as if in apology, and I patted him on the head. I couldn't give him the bacon now, because I didn't want him to think he could act badly, be penitent, and then still get his way. He was like a five-year-old child sometimes.

"It's okay," I told him. "But you'll have to be satisfied with your cat food this morning." He trotted off to the utility room, no doubt in search of sustenance from his food bowls.

I pushed back my chair and stood. I gulped down the rest of my coffee. "Azalea, I'm sorry, but I can't finish my breakfast. Not really hungry anymore."

"I understand, Mr. Charlie," she said. "You going to come home for lunch today? I reckon by then you'll be feeling better and want something good to eat."

I smiled. Azalea was always determined to keep me well fed. "Yes, Diesel and I will be home for lunch, as far as I know. If anything comes up to prevent it, I'll give you a call."

Ten minutes later Diesel and I left the house to walk to the college. We made it to the archive right on the dot of eight thirty. Melba wasn't in when we went by her office, and I hoped I could put off talking to her until later in the day. Going through it all with Kanesha would be exhausting enough.

I felt sick at heart when I unlocked the archive door. The replacement lock hadn't been installed yet, but I didn't figure the thief would be back for anything more. She—or he—was interested only in the diaries, I was sure.

I flipped the light switch, then bent to release Diesel from his leash and harness. He went straight to the window and climbed onto the sill. I headed for my desk, and my eyes lit on four books lying on it.

I stopped, unable to believe what I saw there.

One of the four volumes of Rachel Long's diaries without its archival box.

My legs trembled for a moment, and I couldn't move from the spot. Then I gained control of myself and walked around the desk to sink into my chair. I continued to stare at the book.

My eyes strayed to the shelf. The other three volumes sat there as if they'd never been gone, but without the archival boxes I'd made for them.

This made no sense. Why would the thief steal the diaries one day, only to return them less than twenty-four hours later?

My mind felt stuck in a groove, with that thought going round and round. Then I realized that it was possible that the thief didn't bring them back. Some other person might have found them and decided to return them, for reasons unknown.

I shook my head. Either way, it was bizarre.

What would Kanesha say when I told her?

Thinking of Kanesha made me realize something that had my stomach twisting in knots.

The diaries were evidence in a crime. That meant Kanesha would take them away for testing. Would the technicians who examined them treat them with the care they deserved?

For a moment I was tempted to hide the diaries and not tell Kanesha they'd been returned. That way I could go ahead and start scanning them and find out what was in them that caused all this brouhaha. When I finished, I could say I found them back on the shelves.

Then I realized that wouldn't work, for two reasons. The first, and most important, was that I couldn't bring myself to do it. I couldn't lie to Kanesha like that. The second was that, once the lock was changed, it would be extremely difficult for someone to get into the office to put them back. There wouldn't be a way around that inconvenient fact that I could see.

I checked my watch—already three minutes past nine. Kanesha ought to be here any second now. I sat back in my chair and tried to relax. Hearing the purring cat behind my head helped. Happy to be in one of his favorite spots, Diesel rumbled away as he lay there and stared out the window.

A few minutes later Kanesha walked in. "Morning, Charlie."

I returned her greeting, then said, "You're not going to believe this." I gestured toward the book on my desk. "The diaries are back."

Kanesha stared at me as if she thought I'd lost my mind. She strode forward until she stood less than an inch from the other side of my desk. She looked from me to the book on my desk a couple of times.

"You've got all four of them?" she asked.

I nodded. "The other three are on the shelf there." I pointed to them. "They were in archival boxes when they were taken, but they came back without them."

Kanesha shook her head. "This is the craziest dang thing I've ever seen." She pulled out her cell phone and punched in a number. After a few moments she identified herself and then gave instructions for retrieval of the diaries for forensic examination. Call completed, she put away the cell phone and found a chair.

"I know you have to take these as evidence," I said as I resumed my own seat, "but they really have to be handled with extreme care."

"I understand that," Kanesha said with a faint note of impatience. "The state crime lab is used to handling all kinds of fragile objects. I'll be sure they understand the importance of the diaries, and I'm sure they'll take all due care with them."

That didn't completely reassure me, but I had no say in the matter. "How long do you think they'll take to complete their examination?"

Kanesha shrugged. "Ordinarily it could take several weeks to a few months. They're always busy. But the mayor might be able to call in a few favors and get them first in line. She knows a lot of influential people."

Political clout was a good thing, I reflected, when used for a good reason.

"Helpful that they already have your prints on record." Kanesha grinned.

I decided to ignore that little sally. I was about to ask her a question when I heard a knock at the open door. I glanced past Kanesha to see Lucinda Long in the doorway, her purse on one arm and a canvas bag hanging from the other.

"Good morning, Your Honor," I said. "Please come in. I have some news I think you'll be happy about. Deputy Berry and I were just discussing it, in fact."

The mayor moved forward. "Good morning, Ms. Berry. I've got news of my own that I think will make *you* happy, Mr. Harris." She brandished the canvas bag. "I've found another volume of Rachel Long's diaries."

SIXTEEN

||||||||||||||||||||||||||||||||||||||||

Diesel jumped down from the windowsill to go sidle up to the mayor. Kanesha rose from her chair, and I did, too, as soon as I could gather my jumbled thoughts enough to do so.

"Another volume," I said. "That's exciting."

"I thought you'd be pleased," Mayor Long said as she patted the cat's head. "With the loss of the other four, and not knowing if—and when—we might get them back, this is truly lucky."

She stepped forward, and Kanesha moved to one side. The mayor's eyes lit on the diary on my desk. She stared at Kanesha, then at me. "That looks like one of the missing diaries."

"When I came in this morning," I said, "I found them on the shelves here, as if they had never disappeared."

The mayor shook her head back and forth several times, obviously surprised. "What in the blue blazes is going on here?"

Kanesha motioned for Mrs. Long to take the chair she had vacated, and the mayor nodded. She made herself comfortable, her handbag in her lap. She leaned forward to place the canvas tote and its contents on the front edge of my desk. Diesel, evidently convinced the petting was done, went back to his spot in the window behind me.

Kanesha pulled another chair near the mayor and sat while I resumed my own seat. I was about to speak when Kanesha caught my eye. She shook her head slightly, so I stayed quiet.

"Your Honor," Kanesha said, "I have some news I need to share with you. Pretty shocking news. I was planning to call you this morning after I finished with Mr. Harris, but we might as well talk now."

Mrs. Long's hands tightened on her handbag. Her expression blank, she said, "Go ahead."

"I'm sorry to inform you that Dr. Marie Steverton has died," Kanesha said.

"Dead? What on earth happened? I just talked to her last night." The mayor sounded bewildered.

"She was the victim of a hit-and-run in the street in front of her house," Kanesha said. "A neighbor was wakened by the noise around two a.m. and went out to investigate. He found her, but she was beyond help by then."

"How horrible," the mayor whispered. "What in the name of all that's holy was Marie doing outside at that time of the morning?"

"We are investigating that," Kanesha said. "At present we don't know what would have brought her outside then." Her gaze focused on the tote bag on my desk. Her tone sharpened when she spoke. "Your Honor, where did you get that bag?"

"The bag?" Once again the mayor appeared at sea. "I've had it for some time. I picked it up years ago at a college reunion. Why do you ask?"

"We found one like it, with that same emblem on it, in the street near Dr. Steverton," Kanesha said. "It was larger than yours. It was also empty, although there were traces of something that had been inside it. We're going to have it examined thoroughly, of course."

"This gets weirder by the minute," I said.

"Marie and I were at Sweet Briar together," the mayor said. "It's no surprise she had a bag with the crest on it. But why did she have it with her then?"

"That's what we aim to find out," Kanesha said. "I'm hoping the trace evidence inside will tell us. Your Honor, do you know if Dr. Steverton has any family that we need to contact?"

Mrs. Long shook her head. "As far as I'm aware, no, she didn't have any close relatives. The college may have more information for you."

"I'll be checking with them," Kanesha said. "You mentioned you talked to Dr. Steverton last night. Can you tell me about that conversation, and when it took place?" She pulled out her notebook and a pen.

"Your Honor, would you like some water? Or something else?" I asked. Mrs. Long looked a little wan to me.

The mayor shook her head. "No, thank you, Mr. Harris." She turned to Kanesha. "I'll do my best, but it really was a brief conversation." She paused for a moment, her brow wrinkled. "It was around ten thirty, I think. To be honest, I was a bit irritated with her for calling so late, because I was getting ready for bed after a long and tiring day."

"Did she want something in particular?" Kanesha asked when the mayor paused.

"I was so tired by then I could hardly concentrate," the mayor said. "Marie had a habit of jabbering away without giving a person time to think, much less get a word in edgewise. When she slowed down a bit, I could finally figure out what she was talking about." She shook her head. "She kept asking me if I thought the diaries were worth as much as fifty thousand dollars. I told her I had no idea, and then I asked her why she wanted to know."

"What did she say?" Kanesha asked.

"She just kept going on about a reward, and how that might get them back. *You can afford it, Lucinda.* She must have said that ten times. *Surely they're worth that much to your husband and son.* She also said that several times. She sounded excited, and I got tired of listening to her. I didn't even get a chance to tell her we'd found another volume of the diary." She sighed heavily. "I finally told her I'd think about it. I had to hang up on her, because then she started on about maybe the diaries being worth even more than fifty thousand."

I knew Marie Steverton had pinned her hopes of tenure on the diaries and was no doubt desperate to get them back. How—and why—did she come up with such a crack-brained scheme? I couldn't imagine that the thief took them in hopes of extorting a reward for returning them. That was crack-brained as well.

Then another thought struck me. What if Marie had stolen the diaries and then hit on the plan to extort money from the Longs?

I glanced at Kanesha, but as usual I couldn't read her expression. I felt diffident about mentioning the idea in front of the mayor. I would broach the subject to Kanesha later in private, if she didn't bring it up first with the mayor now.

"Did you think more about the idea of a reward?" Kanesha asked.

"Frankly, no," the mayor said. "I think Marie was drinking

107

when she called me. That fast talking was usually a sign of it. She would go on these binges sometimes when she was upset or worried and start calling people. When she sobered up she didn't often remember making the calls." She shook her head. "So I figured she would have forgotten about such a foolish idea this morning."

"Do you think it was possible she took the diaries herself?" Kanesha asked. "Do you have any idea whether she needed money badly?"

Mrs. Long stared at the handbag in her lap for a few moments. When she raised her head, she said, "I suppose it's possible. But I find it hard to believe Marie would do such a thing. As to whether she needed money badly, I really have no idea. She never approached me for money before." She focused on her handbag again.

"I have to consider all possibilities," Kanesha said. "Can you think of anyone who had a grudge against Dr. Steverton? Someone who intended her harm?"

Mrs. Long shook her head. "The good Lord only knows how Marie could rile people up. She never learned the value of tact and diplomacy. That cost her a number of jobs, I'm afraid. But I can't see anyone being angry enough with her to run her down in a car." The mayor looked wan again.

I couldn't blame her. I found that mental image unsettling myself. Poor Marie Steverton, I thought. A painful way to die.

"Thank you for your time, Your Honor," Kanesha said. "Now, about the diaries that have been returned."

"That is just as hard to believe as someone wanting to kill Marie," the mayor said. "Why take them and then bring them back less than twenty-four hours later? It doesn't make sense."

"No, it doesn't," Kanesha said. "Until we find out who took them and who returned them, we won't know what the motivation was. The problem at the moment is, I need to take them as evidence. They'll need to be examined for anything that could answer our questions. Obviously, Mr. Harris here wants them safely back in the archive as soon as possible. I wondered whether you could talk to some of your contacts and see if the state crime lab can make them a priority."

The mayor looked troubled. "I hate to see the diaries go anywhere, but obviously I understand the need to have them examined. I know a couple of people in Jackson who might be able to help." She stood. "I'll see what I can do. For now, at least, Mr. Harris can work on the fifth volume."

"If you don't mind my asking, Your Honor, where did you find it?" I thought it odd that all five volumes weren't together when she made the first discovery.

"Not at all," Mrs. Long said. "I was curious about the trunk Beck found the others in, and I had a little time after dinner. So I went up to the attic and dug around in it a bit more. I discovered there was a false bottom in the trunk, and this fifth volume was in it."

"I wonder why it was hidden and separated from the others." I stared at the tote bag. Could this fifth volume be the reason there was such interest in the diaries in the first place? Did it contain the elusive secrets that lay behind this whole bizarre situation?

SEVENTEEN

||||||||||||||||||||||||||||||||||||||||||||||||||||||

I decided I was a little too prone to flights of fancy not grounded in fact. There was no telling who originally placed this one volume in the false bottom or what the motivation was. Because of everything that had occurred in the past couple of days, I was overthinking this.

"Thank you, Your Honor," I said. "This volume will be stored safely in the more secure room next door when I leave tonight."

"Excellent," Mrs. Long said. "Now I really have to be on my way. I'm already late for a meeting."

Kanesha added her farewells to mine. Once the mayor was gone we sat again.

"Are they going to do anything about the lock on this door?" Kanesha asked.

"I'm sure they will now," I said. "I think they ought to put cameras up here, too. Probably nothing like this will ever happen again, but it sure would be nice to have the added security."

"I'd be willing to bet Chief Ford has already mentioned that to your boss," Kanesha replied. "This building is way overdue for a security makeover."

I tried to keep the bitterness out of my tone when I spoke, but I doubt I was successful. "Yes, it is overdue, but the college administration has different priorities. If it were something involving the football team, you can bet it would have been addressed long ago. A piddly little thing like an archive with rare or irreplaceable documents doesn't rate beside a sports team."

Kanesha frowned. "You'd think they'd get a better return on their money on the field, if they're spending so much of it on sports."

Our college football team hadn't had a winning season in three years now, and the alumni were not happy. The administration kept shifting money to scholarships for athletes in an attempt to lure gifted ones to Athena. So far it didn't seem to have worked all that well.

"You're right about that," I said. Time to get this conversation back on track. "I'll pack the diaries in a box. I'm sure you don't want to wait until I make new boxes for them."

"No, we don't have time for that." Kanesha nodded. "Use those cotton gloves, and touch as little of the surfaces of the books and those boxes as possible. I doubt we're going to find any fingerprints, but you never know."

"I'll be careful." Her instructions irritated me a bit because by now, I thought, she surely ought to realize I knew enough to be careful. I found an empty box in the supply closet and brought it back, along with the four large manila envelopes the mayor had used to contain the diaries before.

I slipped each book into an envelope with great care, then sealed the metal clasp on the envelope and placed it in the box.

When I finished, I said, "I'm going to pray that the techs at the crime lab will be that careful as well."

"The mayor will see to it," Kanesha said. "She knows the right people to make sure of it, even though she didn't sound all that confident talking to us."

"Okay," I replied. I really hated to see the diaries leave my office again, but I knew it had to be done. "You know, we got sidetracked right away with the sudden reappearance, and then the mayor coming in with her surprise. You never did ask me what you wanted to know about Marie."

"I hadn't forgotten." Kanesha settled back in her chair. "Take me through any encounter you had with Dr. Steverton during the past couple of days."

I took a moment to marshal my thoughts. Then I launched into my recital of events. There was an interlude of about three minutes when Kanesha's deputy arrived to pick up the four diaries. Once he left with the box, I resumed my narrative.

Kanesha did not ask questions until I finished. I appreciated that about her. She was patient and listened, rather than interrupting and perhaps making me forget something.

"I'll be interviewing Ms. Grimes sooner rather than later," she said. "Obviously she and Dr. Steverton were at cross purposes with each other."

"Yes, they were," I said. I recounted my experiences with Kelly Grimes, the ones that didn't directly involve poor Marie. "She impressed me as being as eager as Marie to get hold of the diaries. Did you search her house?"

"Apartment," Kanesha said. "We did and turned up nothing. Based on our searches, I had to conclude that if either woman took those diaries, they managed to hide them real well. Maybe in another location."

"What about Jasper Singletary?"

"According to his campaign manager, he was at a meeting in Jackson at three o'clock. He made it back to Athena around ten last night." Kanesha shrugged. "I have an appointment with him at ten thirty this morning." She checked her watch. "Twenty-five minutes from now."

"In order to be in Jackson for a meeting at three, he would have to have left Athena no later than one," I said. "If he left Jackson around eight he could make it back here by ten, I suppose."

"Yeah, I'd worked all that out myself." Kanesha stood.

"Sorry," I said. "Bad habit of thinking aloud."

"Sure," Kanesha said. "I'll probably come back to you with more questions after I've dug a little deeper into all this. In the meantime, if you find anything pertinent in that diary, let me know."

Diesel meowed and a moment later I felt a paw on my shoulder. I could hear Kanesha's boots on the marble stairs as she descended.

"What's up, boy?" I turned my chair to face the cat on the windowsill. "You want to visit Melba, don't you?"

Diesel meowed again.

"I bet she'll be here in the next two minutes. You just wait and see." I knew Melba's curiosity would be at fever pitch by now. She probably would have seen Kanesha come or go—the mayor as well. I was sure she had already heard about Marie's death.

I turned back to face the doorway. *One . . . two . . . three . . .* I made it to *seventeen* before she popped up.

"What the heck is going on around here?" she asked as she

took the chair in front of my desk. "Hey, Diesel, come give Melba some sugar."

Diesel reached her before she got out the last few words. While she cuddled with the cat, I responded to her question.

"I found the missing diaries in my office this morning. No idea who had them or why they reappeared."

Melba continued loving on Diesel while I told her the rest. As I suspected, she had already heard about Marie's death. A friend of hers owned a house two doors down from the neighbor who found Marie in the street, and the whole neighborhood was abuzz with the story. Melba's friend called her first thing this morning to share the terrible news.

We chatted for a few more minutes about the unfortunate Marie; then I told Melba gently that I was anxious to start work on the one volume of the diary I had available to me.

Melba grinned at me. "I guess I'd better scoot back downstairs before I wear out my welcome here completely." She gave the cat a couple more scratches on the head before she headed out the door.

"Thanks," I called after her.

Diesel muttered at me because Melba left. He lost his source of undivided attention, and he was not happy about it.

"Melba has to get back to work like I do," I told him. "You be good now and get back up in your spot on the window."

He stared at me for a moment before he padded around my desk and climbed back into the window. He continued to make grumbling noises, fainter and fainter, as I focused on my task.

I extracted the fifth diary volume from the mayor's tote bag. I would have to remember to return that to her at some point. After a quick examination I determined that this book was in roughly the same condition as the others. Flaky but intact leather binding, with the same issues from the iron gall ink as the previous volumes. Only about half the pages, I estimated, contained writing. The remainder of the book was blank.

Curious, I checked the first and last entries. Rachel Long had neatly dated each entry, and that was helpful. The first entry had the date of March 9, 1861. The last entry, about two-thirds of the way through the volume, was written on May 17, 1865.

If I recalled correctly, Rachel started her diary in July of 1854. To judge by the dates of this volume, it must be either the second or third of the five in terms of chronology. I wondered why a middle volume had been secreted in the trunk. I was also curious why she stopped writing in this one before she had filled it.

I had to resist the temptation to sit there and read it. The answers to many questions could lie within these pages. It would take me a little while to get used to Rachel's handwriting, but I was confident I could decipher it. I really needed to scan the pages first, however. At least if something happened to this volume, I would have the scans.

That thought caught me a bit off guard. If word got out about this fifth volume, would the person who stole the others try to take this one, too?

EIGHTEEN

||||||||||||||||||||||||||||||||||||||||||||||||||||||

Enough with the questions, I admonished myself. This fruitless speculation wouldn't achieve anything. I needed to focus on the task at hand: scanning the diary.

Once I had created a good digital copy, I could take the time to read the contents to discern whether anything in the volume had relevance to the current situation.

The overhead scanner, attached to its own computer, sat on a table against the wall near my desk. I carried the diary over and turned on the computer and the scanner. When they were ready, I positioned the book and opened it to the first page to scan.

As the scanner worked I could see the image on the computer screen. Based on the first five pages I scanned, I thought I would end up with an excellent digital copy as long as all the pages were as readable as these.

My arms tired quickly from the necessity of holding the diary volume in the correct position. I timed myself at roughly sixty seconds per page, and I decided I should probably take a short break every fifteen minutes. At this rate I could probably scan thirty to forty pages an hour. I hadn't counted the number of pages in the diary that contained writing, but I estimated there were no more than a couple hundred.

Diesel paid little attention while I worked at the scanning station. He had heard the humming noise it made enough times that it held no further interest for him. He did stir when I took my breaks and went back to my desk to check e-mail. Around eleven thirty, when I sat in front of my computer, a large paw tapped me on the shoulder and a loud meow sounded in my ear.

I laughed. "Okay, I give. I'm hungry, too. Let's go home for lunch."

The cat slid to the floor and walked over to the doorway, where he waited for me to come attach his harness and leash. I was halfway there when I remembered the diary. I said I wouldn't leave it in this office when I wasn't here. I put my cotton gloves back on, fetched the volume, and took it to the storeroom next door. The more up-to-date lock on this door should keep the diary safe until I came back to the office.

That task accomplished, we headed home for lunch.

We found a welcome surprise in the kitchen. Laura sat at the table, busily chatting with Azalea. She broke off their conversation to jump up and greet me with a hug. Diesel received scratches on the head and along his spine, and he purred with happiness.

"This is a pleasant surprise," I said. "To what do we owe the honor?"

"I have the afternoon free. No classes to teach, no appointments with students, so I thought I'd come by and visit. I was also hoping I could get Azalea to share some of her recipes with me.

Frank is a wonderful cook, but I don't think it's fair for him to have to do *all* the cooking." Laura grinned.

Azalea beamed fondly at my daughter. "Miss Laura, you know you're welcome to any old thing you want to know about how I cook. You and me can surely come up with something to surprise Mr. Frank."

"The first surprise will be that I actually made anything without burning it or undercooking it." Laura's laugh was infectious, and both Azalea and I joined in. Diesel warbled loudly, determined not to be left out of the fun.

"Mr. Charlie, you sit yourself on down there, and I'm going to have your lunch ready in a minute." Azalea stared pointedly at me, and I sat. "Miss Laura, how about you? Can I tempt you into having some of my chicken and dumplings?"

Laura groaned. "Azalea, nobody ever made better chicken and dumplings than you, so how I can I turn them down?" She sighed. "I'll just have to run a few extra miles this week, I guess."

Diesel, having heard the word *chicken*, walked over to Azalea and sat down near her. He looked up at her with his most beguiling expression and gave her a couple of plaintive meows.

Laura and I grinned, and I waited to see how Azalea would respond.

Azalea put her hands on her hips and stared down at the cat. "You ought to be ashamed. You so fat already. You think I'm going to waste my good food on you." She shook her head.

Diesel meowed weakly. He was trying to assure her that he would expire shortly unless he had chicken.

Azalea snorted. "You are the most pitiful cat that ever I did see. I reckon maybe I can let you have a little bit." She turned back to the stove, and I would have sworn I saw her shoulders quiver. She liked to pretend that Diesel was nothing but a nuisance, but I knew she found him more entertaining than not these days.

Diesel appeared satisfied. He left Azalea's side and transferred his adoring gaze to Laura. She petted him while we talked.

"So what's new with you, Dad?" Laura smiled archly. "Any news on the Helen Louise front?"

I shot her a look, the one I'd given her every other minute during her teenage years. "I'll pretend I didn't hear that. Actually, I've been really busy with work. I guess you probably haven't heard the news about Marie Steverton."

Laura frowned. "That name is vaguely familiar, but I can't place her right now. Who is she, and what did she do?"

"She is, or rather was, a professor in the history department. Women's history."

"Oh, *her*," Laura said with a tinge of exasperation in her tone. "She's the one Frank told me about. He said there was a woman in the history department who had a fit when the college players put on *The Taming of the Shrew*. She even went to the president to try to get it stopped." She paused. "Hold on—you said *was*. What happened?"

"She was killed in a hit-and-run accident early this morning," I said.

"How awful," Laura said. "I heard she drove people nuts, but to think that she died that way. So sad."

"The worst part is, it probably wasn't an accident."

"Another murder?" Laura's eyebrows rose. "Dad, don't tell me you're involved in this."

"Don't start on that," I said, perhaps a bit defensively. I was still sensitive from the ribbing Sean had given me. "If you'll sit there and be quiet, I'll tell you all about what's been going on."

Laura nodded. "I will."

Before I could start my recital, Azalea served us both steaming bowls of chicken and dumplings. I was ravenous, and I remembered that I had eaten only about a third of my breakfast this morning. In between mouthfuls of the delicious food, I gave Laura the salient facts about my encounters with Marie.

By the time I finished, I realized I had put away two bowls of chicken and dumplings to Laura's one. Azalea rewarded Diesel with a small plate of boiled chicken breast, enough to keep him happy for an hour or two before the starvation pangs set in again.

"Those diaries must be hot stuff," Laura said. "Maybe Athena after the Civil War was a nineteenth-century Peyton Place."

"There's no telling what's in there," I said. "The diaries are certainly a hot property. I'm praying, though, nobody else gets hurt because of them."

"Especially *you*." Laura shot me a stern look. "You be careful while you're working on them. I don't want to get a call from somebody telling me you're lying on a bed in the emergency room because you've been conked over the head."

"I'll do my best to avoid your having to get that call," I said. I pushed back my chair. "I need to get back to work. I want to finish scanning the one volume I have by the end of the day."

"You just be careful, Mr. Charlie," Azalea said. "Miss Laura's right. Ain't going to do nobody no good if you end up in the hospital over some old books."

Laura gave me a triumphant smile.

"Yes, ma'am, I'll be careful." Sometimes Azalea made me feel like I was ten years old. I knew she was fond of me in her own way, but I was over fifty, after all. "Come on, Diesel, let's go."

Diesel, still seated next to Laura's chair, looked back and forth between my daughter and me. I could tell he was torn. He loved Laura and didn't see her often enough these days.

Laura understood. She rubbed the cat's head. "You'd better go with Dad, boy. I'd love to stay here the rest of the afternoon and play with you, but I have to leave in about an hour. You go on, and I'll see you again soon."

The cat chirped a couple of times before he got up and walked over to me. "Good boy," I told him. I reattached his leash. Laura rose to give me a hug and a kiss, and I bade her and Azalea good-bye.

Ten minutes later I unlocked the office door and let the cat inside and unleashed him. Then I went to the storage room next door to retrieve the diary.

I woke up the computer and scanner and set to work. I really wanted to finish this by the end of my workday, around five o'clock, if not before.

I didn't know how much time had passed when a voice from the doorway interrupted my concentration.

"Come in, Ms. Grimes," I said. "I'm glad you're here."

"Oh, really, that's a switch." She laughed as she approached me. Her eyes widened when she realized what I was scanning. "You got them back? That's amazing."

I closed the book and stood. "I did get the diaries back. I found them here when I came to work this morning." I ushered her toward the chair in front of my desk. "They are now in the custody of the sheriff's department, on their way to the state crime lab for examination."

"That sucks," she said, obviously disappointed. "How long will they keep them?"

"I don't know," I said. "It could take weeks."

Ms. Grimes swore, and I shot her a look.

"Sorry," she said, although she didn't sound all that penitent. She jerked her head in the direction of the scanner. "So what's that you're working on over there? Some other project?"

"No, it's a fifth volume of the diary that the mayor found last night. She brought it over this morning."

"When can I have a look at it?"

"I don't know," I said. "In light of everything that's happened, I'll have to discuss that with the mayor and the sheriff's department."

Ms. Grimes scowled at me. "You're deliberately trying to keep me from looking at those diaries. Why are you making this so difficult?"

I heard Diesel shifting around on the windowsill behind me. He had picked up on the tension, and it made him uneasy. I turned to rub his head for a moment in reassurance. Then I faced the writer again and did my best to keep my rapidly escalating temper from erupting.

"Tell you what, Ms. Grimes. I'll make a bargain with you. You stop lying to me, and maybe I'll be a little more cooperative."

NINETEEN

||||||||||||||||||||||||||||||||||||||||||||||||||||||

Kelly Grimes's face reddened. "How dare you accuse me of lying." She jumped up from her chair and leaned forward over the desk.

I didn't flinch. I regarded her calmly as I replied, "I dare because you lied to me about being secretly engaged to Beck Long. You might be engaged, but if you are, I'd bet it's to Jasper Singletary."

That took her by surprise. The red faded, and she stepped back. "I don't know what you mean."

"Sit down, Ms. Grimes," I said. "I'm not in a mood to lollygag around over this. Marie Steverton was murdered early this morning, and I'm sure you know that, what with you being a writer."

Ms. Grimes jutted her chin out, and her eyes flashed fire. "I don't appreciate the tone of that remark, *Mr.* Harris. I'm a damn good writer."

"What about journalistic ethics?" I asked. "Aren't you supposed to be fair and honest in gathering information? I looked that up, by the way, on the Society of Professional Journalists website."

The writer stared at me, evidently unable to frame a reply.

"I want to know why you and Jasper Singletary are so interested in the contents of a diary kept by a woman who's been dead for over a hundred years. If it had anything to do with the murder of Marie Steverton, I'm sure the sheriff's department will be interested, too."

Behind me I heard Diesel muttering. I knew he didn't like the tone of my voice. I hated for him to be upset, but I was determined to get through to this foolish young woman. While I waited for her response, I turned my chair toward the window and let Diesel climb into my lap. He sat with his body against my chest, his head rubbing up against my chin. I could feel him start to calm down.

Together we turned back to face Ms. Grimes. "Well?" I said.

The writer sighed. She looked tired. "Okay, so I lied to you about being engaged to Beck Long. I wouldn't have done it, but Jasper asked me to help him. He's feeling desperate because Beck has all the advantages in the race."

"Such as?" I asked. I already knew the answer, but I wanted to hear what she had to say, and how she said it.

She cast me a glance of loathing. "You can't be that naive. You grew up here, right? You know the Long family's had a lock on politics in this town for several generations." She laughed, a bitter, unpleasant sound. "They're corrupt from decades of sitting in power, getting elected just because they have good looks, a lot of money, and facile tongues."

"What does Jasper Singletary have?" I asked.

"For one thing, he graduated third in his law school class. Beck Long barely scraped through. If his daddy hadn't pledged a lot of money to the school, he would have failed. Jasper is smart, Mr. Harris. We need intelligent men like him in our government."

I had heard stories about Beck Long's lack of academic

prowess, so I wasn't surprised to hear Grimes bring up his law school performance. He wouldn't be the first young man to skate by on good looks, money, and a family name.

"If Beck Long gets elected," Ms. Grimes continued in a heated tone, "it'll just be more of the same. Jasper wants to lead this state forward, and he deserves a shot."

Her passionate loyalty impressed me, but I wasn't ready to concede anything. We still hadn't hit the root of the issue.

"I'll take that under consideration," I said as Diesel nestled closer to me. I had to be careful not to get cat hair in my mouth when I talked. "Are you engaged to him?"

Ms. Grimes's shoulders slumped. "Yes, we're engaged, but he wants to keep it private." Her tone sounded a bit resentful, and I suspected she wasn't happy about being kept in the background.

"Why is your fiancé so interested in Rachel Long's diaries? What can possibly be in them that could help him in a race against Beck Long?"

"That's not for me to say," the writer said sharply. "Jasper will have to tell you, but I don't know whether he will. I doubt he'll think it's any of your business."

"It might not be," I said, "but it is the business of Chief Deputy Kanesha Berry. She's in charge of the murder investigation. The diaries are linked to Marie's murder, and to my mind, anyone as interested in the diaries as you and your fiancé are has to be connected somehow."

"How did you figure out about me and Jasper?" the writer asked.

"Did you not see me sitting there in the bakery yesterday?" I asked. "I watched you on and off for quite a while. I had to wonder why a writer—a good one, that is—didn't approach either Beck Long or Jasper Singletary when such a golden opportunity presented itself."

Ms. Grimes shrugged. "You can't be badgering people all the time. Sometimes you simply have to leave them alone in a public place."

"Sure," I said. I figured even Diesel heard the ironic inflection in that one syllable. "Then there was the business of the note you left on your table for him. He did it discreetly, but I still saw him stop by the table and palm the note."

The only response I got from that was a stony expression.

"Is the bookstore a regular rendezvous spot for the two of you?" I asked. "I just happened to stop in there after I left the bakery, and I overheard a bit of your conversation. I recognized your voices. What I heard confirmed my suspicion that you're involved with him and not with Beck Long." I wanted to add that she would have a brief career if she ever went into espionage but I figured that would be twisting the knife a bit too hard.

The silence lengthened, but I had said my piece. Now it was up to Ms. Grimes.

Finally she spoke. "I can't tell you anything, not without Jasper's permission. It's up to him whether he wants to talk to you. He won't have a choice, of course, if you sic the chief deputy on him."

"She already knows there's a connection between him and the diaries," I said.

Ms. Grimes uttered another vulgar word. I pretended I hadn't heard.

She stood abruptly. "I've got to talk to Jasper. He'll be in touch." She turned to go.

"One more thing before you leave," I said. She turned back and scowled at me. "Did you take the diaries, or bring them back?"

She shook her head. "No, if I'd gotten my hands on them, I

would have kept them as long as Jasper needed them." She turned and walked out.

I stared at the empty doorway for a few moments, the cat still in my lap. I didn't, as a rule, browbeat people. I hated confrontations, but on occasion I had no choice. I didn't like being lied to, and that made me angry enough to confront Kelly Grimes.

She confirmed my notion that she was involved with Jasper Singletary and that he was interested in the contents of the diaries. Why, I still hadn't a clue. He might decide to talk to me, or he might go straight to Kanesha.

Whatever happened, I needed to get back to scanning the one volume I did have. As soon as the others came back from the state crime lab, I would work overtime if I had to in order to read them and find out what secrets they held.

I turned my chair back to the windowsill and gently urged Diesel to reclaim his spot. "It's all okay now, boy," I told him. "Everything is fine."

The cat meowed as I lifted him, and I thought for a moment he would resist. Then he climbed onto the windowsill. I gave him a couple of head rubs before I got up and went back to the scanning station to resume my project.

I took fewer breaks during the afternoon and probably strained my neck, shoulders, and back far too much, but by four thirty the scan was complete. I closed the book and set it aside. Next I e-mailed myself the files I had created during the scanning process. They were PDFs, and I could read them easily at home or here in the office.

For the next few minutes I sat and massaged my neck and shoulders as best I could. I felt the tightness of the muscles loosen enough for me to do a head roll. I figured I should stand in a hot shower for a while when I got home. That ought to further the healing process.

Before we left, I took the diary back to the storage room and made sure it was secure. Then Diesel and I were ready to go.

The afternoon was hot and sultry, typical of September. I would be happy when cooler weather arrived, and I knew Diesel would be, too. At least most of the way home was shaded by large, leafy trees.

By the time we reached our destination we were both ready for water. I could hear him lapping it up while I drank my own, standing with my back against the sink.

Azalea had left for the day—she usually finished with her chores by four at the latest—and the house and its quiet solace soothed me. Feeling more relaxed, I contemplated getting my laptop and sitting down to start reading Rachel Long's diary. After a moment's reflection, I decided more relaxation was in order before I glued myself to another computer screen. I also realized I was hungry, despite the big lunch I'd had.

I checked the fridge and was delighted to see there was plenty of leftover chicken and dumplings for dinner. The next order of business, after a second glass of water, was a hot shower.

Forty-five minutes later, muscles looser and neck- and backaches gone, I sat down to my chicken and dumplings. I found a bit more of the boiled chicken breast in the fridge. I doled it out while I ate, and Diesel was a happy kitty. We would both have to run up and down the stairs a few times to compensate for all the food, though.

I had just settled down on the den sofa with my laptop, Diesel stretched out beside me, when my cell phone rang. I glanced at the screen before I answered.

"Hey, Melba, how are you?"

"Charlie, you'll never guess who I ran into at the grocery store on the way home from work today." Excitement bubbled in her voice.

"Let me see now. Far as I know, Brad Pitt isn't in Athena these days. Neither is George Clooney. So I'm stumped." Melba often rhapsodized about the many attractions of these two movie stars, and I liked to tease her when an opportunity presented itself.

"Ha-ha," she said. "Are you going to be serious? Because if you're not, I'm not going to tell you." Her words sounded tough, but I knew she wouldn't be able to hold back whatever it was.

"I'll be good," I said. "Who did you run into?"

"Miss Eulalie Estes," Melba said. "She must be eighty if she's a day, but sharp. I hope I'm in that good of a shape when I'm her age."

I resisted the impulse to make an age-related remark. "I'm glad to hear she's doing so well. She was pretty gracious when they basically forced her to retire and gave me the archive job."

"It was hard on her," Melba said. "She loved that archive, and I'll bet she knows more about the history of Athena than anybody."

"True," I said. "Is that what y'all talked about?"

Melba snorted into the phone. "Yes, that's what we talked about. I happened to mention those diaries, and she got all excited. Said she sure would love to see them for herself."

"I'm sure she can, once they're back in the archive. As far as I know they'll be available to the public, and obviously Miss Eulalie would know how to handle them."

"I really think you ought to talk to her, Charlie," Melba said. "She's never seen those diaries, but if there's any kind of scandal involving the Longs, or anybody who was around in the Civil War, Miss Eulalie will know about it."

TWENTY

I could have slapped my own face. Why hadn't I thought about talking to Miss Eulalie before now?

"You're right," I said. "She's an excellent source, and I should have considered it."

"You're welcome," Melba said. "Why don't you call her right now? You could probably go and see her tonight. She told me she's a real night owl."

I glanced at the clock. Nearly seven, so there was plenty of time for a visit with the retired archivist as long as she was willing. "Another good idea. Is she listed in the phone book?"

"I'd imagine so," Melba said. "I'll get off the phone now. You can tell me all about it tomorrow." She hung up.

The phone book lived in a drawer in the kitchen. "I'll be back in a few," I told Diesel. He raised his head and yawned. He stretched before he settled down to nap again.

Although the phone book served the entire county, it was still slender. I flipped it open and looked for Miss Eulalie's number. Sure enough, it was listed. With one finger to mark the number, I picked up the receiver of the wall phone and punched in the digits.

Miss Eulalie answered on the third ring. "Good evening, Charlie. I had a feeling you might call." She chuckled, a light, tinkling sound.

Caller ID, of course. She wasn't psychic as far as I knew. "Good evening, Miss Eulalie. Yes, I was just on the phone with Melba Gilley, and she encouraged me to get in touch with you."

"Melba is a dear girl, but she does love to talk. I was afraid my lettuce would be completely wilted before I managed to get into my car and drive home." Again I heard that fairy-like laugh. "I was excited to hear, though, about those diaries. What a treasure trove they could be."

"Yes, ma'am," I said. "I'm not sure how long they'll be down at the state crime lab, but once they're back I'll be sure to let you know."

"I'd appreciate it. I do so miss working with primary sources like that." Her wistful tone touched me. I wasn't privy to the decision that resulted in her retirement, but I did feel occasionally that I had somehow usurped her.

Her tone turned brisk. "I imagine, from what Melba said, you're interested in the Long family's history. I probably know as much or more about it than they do themselves, and I'd be happy to share some information with you. I have an idea or two about why there is such interest in the diaries."

"I sure would appreciate it, Miss Eulalie," I said. "When would be a convenient time for you?"

"How about now?" she said. "My dance card is hardly full these days, and you can satisfy your curiosity sooner rather than later."

I laughed. "Yes, ma'am, I certainly am curious. I'd love to come over this evening. Would it be all right if I bring my cat with me? He's not used to being left alone, but if you have any problems with it, I'll understand."

"Not a problem," she said warmly. "I love cats, and I've heard a lot about that giant feline of yours."

She gave me her address, and I realized she lived only a few blocks to the north of me in the same neighborhood. "We'll be there in about fifteen or twenty minutes."

I went back to the den and told Diesel we were going on a visit. He perked up and meowed. For a cat who spent much of his day sleeping, he did like getting out of the house.

I ran upstairs to change, and when I came back down I found him waiting by the front door. Once he was in his harness and leash, we set off on our walk to Miss Eulalie's house.

Now that the sun was going down, the temperature cooled a bit, and the walk was nearly pleasant. We strolled at a casual pace, because I didn't want to arrive sweaty and hot. I found Miss Eulalie's place easily, and as we headed up the walk to her front porch, I admired her beautiful yard. Orderly beds of shrubs and flowers, neatly mowed grass, and tall oak and pecan trees combined to make it a showpiece.

Miss Eulalie opened the door just as I was taking my finger off the doorbell. "Charlie, I'm so glad to see you. Oh, my, he is a big kitty. Y'all come on in." She stepped aside to let us enter. "This is turning out to be my day for company."

"You're looking well, Miss Eulalie," I said. She was a sparrow of a woman, short of stature, slight of figure, but with a personality ten times her size. Her white hair sat in a tight chignon at the back of her head, and her deep green cotton dress set off her pale complexion nicely.

"My goodness, kitty, I bet if you stood on your hind legs you'd be almost as tall as me." Miss Eulalie laughed. "His name is Diesel, I believe?"

"Yes, ma'am." I had to agree. Diesel looked even bigger next to her diminutive frame. "Don't let him knock you over." The cat rubbed against her, and he was strong enough that I worried he could make her fall.

"Nonsense," she said, her hand on the cat's head. "Let's go into the parlor and have a chat." She led the way, Diesel by her side, and I brought up the rear.

Her parlor reminded me a lot of the one at Riverhill, the antebellum mansion that belonged to the Ducote sisters, Miss An'gel and Miss Dickce. From what I could see, the furniture dated from the same era as theirs, right down to the Aubusson carpet on the hardwood floor. A portrait of a floridly handsome gentleman in evening dress—perhaps Miss Eulalie's father—had pride of place over the mantel. Framed photographs occupied most of the flat surfaces in the room.

Miss Eulalie motioned for me to take a seat in a club chair while she chose a sofa. "I see you've noticed all my pictures," she said. "Family and former students and their families."

I recalled that she taught history at the high school for twenty years before she decided to become a librarian and archivist. Even though I entered high school about a decade after she left teaching, I heard any number of stories about her and how tough but wonderful she was. From what I heard, I often wished she had been my teacher.

I told her that, and she beamed at me as she continued to

stroke the cat's head. Diesel sat on the floor beside her, and I was glad he hadn't tried to climb on the sofa with her. The deep ruby velvet of the upholstery would show the cat hair starkly.

"I have iced tea and cookies." Miss Eulalie indicated a tray near her on a side table. "Please have some."

"Thank you," I said. After the walk, the cold drink was welcome. I went over and picked up a glass and stared down at the plate of oatmeal raisin cookies. I had a weakness for them, and they looked homemade.

"I made them this morning," my hostess said. "Please, have as many as you like."

"Thank you." I gave in to temptation and placed three on a small serving plate. I took my food and drink, along with a linen napkin, back to my chair.

"Now, I didn't ask Melba for any details about this fuss over those diaries," Miss Eulalie said with a grin, "because I wanted to get home from the grocery store the same day I went."

I laughed. "I know what you mean. I think the whole business is strange, frankly. When the mayor brought them to me, she said she thought they might be helpful with her son's state senate campaign. Then I found out that Jasper Singletary was interested in them, too, for much the same reason. Now, I can just about see the point with the Longs, but how could it affect Jasper Singletary?"

Miss Eulalie looked thoughtful as she sipped her tea. "There's been bad blood between the Longs and the Singletarys for decades," she finally said. "Even I don't know the details, but I gather it dates from the nineteenth century."

"That's a long time to hold a grudge." I munched on the second cookie. They were so delicious I could easily devour the whole batch. I told myself firmly that three was more than enough. My eyes kept focusing on the plateful, however.

"Yes, it is. Ridiculous, if you ask me. Now, have more cookies if you like." She glanced at the lone cookie on my plate. "The Longs have always been wealthy, of course, and as far back as I know of, the Singletarys have been just the opposite. Small farmers who have to struggle every year and who somehow never seem to get ahead." She sighed. "That kind of disparity rankles, I suppose, and that's what has nurtured the feud all these years."

"If the Singletarys hate the Longs because the Longs are rich, do they also hate people like Miss An'gel and Miss Dickce Ducote?"

"Not that I'm aware of," Miss Eulalie replied. "They have reason to be grateful to An'gel and Dickce anyway." She noticed my look of inquiry. "They gave Jasper the scholarship that put him through Athena College."

That sounded like the sisters. They did so many good things in Athena, it was hard to keep track. They performed their charitable works as quietly as possible because they never sought the limelight. I said as much to my hostess, and she agreed with a smile. I realized then she was a contemporary of the Ducotes and had probably known them all her life.

"I guess it's possible the diaries might reveal the source of the bad blood between the two families," I said. "Maybe it's so scandalous that one side thinks the other might be embarrassed badly if it came to light."

"Thereby affecting the state senate race." Miss Eulalie frowned. "Sounds outlandish, doesn't it? But roots and memories run deep here, and if it's terrible enough, it could have an effect."

"Terrible enough to kill for?" I asked, thinking of poor Marie Steverton.

Miss Eulalie nodded. "Where family pride is involved, especially in the South, never underestimate the lengths someone will go to protect their name."

"I can't wait to work on the diaries," I said. I got up to help myself to two more oatmeal raisin cookies. I told the little voice in my head to shut up about the calories. "In the meantime, the mayor found a fifth volume. I scanned it today, and I'll read through it to see what it might be able to tell us."

Miss Eulalie nodded. "Yes, I heard about that. I also have something that might shed light on this. Did you know that Rachel Long's grandson's wife wrote a memoir of the old lady?"

"Yes, ma'am," I said. "The library at the college had a copy, but it's apparently been lost."

"How aggravating," Miss Eulalie said as she rose from the sofa. "I happen to have a copy, though, and if you'd like to borrow it, you're perfectly welcome. I read it many years ago."

"Thank you. I would like to," I said.

My hostess nodded. "Sit there and enjoy your cookies. It's in my study. I'll fetch it."

Diesel had been remarkably well behaved so far, but the moment Miss Eulalie left the room he came over to me and begged for a bite of my cookie.

"Sorry, boy," I said. "The raisins are bad for you. No cookie for you."

He meowed and stared at me, so I repeated what I told him. He turned and went back to his spot next to the sofa, tail high in the air.

Miss Eulalie returned then, empty-handed. Her expression was blank. "I'm sorry, Charlie; you must forgive me. I seem to have misplaced the memoir." With her right hand she fidgeted with a broach pinned to her bosom.

"That's too bad," I said. Something didn't seem quite right with her. She appeared flustered.

"I'll keep looking for it," she said. "I apologize, but I'm coming down with one of my bad headaches."

"I'm sorry, Miss Eulalie. I hope you feel better soon. Diesel and I will get out of your hair. Thanks for the delicious cookies and the information."

"Thank you for your visit," my hostess said. She remained silent while she escorted the cat and me to the front door. I turned on the verandah to bid her good night, but she had already shut the door.

That was a rude thing to do, and Miss Eulalie would never be rude—unless she was powerfully worried about something.

In this case, the missing memoir. I didn't think it was a coincidence.

TWENTY-ONE

||||||||||||||||||||||||||||||||||||||||||||||||||||||||||||||||||||||||

I didn't believe for a minute that Miss Eulalie had misplaced her copy of the memoir of Rachel Long. She was every bit as sharp as the Ducote sisters, and I'd bet she could easily find any book in her study. She wouldn't have been so flustered over simply mislaying a book.

She couldn't find the memoir because someone took it. I'd also bet she knew *who* took it, and that was what upset her. Obviously a person she considered a friend; otherwise she would have been angry and not so eager to get me out the door.

By the time Diesel and I reached home, I had settled on two likely candidates: Lucinda Long and Jasper Singletary. I didn't have to think twice about the mayor—Miss Eulalie probably taught her in high school. I couldn't be completely sure about Jasper, but if I went by her tone of voice when she told me about how the Ducote sisters helped him get through college, she had warm feelings for him. I sensed tacit approval of him in her manner.

What should I do about it? I wondered as I released the cat from his harness and leash. Diesel loped off toward the utility room. I wandered into the kitchen and sat at the table, lost in thought.

I could give Miss Eulalie a call tomorrow afternoon to ask whether she had found her copy of the memoir. I hoped that she wouldn't put herself in danger by confronting the person who removed the book from her house. *Should I call her and warn her?*

I mulled that decision over for the next quarter hour. Diesel returned and stretched out on the floor beside my chair while I pondered the situation.

Was I making too much of this? Surely Miss Eulalie wouldn't be in danger. I was letting my imagination go into warp drive.

Then again, if the person who took Miss Eulalie's copy of the memoir was the same person who ran over Marie Steverton, then Miss Eulalie could well be in harm's way.

Finally I decided that I couldn't risk anything happening to that little old lady. I looked up her number again and punched it into the phone.

The phone rang seven times, and I was about to hang up and call Kanesha when Miss Eulalie answered.

"Thank goodness," I said. "This is Charlie again. I hope you're not going to think I'm crazy, but I'm worried about your safety because of that missing book. Miss Eulalie, did you really misplace it, or did someone take it from your house?"

I heard a sharp intake of breath from the other end of the line. Then Miss Eulalie laughed. "Charlie, my goodness, you *are* one for getting excited about the oddest things. I was about to call you to let you know I remember what happened to my copy of the memoir. I put it in the Long collection several years ago, and I forgot all about it." She laughed again, but I thought it sounded a bit forced—definitely not the fairy-like tinkle I remembered from our earlier conversation.

"I'm glad to hear it's safe," I said. "I hope your headache is better."

"My headache? Oh, yes, it's much better. Thank you for being so kind as to ask. Now I really mustn't keep you any longer. Good night."

I barely had time to bid her good night in return before she hung up.

I put the receiver back on the hook and returned to my seat at the table. I had the oddest feeling that Miss Eulalie had lied to me. The first thing I'd do tomorrow at the archive would be to delve through the Long collection to find that memoir. I would also check the accession records. If Miss Eulalie had indeed donated her copy, there should be a note about it. I knew from my experience with her recordkeeping that she had been meticulous during her tenure.

If she lied to me, then why had she done so? Was she protecting someone? Mayor Long? Jasper Singletary? Or someone else, someone I hadn't considered?

Now *I* had a headache. As curious as I was about the contents of the diary pages I scanned today, I would leave them for tomorrow. A good night's sleep might bring clarity, clarity that I needed.

I knew Helen Louise would not be calling me tonight. She was catering a private dinner party and probably wouldn't be home until at least eleven. She would be too exhausted to talk.

"Come on, boy," I said to the cat at my feet. "Let's get ready for bed."

I heard my cell phone ring the next morning right when I stepped out of the shower. I dried myself enough that I wouldn't drip water everywhere and hurried into the bedroom to answer the call. I caught it in time.

In response to my greeting, the caller said, "Good morning, Mr. Harris. Jasper Singletary. I'd like to talk to you in private as soon as possible. Are you available this morning?"

"I'd very much like to talk to you, too, Mr. Singletary," I said. I thought he sounded tense. "I'm available this morning. When and where would you like to meet?"

"How about your office at eight forty-five?"

I glanced at the clock. I had time for a quick breakfast before I would need to head to the archive. "That will be fine."

He rang off.

While I dressed I thought about the coming interview. Kelly Grimes had no doubt given him an earful about my recent conversation with her. I hoped he wouldn't be hostile, but I certainly didn't expect him to be overly friendly. Nothing like a good confrontation to start the day, I thought morosely.

Azalea had my breakfast on the table when Diesel and I walked into the kitchen. Cheese grits, bacon, and toast this morning. I loved her buttery cheese grits, but I groaned inwardly at the thought of all the calories.

"Good morning," I said. "Breakfast looks delicious as usual."

"Morning, Mr. Charlie," Azalea said. "You, too, cat." She stared down at Diesel as he looked back and forth between her and me. He wanted bacon, and he didn't mind who gave it to him first.

"I'm going to have to make this fast," I said as I picked up my coffee. "I've got an appointment at eight forty-five." Azalea would cluck over me if she thought I was eating too quickly.

"All right," she said.

I had a sip of my coffee, then a bite of the heavenly grits. "So good. Do you know the Singletary family? I don't remember them from when I was growing up. Now, of course, Jasper Singletary's in the paper all the time lately."

Azalea nodded. "They been around these parts a long time. Go way back, just like the Ducotes and the Longs and some of the other old families. Always been poor, though. Mr. Jasper's the first one of them who amounted to anything, you ask me." She sniffed. "Mostly sorry folks, always moaning and carrying on because they're poor. Still farming that sad old place where they hardly ever made no money."

"I don't think I've ever met any of them," I said, "though I've seen Jasper a few times in public. He seems like a smart, hard-working young man. I wonder, though, if he stands a chance in this election against Beck Long."

"He might do better than you rightly expect. People are talking about him being a good man," Azalea said. "Now, Mrs. Long is a nice lady. Reckon Mr. Long is a fine man himself, but their son, well, he got himself in some messes back when he was in school. He's still kind stuck on himself; that's what I hear."

"Typical rich boy acting up and then his parents get him out of it, I guess." I pinched off a piece of bacon for Diesel, then popped the rest of the slice into my mouth.

"My friend Ronetta's been their housekeeper since before that boy was born," Azalea said. "Ronetta told me Mr. Long never would make that boy mind. Now, that ain't no way to raise a child. They got to know what they can do and what they can't. If you don't teach 'em that, you're just asking for trouble."

I agreed with that wholeheartedly. I liked to think that my wife and I instilled our children with good manners and self-discipline.

They had their moments growing up, particularly during their teenage years, but I never had to get them out of serious trouble.

"Looks like he's finally straightened up," I said. "I haven't heard any talk about him acting badly these days."

"I reckon he finally grew up and got some sense," Azalea said. "He's been living in Atlanta for a while. Didn't come home until last year when he decided he wanted to be a politician."

I spooned up the last of the grits and gave the cat one final piece of bacon. "If he got into trouble in Atlanta, I guess nobody here's heard about it." I drained my coffee cup and pushed back my chair. "I need to get going. Thanks for breakfast."

Azalea nodded. "You're welcome. I'll be leaving before you come home for lunch, but it'll be waiting for you."

I thanked her again. Sometimes she told me what she was making; other times she let it be a surprise. Today must be a surprise day.

Diesel and I were out of the house a few minutes later. The morning was hot and humid—as it often was this time of year—and we did not hurry. We still made it to the office several minutes ahead of my appointment. Shortly after we both settled in our accustomed places, I heard a knock at the door.

I stood. "Good morning, Mr. Singletary. I'm glad to meet you. Please come in."

He advanced into the room, and I moved around the desk to shake his proffered hand.

"Morning, Mr. Harris. I appreciate you taking the time to meet with me."

He glanced past me, and his eyes widened when he spotted Diesel. The cat climbed down from the windowsill and came over to greet Singletary. Diesel sniffed at his hand before rubbing his head against it. For the cat, that was the seal of approval. I was afraid he would try to rub himself against Singletary's dark trousers, but he went back to his spot in the window.

"Handsome animal," Singletary said. "I've never seen a cat that big before."

That was my cue to explain about Maine Coons, and by now I had it down to a few sentences. Singletary nodded when I finished, and I could tell he was impatient to get on with things. I indicated he should take the chair in front of my desk before I returned to my seat.

Face-to-face as we now were, I could see the firm jaw, the intense expression, and the broad shoulders, all of which made me aware of an aura of power this young man exuded. He was ambitious—I knew that—and determined. But would he stop short of murder? Or would he do anything to get what he wanted?

"Kelly Grimes told me about the conversation she had with you yesterday. She was upset." His voice was deep, and his drawl betrayed his Mississippi origins. Mine had come back since I moved home again, after many years in Texas, but his was more pronounced.

"Yes, I was pretty hard on her." I intended to face potential complaints about my treatment of Ms. Grimes head-on. "I will tell you exactly what I told her. I do not appreciate being lied to, and I consider what she did a breach of her professional ethics. I ought to report her actions to the editor of the paper, but I'm willing to let it go, unless I catch her lying to me again about anything."

"Fair enough." Singletary nodded. "I asked for Kelly's help in doing research, Mr. Harris. I did not know until after the fact that she pretended to be my opponent's fiancée." He shrugged. "I don't see that her ruse was necessary, but I can assure you, both she and I will be straightforward with you from now on."

"I appreciate that," I said. "I have to say I am completely at a loss to understand why you are so interested in these diaries. Why have you and Ms. Grimes been so determined to get a look at them?"

"I must ask you to keep what I am about to tell you to yourself, if at all possible."

His intense expression made me even more curious about his interest in the diaries.

"Unless it has some bearing on the murder of Marie Steverton," I said in a firm tone, "I will of course respect your wishes."

He stared hard at me for a moment. Then he nodded. "All right." He paused for a breath. "Here's the deal. I'm looking for proof that Rachel Long was a murderess."

TWENTY-TWO

His response shocked me. I wasn't sure what I expected, but it surely wasn't that. I stared at Jasper Singletary and he gazed steadily back.

"Murderess?" I shook my head. "That's a terrible accusation to make. Who is she supposed to have murdered?"

"Three members of my family, all children," he said, his tone grim. "Four, really, if you count the mother who died of a broken heart."

"What members of your family? I don't know anything about your ancestors, so you're going to have to explain this to me." I leaned back in my chair. I felt a paw on my shoulder. As usual, Diesel picked up on the fact that I wasn't my typical calm self. I rubbed his paw to reassure him while I kept my eyes focused on Jasper Singletary.

"Sure, but this will take a few minutes, so you'll have to bear with me," he said. "This goes back obviously to Civil War days.

My family owned a good-sized farm—we still own it, actually, even though it's a lot smaller now—that abuts the Long property, so the Singletarys and the Longs have been neighbors for over a century and a half." He laughed bitterly. "Some neighbors *they* are. Anyway, my three times great-grandfather, also Jasper, married twice. He and his first wife had one son, my two times great-grandfather, Franklin. First wife died in 1855 when Franklin was about ten years old, and Jasper remarried less than a year later. He and the second wife had three children, little stair-steps. First one came along when Franklin was twelve, and the third one when he was fifteen.

"Is that all clear so far?" he asked. When I nodded, he continued. "Good. Well, Jasper had married late the first time, and he was already in his forties when Franklin was born. By the time the war came, Jasper was too old to fight. He had heart trouble of some kind, according to my great-aunt Caroline, my grandfather's sister, and that kept him at home even though other men his age ended up fighting.

"Jasper doted on all his children, particularly the little ones. Franklin was ready to enlist right after Mississippi seceded, but he was only sixteen. He also had the same heart trouble Jasper had, and Jasper refused to let him go."

He paused, and I decided to interject a comment. "I'm sure that was frustrating for Franklin, seeing so many others his age going off to fight." I shook my head. "Early on, they all thought it would be over in a couple of months, at the most."

"It's a good thing Franklin didn't go." Singletary smiled briefly. "Otherwise I wouldn't be here. I'm happy to say also, in case you were wondering, I didn't inherit the heart defect they both had."

"I'm pleased to hear that," I said. "You've set up the situation with your ancestors. How do the Longs fit into all this? Particularly Rachel?"

"About this time, right after the war got started, probably in June of 1861, Jasper had a serious bout of heart trouble. I figure he had a stroke or two, and that left him unable to do much work. They did have one hired hand, a distant cousin of Jasper's, but he was young enough and enlisted right away. Jasper didn't hold with slavery, so everything fell on Franklin, his stepmother, and the little ones."

"Admirable, but certainly unusual in Athena at that time," I said. "That must have been difficult for your family, not having help."

"It was, and things got worse. Jasper didn't improve, and the family was having a hard time. He wouldn't ask anybody for help, although there were some cousins who did what they could. With the war on, things got harder for everybody. Jasper still couldn't work that fall, and Franklin didn't have the stamina to do all that he needed to do. Jasper's wife, Vidalia, decided to go to Rachel Long and ask her for help. Their clothes were in rags, they had barely any food, and Vidalia was desperate. Jasper was too proud to ask the high-and-mighty Longs for anything, so she went behind his back and did it for him."

He sounded angry, but I didn't know whether it was with his namesake for his stubbornness or with Vidalia for going behind her husband's back. Pride could be a good thing, but not if it meant letting your wife and children starve to death.

"How did Rachel Long respond to Vidalia?" I asked. Given his charges against Rachel, I was prepared to hear that she turned her back on the Singletarys and let them all starve.

"Lady Bountiful went swanning over—my great-aunt's words,

you understand—to dispense charity in the form of clothing and food so the pitiful Singletarys wouldn't be on her conscience. In the meantime, her father-in-law, Andrew Adalbert Long, Sr., decided this would be a good time to talk Jasper into selling him some land he'd had his eye on for the past twenty years."

"Did Jasper sell?" I asked.

My visitor shook his head. "No, not then. He did later, but I'm getting ahead of the story. Jasper almost had another stroke when he found out Vidalia went begging, but she and Franklin didn't listen. They and the little ones needed the food, and the little ones needed warm clothing. So at first they thanked Rachel. After that initial visit, she didn't come again, but she did send her maid, a slave from her family's plantation in Louisiana, over a few times with more food." He grimaced. "This is the part of the story I don't get, but my great-aunt said she had it straight from Franklin, her daddy, that Rachel Long's maid was a conjure woman."

"A lot of people in those days believed in voodoo," I said, "and they often associated it with Louisiana."

Jasper nodded. "I know that, but I still find it hard to believe myself. The strange thing was, when the maid started visiting, the children and Vidalia all turned sickly. They weren't strong to begin with because of malnourishment, although the food from the Longs helped. The little ones all died within the space of a week."

"Wasn't a doctor called? Couldn't anything be done for them?"

"The only good doctor in town had gone to serve as an army doctor," Jasper said. "All they had left were a couple of midwives who knew about herbal medicines. They couldn't figure out what was wrong with the children."

"You said the mother died of a broken heart. When did Vidalia succumb?" I asked.

"Several months later, in the winter. Jasper died the next spring, leaving Franklin on his own. In the meantime, while Jasper was out of his mind with grief over the little ones dying, Andrew Long came in and talked him into selling the land for far less than it was worth. Franklin was out in the fields when it happened, and Vidalia was on the verge of dying herself. Neither one of them knew what was going on."

"In your great-aunt's mind, then, Andrew Long cheated her grandfather and father out of land."

"That's about it," Jasper said. "Aunt Caroline believed, like her daddy did, that Rachel Long had her maid poison the children to drive Jasper crazy. All so Andrew could get his hands on a hundred acres."

What an appalling story, I thought. *Could any of it be true?* I could believe that Rachel's father-in-law was an opportunist and decided to get what he wanted when Jasper was at a weak point. But to believe that Rachel, through her maid, poisoned those little children to help her father-in-law cheat Jasper Singletary? That sounded far-fetched, at best. The death rate for children—particularly for children who didn't have enough of the right food to eat—was high during that time. They probably died of natural causes.

"I know what you're thinking," Jasper said. "Children died routinely back then. Starvation, acts of war, you name it; the civilian death rate skyrocketed while the war raged on. But the war hadn't yet reached Athena when these children died."

"If I remember correctly, the Union Army finally came to Athena in November 1862," I said.

"That's correct," Jasper replied. "That was a year after the children died. And Vidalia. She lasted less than half a year after burying her babies."

"One tragedy after another," I said. That sounded weak to me, but I couldn't figure out what to say to the man about the sad deaths of his family members more than a hundred years ago.

"That's the luck of the Singletarys." His tone held a bitter edge. "That's the way it's been ever since, but I'm aiming to change all that. I am going to win this election and prove that I have what it takes. Beck Long and his hallowed family name aren't going to stand in my way."

Again, I didn't know quite how to respond to that. I hadn't decided yet on my choice in the election, and I didn't want to get into a discussion of it right now. I waited a moment to see whether he would continue. When he didn't, I said, "Given all you've told me, I would say you're hoping Rachel Long's diary will contain some proof of these allegations."

"Yes," Singletary replied. "There may be some clue in there to tell us what really happened."

"If there is any kind of proof in the diaries that Rachel Long and her maid were responsible for those deaths, what will you do?"

The hopeful politician narrowed his eyes. "Blacken the Long name so that they finally pay for their sins." He smiled broadly. "And put myself in office."

TWENTY-THREE

I could read nothing but malice into Jasper Singletary's words. If it were indeed true that Rachel Long and her maid were somehow responsible for the deaths of Singletary's family members, I could understand his wanting to have the truth known.

The rancor he felt toward the Longs—that was harder to understand. Had the Singletarys made the Longs the scapegoats for every misfortune they suffered since the Civil War? For that to be true, I reckoned, the Longs would have to have been actively persecuting the Singletary clan for more than a hundred and fifty years.

Or had the bitterness of that one terrible winter eaten into the Singletary family's collective soul and kept the hatred alive all this time?

That sounded melodramatic, but bitterness corroded. I was curious to find out what other incidents could have kept the feud fresh one generation after another. Another talk with Miss Eulalie was in order, and I might consult the Ducote sisters as well. If those three ladies couldn't answer my questions, I doubted anyone could.

While I woolgathered, Jasper Singletary stared at me, his impatience obvious.

"I understand that you want to know the truth," I said, "but have you considered the possibility that the diaries may contain no proof whatsoever that these allegations are valid?"

"Yes, I have thought about it," Singletary replied. "If the proof I need isn't in the diaries, I'll keep looking. One way or another I will prove that the Long family harbored a murderer, no matter how long ago it was."

"How dare you say such a thing."

Neither Singletary nor I was aware that the mayor stood in the doorway. She had obviously heard the young man's words. Her eyes glinted with anger as she advanced into the room. To my surprise, she wasn't alone. The tall figure of her son loomed behind her.

Singletary got to his feet and regarded Mrs. Long coolly. "I dare say it, Your Honor, because according to my family, it's the truth. Only, the Long family has been able to cover it up all these years." He shrugged. "Maybe now the truth will come to light."

Beck Long stepped past his mother, who for once seemed at a loss for words. "Listen here, Singletary, I know you're desperate because your campaign is going nowhere. Unless you want to have your behind hauled off to jail for libel, you'd better stop spouting crap like that."

Singletary laughed harshly. "Your family really did waste money by sending you to law school."

Long's face reddened. He turned to his mother. "What is he talking about?"

Mrs. Long's expression was enigmatic as she regarded her son.

"The events he's talking about must have taken place well over a century ago, so anyone he's accusing of the crime has been dead a long time. You can't libel the dead, so he can accuse Rachel Long or anyone else from her time of being a murderer."

"Oh, yeah, that," Beck Long said. "Well, he's still trying to ruin our family name. That ought to count for something."

Singletary turned to me. "Thank you for your time, Mr. Harris. I look forward to hearing from you." He turned back to nod at the mayor and her son. "Sorry I can't stay and chat, but I have meetings to get to." He strode out of the room.

All during the foregoing exchange, I could feel Diesel becoming more and more restless. The tension in the room had mounted steadily, ever since Singletary began telling me his story. Now, with this open hostility, he was not happy. He climbed down from the windowsill and crowded against my legs. I rubbed his head to try to reassure him. He began to relax.

The mayor came forward and sank wearily into the chair Singletary had vacated. Beck Long hovered over her.

"Mama, what are we going to do? We can't let him run around and start telling people those lies."

"Find a chair and sit down," Mrs. Long said in a sharp tone. "I will take care of it, like I always do." She turned to me. "Mr. Harris, have you had a chance to read through the diary I brought you yesterday?"

Was I supposed to pretend the nasty scene hadn't happened? I couldn't help but admire the mayor's cool in the face of such unpleasantness. At the same time, I was not much impressed with her son.

"No, Your Honor, I haven't," I said. "I was able, however, to scan all the pages to create a digital copy. My plan for today is to read through it."

"You're not going to let anybody else have a copy of the file, are you?" Beck Long stared hard at me.

"If the family chooses to have the diary remain private for now, then no, I won't let anyone else have a copy of it," I said. "Perhaps it might be better for me to return the diary to you, along with a copy of the scan, so that you can decide whether you want the contents known. Frankly, if I were to read it and find evidence to support Mr. Singletary's allegations, I would be in an awkward spot—and I prefer not to be."

Beck Long started to speak, but his mother held up her hand. He closed his mouth and leaned back in his chair, his expression sulky.

"No, Mr. Harris, my husband decided to share these diaries, and we are not going to renege on that agreement now. I cannot believe you will find anything to substantiate that wild story Mr. Singletary has come up with. Frankly, the sooner the contents are public knowledge, the better. Singletary may be sorry he ever wanted to know what's in them. His family have been lazy, good-for-nothing whiners for generations." Her face hardened. "I'm tired of them blaming the Longs for their troubles."

Beck brightened during his mother's speech. By the time she finished he was grinning and nodding his head. "That's it, Mama," he said. "We'll show those lousy Singletarys a thing or two."

Thus far during the state senate campaign I had not heard any speech given by Beck Long. I had a feeling I hadn't missed anything significant, were I to judge by his remarks to his mother and Singletary. Could he really be as dim-witted as he sounded this morning?

The mayor ignored her son's comment. "How long do you think it will take you to read through it?"

I shrugged. "Barring unforeseen complications, I should think sometime today. When I examined the first volume the other day, I found the handwriting easy enough to decipher."

"Excellent." Mrs. Long smiled as she rose. "Come along, Beck. We should let Mr. Harris get on with it. I'll discuss with you later, Mr. Harris, about getting a transcript made of the diaries."

I stood to bid the Longs good-bye. Diesel climbed back onto the windowsill. He seemed not at all interested in either the mayor or her son. Perhaps he was still uneasy from all the tension, though it had rapidly dissipated.

Seated once more, I turned to the computer to retrieve the files I had made of the scans. The scanner was high resolution, so I anticipated little trouble reading the pages, as long as I had scanned them properly.

The mayor's confidence in the diary's contents impressed me. After I thought about it a moment, I decided she might have read at least this one volume before she brought it to me.

If her confidence were misplaced and I did find something damaging or incriminating, I would of course inform Mrs. Long. After that, what could I do?

I had no quick and easy answer to that question—particularly if the incriminating information somehow connected to the present-day murder of Marie Steverton. I would face that situation if it occurred.

In the meantime, I was more eager than ever to read, and I settled into my chair and started on the first page. One advantage of reading the pages from scans was the ability to increase the size. With the diary itself I'd have had to use a magnifying glass. In this case the computer made things much easier.

With the enlargement I found Rachel Long's handwriting not at all difficult to read. The fact that the pages were in such excellent condition helped as well. The ink seemed clearer from what I remembered of the other volumes.

Rachel had a chatty, informal style that reminded me a bit of Mary Chesnut's diary. There was a sense of immediacy, almost as if Rachel were recording things right as they happened, rather than afterward.

The first entry, dated March 9, 1861, was exactly two months after Mississippi seceded from the Union, the second state to do so. South Carolina went first, I remembered. Rachel wrote:

Mr. Lincoln became President five days ago, though of course he is not OUR president. That honor has fallen to Mr. Jefferson Davis, and we in Mississippi are proud that this fine man is from our state. I believe, and in this Mr. Long concurs with me, that Mr. Davis will prove himself worthy.

She went on to express the typical Southern bravado, that if war broke out it would indeed end quickly, thanks to the fine men of the South who could outfight their Northern counterparts easily.

In the early stages they believed it little more than a game, or so I had always thought. Johnny Reb would whip the North quickly, and the South would go on its merry way as a newly formed and separate nation. Five years—and hundreds of thousands of deaths and other casualties—later, the Union was stitched back together.

I read steadily for the next half hour, fascinated by Rachel's observations of daily life. The mood in the South remained euphoric, even after the incident at Fort Sumter in mid-April 1861.

In an entry dated May 26, 1861, Rachel noted news that the Union Army had crossed the Potomac and captured Alexandria,

Virginia. Rachel expressed confidence that the city would soon be retaken by Confederate troops.

Two days later she made her first mention of the Singletary family.

Word has reached us that our wretched neighbor, Mr. Jasper Singletary, has once again fallen ill with his heart troubles. Though he is certainly the most quarrelsome and obstinate creature that Our Dear Lord ever placed upon this earth, I cannot wish him to suffer, for then his poor wife and children will have even less. I have upon occasion visited with Mrs. Vidalia Singletary, and she is a sweet but timid creature, and I fear that she is used most roughly by her husband. Mr. Singletary would no doubt suffer another fit of apoplexy were he to discover that I have sometimes taken food to give to his wife. I cannot bear the sight of those wretched little children with their bony knees and dirty faces.

I sat back and rubbed my eyes, already tired from gazing at the screen so intently for more than thirty minutes. This last entry certainly showed Rachel Long in a positive light. Her charitable interest in the Singletary children spoke well of her, and there was no indication thus far that she bore the least ill will toward the family.

Diesel saw me stretching, and he stretched as well. I got up from the chair and walked back and forth between the desk and the door a few times. The office phone rang while I was walking.

"Hello, Charlie," Kanesha Berry said. "I have some news for you. I'm pretty sure I know who took those diaries from your office."

TWENTY-FOUR

"The evidence isn't conclusive yet," Kanesha went on after a brief pause. "I'm satisfied, though. I'd already figured Marie Steverton as the thief."

"I can't say I'm surprised," I responded. Marie was one of two obvious candidates, the other being Kelly Grimes. "You obviously have some kind of proof. Can you tell me what it is?"

"As long as it doesn't go any further," Kanesha said.

"Of course," I replied, a bit nettled that she even felt the need to mention it.

"Maybe you remember I mentioned we found a canvas bag in the street with the body," Kanesha said. "There was residue in it from something, and I suspected it was flakes from the binding of those diaries."

"Was it?"

"Yes, the flakes match, although the report isn't official yet."

"You're sure the bag belonged to Marie?" I asked. I couldn't resist needling her slightly in return for her earlier question.

"Had her name embroidered on a tag inside," Kanesha said.

"I wonder why the person who took them from Marie left the bag behind." I paused as another thought struck me. "Have you made any progress on finding the car that ran Marie down?"

"Nothing significant," Kanesha replied. "The neighbor who saw the car disappearing wasn't close enough to read the license plate number or really tell what make and model it is. All he could come up with was large and dark. And that it was a car, not a pickup."

"Was there any damage to the car?" I asked.

"Pretty likely," she said. "We found fragments that might have come from the vehicle. Also there will probably be minute paint fragments on the deceased's clothing. They might even be able to figure out a make and model from that. In the meantime, we're considering all possibilities."

"That's good. Do you have any idea when they'll be finished with the diaries and I can get them back?"

"You should have them in your hands sometime Friday afternoon," Kanesha said. "The mayor really pulled some strings, because they made this investigation a top priority."

I couldn't tell from her tone whether Kanesha was impressed or annoyed by this exercise of political heft.

"I'll be glad to have them back," I said. "In the meantime I finished scanning the volume the mayor brought the other day. I've been reading it, and it's interesting."

"Found a motive for murder yet?" Kanesha asked. This time I interpreted her mood easily—skeptical.

"Not yet." I wished I could share Singletary's tragic story with her, but I'd given my word.

"Give me a call if you do." Kanesha ended the call.

I put the receiver down and turned back to the computer. Diesel warbled, and I focused on him instead. He batted a paw toward my arm, and I recognized the demand for attention. I stroked his head and along his back a few times. He meowed loudly, and I also recognized that sound. He was hungry.

A quick check of my watch told me why. At eleven fifteen it was close enough to lunch for us to take a break and head home to eat. "Come on, boy, I'm a little peckish myself."

After a meal of scrumptious homemade chicken pot pie for me and more boiled chicken for him, Diesel and I made it back to the office around twelve fifteen. Melba's door was closed, and that meant she was out to lunch. She would no doubt appear upstairs at some point in the afternoon, but not, I hoped, until I had made considerably more progress with Rachel Long's diary.

The cat settled into this favorite spot while I called up the file. I found my place and started reading. Moments later, I hit upon another mention of the Singletary family.

Vidalia Singletary came to see me today while Father Long was occupied elsewhere, and that is just as well, for he finds the sight of the poor woman distasteful—almost as distasteful as that of her husband, for whom he has little good to say. That pains me, for I would have my husband be of a more Christian disposition toward these unfortunates. Vidalia appeared near exhaustion, and she burst into the most pitiable tears the moment I first spoke to her. It took me some several minutes to calm the poor woman enough that I might hear the extent of her troubles. The sum of them was simply that her husband was still too weak to work the farm.

Franklin, the son by Mr. Singletary's first wife, is rather a feckless boy and moreover is not himself strong, apparently suffering from a similar complaint of the heart as his father.

How could I not take pity upon one so wretched? My soul would be worth nothing in this life or the next were I not to help those so much less fortunate than we. Although I do see that difficult times are coming for us all, as we are feeling the effects of that d——d blockade (the Lord forgive me for swearing, but we are vexed terribly by this) of our ports. Yet with the shortages here, I know the situation is much more dire for Vidalia and her little ones. Vidalia herself is in rags, and the children fare little better.

In addition to victuals I also gave her a large bolt of cloth from which to make suitable garments for herself and the children. My charity is perhaps not as pure as the Lord would command, for I gave her the bolts of green tarlatan sent to me by my cousin Marianna from London. The shade is most complimentary to me, but the fabric does have a rather peculiar smell. I would rather not see it go to waste, and there is enough for Vidalia to make at least two suits of clothing for each of the children as well as a simple dress for herself.

I sat back for a moment and rubbed my eyes. Rachel Long still sounded like a charitable woman, even though one act of charity consisted in giving away something she did not particularly want herself. She had no intention to use the cloth, so she might as well give it to someone who could, odd smell aside. A few good washes, and the odor probably went away. I noted again the name of the fabric, tarlatan, and jotted it down on a notepad. I didn't recall having heard that term before, and I would look it up later. Perhaps

I could throw it into a conversation and impress Laura, who always found my lack of knowledge of women's fashions amusing.

Back to work, I admonished myself. I focused on the screen. A few days later, on June 10, 1861, Rachel confided disturbing news to her diary.

Today Vidalia Singletary sent word by her husband's son Franklin that her children are ill and she does not know how to doctor them. She begged me to come, as she herself is falling ill as well, but though it caused me much distress I could not go. Mother Long is suffering terribly from a fever, and I dared not leave her side. If only Doctor Renwick had not abandoned us all, but I know our valiant boys on the front lines have need of his skills, too.

I could not ignore Vidalia's plea however so I instead sent my maid Celeste. The girl learned something of the ways of healing from her grandmother and mother on my own grandmother's plantation in Louisiana. She is knowledgeable enough about herbs and so should be able to dose the children with something to alleviate their distress. I will of course pray for the speedy recovery of Vidalia and her children. Her husband, I fear, is past help by now.

I felt heartsick reading this. Rachel seemed to be a truly tender and caring woman, but without a doctor and with her own sick mother-in-law, she evidently did the best she could.

How skilled at herbal medicines was Celeste, though? I wondered also how old Celeste was. Rachel seemed to think the girl knew enough to help. According to present-day Jasper, however, Celeste did not help Vidalia and the children. Instead, or so he believed, she harmed them. Had she done so deliberately? Or accidentally, through lack of real skill and knowledge?

Only Rachel's diary might hold the answers. I scrolled down to the next page and continued reading. Nothing about the Singletarys in the next couple of entries. Rachel had little time for her diary, for it seemed that her mother-in-law hovered near death's door for several days before rallying miraculously. An exhausted Rachel turned the elder Mrs. Long's care over to one of the slaves and went to bed herself with a fever, no doubt brought on by exhaustion.

A few days later Rachel recovered and began writing more profusely in her diary. On June 15, 1861, she mentioned another plea for help from Vidalia. Once more Rachel dispatched Celeste with food and medicines.

Rachel's diary entries became sparse again. She noted the blockade and the resulting shortages, not to mention the difficulty of the planters in getting their cotton and other products to market. Cotton was king, but only if the planters could sell it for a good price.

Throughout the fall of 1861, there were rumors in Athena that the Union Army was approaching, and Rachel worried over the news. From what I remembered reading, there were no real battles fought in Mississippi between the armies until a year later, so their fears would not be realized for a while.

Rachel frequently expressed anxiety over her husband, a major in one of the Mississippi cavalry regiments. He was a graduate of West Point, I was surprised to learn. She seized upon every letter from him, she wrote, "and read with feverish anxiety until I was assured he was well and had not been in any way injured."

The next entry after that surprised me enough that I exclaimed,

"Good grief," and startled Diesel. He warbled, and I reached over to pat his head while I read once again the words that shocked me.

Celeste, the wretched girl, has been behaving oddly these past weeks. Finally she has come to me with a confession that I can scarcely believe. It seems that those times when I sent her to aid Vidalia Singletary and her children, Celeste behaved shockingly. She claims that she was seduced, but Franklin Singletary has never impressed me as a particularly forceful nor articulate boy. I suspect that Celeste is wholly to blame for her current condition for I have known her to be of a flirtatious nature before now.

TWENTY-FIVE

||||||||||||||||||||||||||||||||||||||||||||||||||||||||||||||

Though Rachel Long did not use the word *pregnant*, I knew that was what she meant by Celeste's *condition*. Franklin Singletary was the father of a slave's child.

I wondered whether *that* bit of family history had been passed down to the present generation.

In the next few entries Rachel made no mention of Celeste or the Singletarys. Then came the sad news, on November 16, 1861.

Franklin Singletary came today to tell us that the three younger children died in the night. They remained feeble, their sickness unabated, since the summer. The weather of the past weeks was harmful to them, I am certain. Cold, wet, damp, it could not have helped their poor frail lungs. I take some comfort knowing that at least they had warm garments from the cloth I provided. Franklin reports that Vidalia is so

weak she cannot move from her bed and his father is pros-
trate with grief at the loss of his children.

Franklin most humbly begged for assistance to dig the graves,
for his father has no workers to aid him. Jasper Singletary was
most vehement against the use of slave labor, an attitude that of
course did not aid his cause among his fellow citizens. Father
Long kindly offered him the use of two of the young, strong field
hands, and they went with Franklin to perform the sad duty.

Even at the distance of one hundred and fifty years, I felt the
grief of such a tragic loss. Poor Jasper Singletary. No wonder the
man was out of his mind—or that his wife died of a broken heart.
I couldn't imagine anything worse than outliving one's child, let
alone three children.

I had to take a break from the diary. My head needed clearing
after reading such a heartrending story. Diesel, bless him, sensed my
distress. He chirped and leaned from the windowsill to butt his head
against my shoulder. He continued to chirp and purr while I stroked
him. I felt better after a couple of minutes of special Diesel therapy.

I still didn't feel like going back to the diary. There was only so
much pathos I could take in a day. As Diesel settled back on the
windowsill to clean his front paws, I debated what to do. There
were always books waiting to be cataloged, but there was another
task I suddenly remembered needed doing.

"I'm going next door, boy," I told the cat. "You stay here and
nap." Diesel answered me with a sleepy meow and a yawn.

With all the other things on my mind, I had forgotten about
searching through the Long collection to find the copy of Angeline McCarthy Long's memoir of Rachel Long that Miss Eulalie
said she donated.

In the storage room next to my office I unlocked the door and switched on the lights. I left the door slightly ajar in case Diesel came to look for me. I remembered where the Long collection was shelved and headed to the far end of the room from the door.

I surveyed the shelves and made a mental calculation of the collection—probably around twenty linear feet, I reckoned. That was a good-sized collection. Much of it consisted of correspondence, but there were also copies of wills and deeds, along with maps of the Long family's extensive property both around Athena and in the Mississippi Delta. I located the finding aid to the collection put together by Miss Eulalie on one of the shelves and started skimming through it.

The contents of each box was listed under the various categories. I found no mention of books in any of the boxes, but the list for the final box in the collection noted it simply as *Miscellany*. Accordingly I moved to the shelf that housed the box and pulled it down, noting that it was lightweight.

After slipping on a pair of cotton gloves, I opened the box on the worktable and delved through the contents. There were three books inside, but none was the memoir I sought. They appeared to be old schoolbooks from the early twentieth century. Interesting, but not pertinent to my present search. I also found three briar pipes, each in a box with a label denoting the owner, Adalbert Long. I wasn't sure where he fit into the family tree, but I remembered that the name Adalbert cropped up frequently among the Longs. The final object was a file folder that contained several pieces of sheet music. I checked their copyright dates, and they were of 1890s vintage. Again, interesting but not pertinent.

I replaced the box on the shelf and considered whether I should go through all the boxes in the collection to search for Miss

Eulalie's copy of the memoir. I couldn't believe the former archivist would have put the book in another box and not have noted it in the finding aid. Still, I decided, I had better check.

Fifteen minutes later, having gone through all the boxes, I came up empty-handed. Either Miss Eulalie had knowingly lied to me or someone had removed her copy of the memoir from the collection. I didn't like to think of Miss Eulalie as a liar, but she was probably protecting someone. The question was whom.

I peeled off the gloves and discarded them before I locked the storeroom and went back to the office. I found Diesel still asleep on the windowsill. He raised his head groggily and yawned when I resumed my seat at the computer. I patted his head a couple of times, and he settled down to sleep again.

I called up the website of the Mississippi Department of Archives and History. I wanted to search their online catalog for a copy of the memoir. No luck, however. Then I searched an online database that claimed to be the world's largest online catalog. Again, nothing.

The memoir of Rachel Long was indeed a rare item. I would have to ask the mayor whether the family had a copy. I knew there was a large library at Bellefontaine, the antebellum mansion that had been home to the Longs since the 1830s. If they didn't have a copy, I would have to hope one of the two missing copies turned up. Otherwise I would never know what clues it might contain to the bizarre events of the past few days.

I needed to get back to the diary for now. I would deal with the memoir later. I found my place and began to read.

Two weeks after Rachel recorded the death of the three little Singletarys—how sad that she didn't even mention their names, I thought—she noted the death of Vidalia Singletary.

As a mother myself I understand the grief of a woman who has lost all three of her children at once. I doubt that I could withstand such a horror, and it is no wonder to me that poor Vidalia did not have the will to live through this harsh winter. Far better to be reunited with her loved ones in the Kingdom of Heaven than to suffer their loss in this sad and frightening world. As the war continues I wonder how we will continue the fight and whether our cause is worth such bloodshed and loss.

I felt Rachel's anguish, and I could have told her that no, it wasn't worth it. The loss of all that life, those years of privation and hardship, weren't worth it, particularly to preserve such a heinous system in which persons were property just like plows and chairs.

Rachel continued to mention the harsh winter and the difficulties caused by the weather. Her parents-in-law suffered particularly, her mother-in-law struck down by pneumonia. She died two days after Christmas. Rachel recorded the fact but did not elaborate, saying only that her own husband would be devastated when he received the news. He was last known to be in Virginia, and she had written but had no idea when, or if, the letter would reach Major Long.

The entry for January 3, 1862, contained startling news. I shared Rachel's shock, once I read through it completely.

Franklin Singletary came to speak to Father Long today, and though I was not privy to the conversation, Mr. Long later shared with me the gist of it. Father Long is most anxious that I should agree with the scheme that Franklin has proposed, but I am reluctant. In the end, however, I fear I shall have no choice because Father Long is so insistent.

Franklin is obsessed with Celeste, it seems, and with the child she will bear him. He has proposed to Father Long that he and his father will cede one hundred and fifty acres from their farm in return for Celeste and her unborn babe. Franklin will take the necessary steps to have Celeste declared a free-woman. While I admire his determination to win freedom for Celeste—a state to which I have no objection—I am fearful of the outcome. Celeste is light in color and may almost pass for white, owing to the fact that both her father and grandfather were white men who had relations with her mother and grand-mother, but by law she is black. Franklin cannot marry her, because the law forbids it. He may call her his wife, but in law she cannot be, and any child of their union will be illegitimate.

I wonder that Jasper Singletary has agreed to this, for he has for many years resisted the attempts of Father Long to buy this same land. Jasper has lost all hope, it seems, because of his tragic losses, and perhaps that is why. Father Long insists that my husband would agree that I should sell Celeste for this parcel of land. Celeste herself has begged me, and I find I cannot withstand such pleas, no matter my worries for her welfare and that of her child. They will be desperately poor, with little good farmland left, and they will face the opprobrium of the townspeople. I foresee nothing but ill fortune awaiting them.

I hadn't yet finished reading the diary but I closed the file and turned away from the computer. I wondered how the current Jasper Singletary would feel when he read all this. It could come as a great shock to him that his great-great-grandmother was a freed slave.

TWENTY-SIX

‖‖‖

"Let's go home, boy," I told Diesel. Though it was only a few minutes past four, I felt ready to get away from the archive and think about something besides the Longs and the Singletarys and their tangled histories.

Diesel slid down from the windowsill and went over to the door while I powered down the computer and gathered my things. Minutes later we were down the stairs and ready to walk out the front door, when Melba hailed me from her office. I suppressed a sigh and turned to greet my friend as she hurried out to where we stood. I had hoped to sneak out without her seeing us because I couldn't tell her what I had read in the diary. Melba had an unfailing instinct, however, for the times when I tried to duck out on her.

"How're y'all doing?" She bent to rub Diesel's head and coo at him.

"Fine, but tired," I said.

Melba straightened. "What have you been doing that's so

tiring besides sitting up there in your chair all day? I've been run off my feet or else I'd've been up there to visit earlier."

"Staring at a computer screen," I said. "That always tires me out and gives me a bit of a headache." I did have a headache, so I wasn't making a play for sympathy, hoping she would be satisfied and let us go without further questioning.

"I've got aspirin in my desk." Melba turned and walked back into her office.

I had no choice but to follow because I knew she would be offended if I didn't accept the aspirin.

"Here." She held out two of the pills and went over to the watercooler to fill a paper cup for me.

I took the pills with the water and thanked her. Diesel warbled anxiously. I was sure he felt my tension, and I made a conscious effort to relax. I was being silly, trying to avoid talking to Melba.

She beamed at me. "By the time you get home that aspirin ought to kick in, and you'll feel better. Sit down a minute before you head into that sticky humidity out there." She gestured toward the visitor's chair by her desk.

I waited until she sat before I complied with her order. Diesel rubbed himself against her legs, and she scratched his head and neck.

"Anything new on the murder?" Melba asked.

"Not that I know of," I said. "This is one time when I'm probably not going to be much help to Kanesha." I didn't think I'd found information in the diary all that significant to the investigation. It could certainly lead to embarrassment on Jasper Singletary's part depending on how he felt about his heritage, but I wasn't sure it was connected to Marie Steverton's death.

"You do know something," Melba said with a shrewd glint in

her eyes. "I reckon, though, you're not going to tell me because it's confidential, right?"

I nodded. "Right. Anything I find in the diaries I have to discuss with the mayor first, and then with Kanesha, if it's at all pertinent. If the mayor decides to let the diary be publicly available, well, then I can tell you."

"Fair enough," Melba said. "I bet you there's going to be something juicy in there somewhere. Every family has skeletons in the closet, but nobody's been able to find the ones the Longs are hiding." She grinned broadly.

"I thought you were a big supporter of the mayor's," I said. "Sounds to me like you're hoping there'll be mud to sling."

"Lucinda's a Long only by marriage," Melba said. "And I do support her. I just don't have much use for her son." She shook her head. "That boy didn't get a full serving of brains the day they were handing them out. If he wasn't so dang good-looking, nobody would think twice about voting for him."

Based on the scene I witnessed earlier today, I couldn't disagree with Melba. "I haven't heard him speak that much," I said. "But what little I have heard hasn't impressed me."

"Guess that's why Lucinda is doing all she can to help get the boy elected. I don't know why she didn't run herself. She'd be a lot better state senator than her son."

"That may be," I said, "but she isn't running."

Melba shrugged. "I reckon her husband is the one pushing to get the boy in office. He served a couple terms a while back in the state house of representatives, and he's probably aiming higher for his son. Trying to keep up the Long legacy."

"It'll sure be interesting to see how this race turns out." I stood. "Thanks again for the aspirin, but Diesel and I need to head on home. We'll see you tomorrow."

Melba gave the cat a few last head rubs before she bade us both good-bye. Despite the heat of the afternoon I was glad to get out of the building before I let something slip to Melba that I shouldn't.

I thought about our conversation on the short walk home. Having been close up with Beck Long and then hearing Melba's assessment of him, I gained a better understanding of why Mrs. Long believed the diaries could help. Emphasis on the Long family's history and accomplishments for generations might dazzle voters enough that they would overlook Beck's deficiencies.

Wouldn't be the first time that image had trumped ability in public office, I thought sourly. I really needed to pay more attention to state politics in order to make an informed decision come election day. Guiltily I recalled my father's opinion on voting. *If you don't vote, Son,* he told me on several occasions, *you've got no right to complain when you disagree with what's going on.* As in many things, my father was absolutely right. Up until his final illness, when he was bedridden and couldn't go to the polls, he had cast a vote in every election after he first became eligible.

My cell phone rang as I unlocked the front door. I waited to answer it until both Diesel and I were inside basking in the cool air of the house, with the door shut behind us. I recognized Kanesha Berry's cell phone number on the screen.

After I answered and said hello, she got right to the point. "Good news. Those diaries will be back tomorrow morning."

"That is good news," I said, though it made my eyes tired and my head ache to think of reading through all those pages of Rachel Long's handwriting.

"You made any progress with the other volume the mayor brought you?" Kanesha asked.

"I scanned all the pages, and I've been reading them today."

"Find anything interesting that could possibly be related to the investigation?"

I hesitated. Should I wait to talk to Mrs. Long first? She had, after all, given the diaries to the archive without restriction on use—except, of course, for the grant of exclusive access to Marie Steverton, now moot.

"You must have found something." Kanesha's sharp tone made me realize she interpreted my hesitation correctly.

"Yes, I did," I said. "I'm not sure it really has a bearing on the murder, but I think you should know, in case it turns out that it is important."

"Good," Kanesha said. "How about I swing by in about fifteen minutes? Are you still in the office?"

"No, I'm at home," I said. "Got here right as you called. Fifteen minutes is fine."

"I'll be there." She ended the call.

I put my cell phone away and removed Diesel's leash and halter. "Come on, boy, let's go have a snack."

The words hardly left my mouth before the cat darted away. I knew his destination. Litter box first, then water and food.

I put a pot of coffee on because I knew Kanesha drank a lot of it. Must be an occupational hazard, I mused. I also found some of her mother's cookies we could enjoy.

Kanesha turned up at the front door on the dot, and I let her in. She thanked me for the coffee and cookies, and she drank and munched while I told her what I found in Rachel's diary.

Her expression remained enigmatic throughout my narration.

When I finished, she said, "That was pretty clear. Sounds to me like Mr. Singletary may not be happy when he finds out about this. Although you'd think he'd already know."

I shrugged. "I guess the family members who knew kept quiet about it, and the later generations didn't find out."

Kanesha frowned. "Still pretty odd, though. You'd think somebody outside the Longs and the Singletarys would have found out. Athena wasn't a big town back then, and I'm sure it wasn't any different then than it is now. Everybody seems to know everybody else's business. How could they keep a thing like that secret all these years?"

TWENTY-SEVEN

"That's a good point," I said slowly. "I'd never heard anything much about the Singletarys, though, until all this election business started up."

Kanesha frowned. "I don't remember Mama talking much about them, either, and she knows all the old families in town."

"Maybe I ought to give Miss An'gel and Miss Dickce a call," I said. Diesel perked up when he heard those names. He chirped several times, and Kanesha smiled.

"He knows who you're talking about, doesn't he?" She stood. "Why don't you talk to Miss An'gel and ask? They know a lot about families around here that they never let slip. I need to get back to the office."

"I will." I escorted her to the front door. "I hope something breaks soon so you can wrap this up. I don't like to think about a killer running around free."

"You think I do?" Kanesha regarded me grimly. "The president of the college is having fits over this, and the mayor is calling every couple of hours to hear the latest. There's a lot of pressure to get this solved quickly."

"Everybody wants results yesterday," I said. "I know you're doing the absolute best you can."

Kanesha nodded. "Thanks. Let me hear from you if you come up with anything. I'll take any lead I can get right now." She turned and strode down the path to the street.

I shut the door and walked back into the kitchen. Diesel stood on his hind legs, one front paw extended toward the plate where a lone cookie sat.

"No, bad kitty," I told him as I hurried forward to grab the cookie away from him. I couldn't believe I'd been so careless as to leave the cookie within reach. "I told you these aren't good for you. Cats aren't supposed to eat raisins."

Diesel meowed loudly as I pulled the cookie away in time. I took it to the sink and put it down the garbage disposal. Diesel warbled in protest loudly enough that I heard him over the grinding of the disposal. I switched it off and turned to look down at my cat. He seemed cross.

"Too bad," I said. "If you want a snack go eat more of your crunchies."

Diesel turned away and marched off, tail in the air. He didn't head for the utility room, though. Instead he made for the stairs. I figured he was going to sulk in my bedroom.

Diesel didn't pout with me that often, and the good thing about it was that he wasn't destructive when he did. I would give him a couple of his favorite cat treats at dinner, and that would improve his mood.

I called Miss An'gel's cell phone but had to leave a message. I explained briefly the reason for my call, then rang off. The Ducote sisters spent most of their time doing volunteer work in Athena and the surrounding area. Meetings of various committees and boards kept them busy, so I wasn't surprised not to get an answer right away. Miss An'gel would return my call as soon as she could.

In the meantime I pondered how I would spend my evening. Too early yet for dinner, so what to do? Kanesha said the four volumes of Rachel Long's diary would be returned tomorrow morning, and that would mean a heavy workload. I sighed. I wasn't eager to plunge back into the one volume I had scanned, but I might as well. The sooner I got through them all, the sooner I might discover a clue to the present-day murder if one existed.

I went into the den and powered up my laptop. I got comfortable on the sofa and opened up the file I sent myself yesterday. I paged down until I found the last entry I'd read in my office.

The next entry came three days later.

The transaction is complete. Celeste thanked me most prettily, and I wished her well, keeping my misgivings to myself. The Good Lord only knew her fate, and I prayed that He would be merciful to her and to Franklin and their babe. I gave her two of my mother-in-law's dresses and an old woolen cloak of hers as well, in addition to the things I had already provided her during her service to our family. I shall miss her, I must confess, for she has been a cheerful presence in this sad and unhappy house.

For the next couple of weeks Rachel wrote of daily life during a hard winter. Their stores of food diminished at an alarming rate, and Rachel prayed they would be able to find provisions in town. She longed for the spring and its warmth and for the chance to plant vegetables to sustain them throughout the year.

On January 27, 1862, Rachel noted the death of Jasper Singletary, "too worn down by illness and despair to linger in this world." She would pray for his soul, that he had been reunited with his loved ones in Heaven. She made no mention of Franklin and Celeste.

After that Rachel evidently had little time or energy for daily attention to the diary. Two or three days often passed without any record of her activities. When Rachel did take time to write, she had little to say other than to mention problems with food and other supplies. Often she concluded with the words "and may the Lord provide as He will."

The bleakness of life in wartime came through poignantly in these pages. I admired Rachel's fortitude in facing each day and somehow struggling through. I felt I knew her a little, and I could not see the Rachel I found in these pages as a coldhearted killer— a woman who plotted the deaths of four people in order to help her father-in-law take the land he wanted from a bereaved husband and father.

She occasionally mentioned her own child, a son of four named after his father and grandfather, Andrew Adalbert Long III. He was a bonny child, she said, and she took comfort in his youth and energy. She sometimes ate little in order that he would have enough, particularly during the cold winter when they had to be careful with their supplies. She longed for her husband's safe return, and the pain of not knowing either his whereabouts or the state of his health affected her sleep.

She wrote little of political events or even of news of the war. Her attention centered on the situation at home. I thought perhaps she avoided recording news of the war because she couldn't bear confiding such sad tidings to her diary. That would make it all seem even more real. I knew that it would have to me.

I read on.

In November 1862 rumors spread that the Union Army was headed for Athena, and the town, though evidently panicked, did what it could to prepare. Rachel had already hidden many valuables away from the slaves—those who hadn't run away by then—and hoped they would be safe. Later she recorded that, though the army did come to Athena and cause considerable damage, they did not penetrate far enough south to find Bellefontaine. The Longs escaped the worst of the Union depredations, unlike the poor townspeople.

I skimmed after that because there were no substantial entries to read. Even Rachel's mention of her father-in-law's passing in September 1863 merited only two sentences. The privations of wartime had grown even worse by then, and I wondered how they managed to survive. I knew Rachel lived for many years after the war, as did her son. I didn't know about her husband, though, and whether he survived the war.

I decided to look it up. I did a search on Andrew Adalbert Long, Jr., in the library's online catalog because I knew the information should be in the record for the collection. The information came up right away. To my surprise I discovered Andrew Junior died in 1863. *Before or after his father?* I wondered.

I would have to check the diary to see what Rachel recorded about her husband's death.

The house phone rang, and I set my laptop aside to get to my desk where the instrument sat.

"Good evening, Mr. Harris," Mrs. Long said. "I hope you

won't mind my calling but I'm afraid curiosity is getting the better of me. Have you been reading the diary?"

"I don't mind at all, Your Honor," I said. "I have been reading, and I have discovered a lot of interesting information." I wondered how she would react to the news about Jasper Singletary's great-great-grandmother Celeste.

"Excellent," she said. "Can you give me a summary? I have about twenty minutes before I have to leave for a dinner being held in my son's honor."

"Sure," I said. I gave her a quick, general report about the nature of the entries in the diary. After a pause for breath, I related the strange story of Rachel's connection with the Singletary family and her attempts to help them.

"Interesting," the mayor said. "Perhaps this will stop young Mr. Singletary from making some of these wild claims of his."

"Maybe," I said. "There is more, however." I told her about Franklin and Celeste.

When I finished, the mayor's reaction shocked me.

She laughed. "Oh, this is priceless. He's been having a fit to get his hands on these diaries, and now he's going to be sorry I ever found them. His campaign is in big trouble now."

TWENTY-EIGHT

|||||||||||||||||||||||||||||||||||||||||||||||||||||||||||||||||||||||||||||||||

How should I respond to the distasteful, gleeful malice I heard in Mrs. Long's voice? She was making the assumption, I supposed, that Singletary would lose votes if it were known that he was of mixed race. One never knew how voters would react to anything. In the twenty-first century I wondered whether this could be a factor in the race.

I had to admit, however, that I'd had some of the same thoughts the mayor expressed to me—only I hadn't been chortling over them.

Finally I said, "At the beginning you stated that these diaries should be available to the public. I have already discussed the contents of this volume with Chief Deputy Berry. Do you still want the contents publicly available?"

"By all means," the mayor said. "The public has a right to know the background of the candidates running for office. Then it's up to them to decide what's important."

That sounded smugly self-righteous—not to mention self-serving—to me, but I didn't care to get into an argument with the mayor over it.

"In that case I will give Mr. Singletary a file of the digitized pages," I said. "In the event that this could affect his campaign, he should know as soon as possible. I think that's the only fair thing to do."

"Agreed," Mrs. Long said. "Now I really have to get going. I'll check in with you again tomorrow. I heard the other books will be back in your office sometime in the morning."

The phone clicked in my ear, and I put the receiver back in its cradle. I didn't like to think so, but I believed that the issue of class had reared its nasty head. The Longs were among the elite in Athena, if not the entire state of Mississippi, whereas Jasper Singletary came from a poor family. The Singletarys had been in Athena for generations, but they didn't have money or political clout. Mrs. Long might add a third lack to those two: breeding. The Longs considered themselves patricians, and there came with that status a sense of entitlement, at least on their part. That bothered me, but there was nothing I could do to change it.

I went back to the laptop and searched for a phone number for Jasper Singletary's campaign headquarters. I didn't want to go through Kelly Grimes. Instead I thought I should share the file only with the man himself. Number located, I punched it in on the house phone and waited for someone to answer. A harried-sounding woman picked up after five rings.

I gave her my name and stressed the urgency of my call. "He is interested in this information, and I know he will want to know about it as soon as possible."

She promised to pass the message along, but I put down the

receiver wondering when Singletary might actually receive the news of my call.

I should not have doubted the poor woman, as it turned out. Singletary called me about fifteen minutes later, when I had my head stuck in the fridge trying to decide what I wanted for dinner.

"You have news for me, I hear," Singletary said after a quick greeting.

"I do. I would like to send you a file with the scanned pages from the diary," I said. "I think you'll find the contents interesting."

"Did you find the evidence I need?"

"No, I didn't," I replied. "I really think you need to read this for yourself, rather than have me try to tell it all to you over the phone."

Singletary expelled a sharp breath. "All right, then." He gave me an e-mail address, and I jotted it down.

"Does anyone else read the mail sent to this address?" I asked. I wanted to be sure that he, and he alone, read this. He might want to think about the contents before he acted upon them.

"Yes," he said. "Has anyone else seen this?"

"No one else has seen it," I said, "but I did share the contents during conversations with Mrs. Long and with Chief Deputy Berry. I don't see that there's any connection to the current murder investigation, but there is family history that you should know about, if you don't already."

He did not respond for several seconds. "Go ahead and send me the file." He ended the call.

I speculated that the abrupt hang-up meant he was angry I had talked to Mrs. Long and Kanesha. Well, so be it. I sat down and pulled the computer into my lap. It took less than half a minute to send the file on its way to Jasper Singletary. I powered down the laptop and set it aside. Time for dinner, I decided.

While I ate the chicken salad Azalea left for me and doled out cat treats to Diesel, I thought about the Singletary family and the source of their hatred for the Longs. I could understand that Franklin and Celeste did not want to tell their children about how father traded land for mother and instead might present the transaction as a nefarious deal arranged by Rachel's father-in-law. But how could the knowledge that Celeste was once a slave be lost to collective memory?

The townspeople would surely have known, and given the mind-set of the time, I couldn't imagine that there wasn't gossip about the couple. Gossip that would have persisted over the years, at least for a generation or two.

I hoped Miss An'gel would call soon. In the meantime I had to think of a discreet way to ask her about the Singletary family and what would be considered miscegenation in the family tree. I knew Miss An'gel would not press me for details that I couldn't share, but I still had to take care with what I said.

By the time she called the kitchen was clean and Diesel and I were upstairs. I was reading while he snoozed beside me on the bed.

"Good evening, Miss An'gel. How are you?"

"Doing fine, Charlie. How are you and that beautiful kitty of yours?"

"We're fine, too. Diesel is stretched out beside me napping, though he did perk up when he heard your name."

Miss An'gel laughed. "Give him a few rubs on the head for me and Sister. You said you wanted to talk to me about a local family. What's going on?"

I gave her a quick précis of the situation with the diaries and the murder of Marie Steverton. "Mrs. Long thought there might be information about the family that could help her son in his election bid. In the one volume I've read so far, I haven't spotted anything."

"That boy will probably skate through on the family name," Miss An'gel said. "I don't think he'll do any harm in state government, but he certainly won't accomplish anything significant." She sighed. "Young Singletary, on the other hand, is bright and capable, but he doesn't have the cachet of a distinguished family like Beck Long. That could hurt his chances."

"About the Singletarys," I said, thankful she had given me a segue to my question, "other than the fact that they have been poor farmers for several generations, is there anything you might know of in their family tree that voters might find, well, objectionable?"

"What a fascinating question," Miss An'gel said. "I'm sure there is a story behind it, but I suppose you can't tell me why you're asking in such a delicate way."

"No, ma'am, I can't, at least not yet," I replied.

"Let me think for a moment." The line went silent for about fifteen seconds. "No, nothing. Other than bitterness against the Long family over some land deal around the time of the Civil War, I can't think of anything."

"What do you know about that land deal?" I asked.

"My mother told us the story when Sister and I were young," Miss An'gel said. "I suppose Mother had it from our father, who had it from his father. Our grandfather was born in 1870, so he would have heard something about it from his father, who fought in the war." She paused. "The story doesn't reflect well on the Long patriarch at the time, one of the many Andrews they've had in the family; I forget exactly which one. The way Sister and I heard it, Andrew Long had his eye on some land the Singletarys owned and had tried to buy it several times. Early on in the war,

Singletary—I think he was a Jasper—fell ill and was desperate for money to feed his family. Long saw his chance, swooped in, and offered the lowest price he could and bought the land. Singletary died right afterwards, I think, and his son had lost some of his best farmland."

"Was there anything else about the land deal that you might have heard?" I asked.

"No, not that I can remember," Miss An'gel said. "One of the reasons Mother told us was because our father had apparently told her not to do business with the Longs because they're cheap and always looking to get the most they can for next to nothing." She laughed. "Don't you dare tell anyone I told you that, now."

I smiled. "Of course not. Thanks for sharing that story with me, Miss An'gel. I really appreciate it."

"You're always welcome," she replied. "And one of these days, I hope, you're going to tell me what this is all about."

"It won't be long, probably," I said. "Please give my best to Miss Dickce."

"I sure will," Miss An'gel replied. She said good-bye and ended the call.

I put the phone aside and regarded the yawning cat beside me. "Miss An'gel was helpful, but what she told me leaves me with questions I can't answer."

The cat looked at me and warbled. Then he stretched for a moment before snuggling down and closing his eyes.

I had a habit of telling Diesel things as if I expected a helpful answer, but I realized I was mostly just verbalizing my thoughts. Thinking aloud helped sometimes.

I found it fascinating that the facts surrounding the transaction of swapping Celeste for the land had apparently never been known to anyone other than the Longs and Franklin and Celeste. How had they managed to keep it a secret?

The only thing I could come up with for an answer was that none of the townspeople knew that Celeste was a slave. That was possible, I supposed, but not likely. The Longs' other slaves would have known, and after the war, when they were all free, surely there would have been talk among them about Celeste.

The phone rang. I glanced at the screen.

"Good evening, Kanesha."

She returned my greeting. "I have two items of interest to share with you." Her tone sounded grim, and I braced myself for bad news. I hoped it wasn't another murder.

"First off," she said, "I am looking at the forensic report on the diaries. According to this, at least ten pages were removed recently from one of the books."

I barely had time to take that in before she continued.

"The other thing—and I have to wonder if these two are connected—I had a call from Chief Ford at the college. Someone broke into Dr. Steverton's office and ransacked it."

TWENTY-NINE

||||||||||||||||||||||||||||||||||||||||||||||||||||||||||||||||||||||

I took a moment to mull over what Kanesha told me. I could see a connection between the removal of the diary pages and the searching of Marie Steverton's office.

"Here's what I think," I said. "Marie removed those pages. Then the killer found out and decided to search the office looking for them."

"That's what I'm thinking, too," Kanesha said.

"When was Marie's office ransacked?" I asked.

"Chief Ford couldn't pinpoint a time," Kanesha replied. "It obviously happened after we looked through the office the morning her body was found. That was around nine thirty. We sealed the office, and it stayed sealed—until the history department secretary happened to notice around five yesterday afternoon that the seal had been tampered with. She called Chief Ford, and he found the office turned over."

"I wonder if the searcher found what he was looking for," I said.

"We don't know," Kanesha said. "Neither the secretary nor the head of the department could tell us whether anything was missing. The secretary said the office was messy to begin with, and the only valuables she knew of were the computer and a CD player. Both of them were still in the office."

"Whatever is in those missing pages must be significant," I said. "Marie had to have been the person who removed them. Otherwise it doesn't make much sense."

"I agree," Kanesha said. "I wish I could narrow down the time frame for the office search. It must have occurred during the night, because it's next door to the secretary's office. She would have heard someone moving around in there otherwise."

"Marie obviously had an excellent hiding place, because you didn't turn up the diaries when you searched her house," I said. "Maybe the missing pages are in the same spot, wherever it is."

"I sent two deputies over to search the house again tonight," Kanesha said. "They reported no signs of forced entry or of a search but they're still looking for the pages."

"I hope they turn up," I said. "The contents have to be pertinent to this crazy situation somehow."

"I expect so," Kanesha said. "If we find them, I'll be in touch." She ended the call.

I wondered what Marie could have found in the torn-out pages. If the information in those pages could damage someone—either the Longs or Jasper Singletary—then obviously the killer would want to find and destroy them.

Perhaps Marie tried her hand at blackmail; but if she had, she paid the ultimate price. At least this train of thought produced a believable motive for her death—if I accepted that the missing pages contained seriously damaging information.

Jasper Singletary claimed that Rachel Long deliberately poisoned his ancestor's wife and children. Would Rachel have confessed something like that to her diary? That would have been a stupid move, and from what I'd read today, I didn't think Rachel was a stupid woman.

I went back to an old question—why was one volume of the diary hidden and not kept with the other four? Did the hidden one—that I had read today—contain information missing from the others? There had to be a reason it was separated and placed in the false bottom of the trunk.

There were too many questions. My mind buzzed from all the possibilities, none of which seemed to offer a solid answer.

I felt too restless, too mentally unsettled, to choose a new book to read. I checked the time. Eight thirty. At least ninety minutes or more before Helen Louise would call.

"I'll be back in a minute," I told the drowsy cat beside me. He blinked at me and yawned.

I retrieved my laptop from the den and brought it back to the bedroom. I had some pages left to read of Rachel Long's diary, and I might as well finish them tonight. I recalled having read about the death of her father-in-law in the fall of 1863 and then searching for information about her husband's death. I hadn't gone back to the diary to find out what Rachel recorded about the loss of her husband.

I found mention of it in an entry dated October 15, 1863.

Two weeks ago we laid to rest my precious Andrew, only days after we mourned the passing of his father. Father Long lost heart, seeing his son in such grievous condition, and the news of the war compounded his sorrow. I must remain strong and pray that the Lord will guide me now. My boy is too young for the responsibility of caring for his inheritance, and I cannot fail him, though I cannot see how we will last through the winter.

Poignant words, but I knew that Rachel had survived, along with her son. They made it through the war and somehow found the way to prosperity again. In her way, I thought, Rachel must have been a formidable woman. With the deaths of her father-in-law and her husband, she had a heavy burden. I recalled that her son, Andrew III, was only about five or six years old at the time.

I finished the pages about twenty minutes later. Rachel's record-keeping grew sparse. She had little time to think about writing in her diary. The final entry came on May 17, 1865.

Word reached Bellefontaine today that General Lee surrendered to General Grant in Virginia. The war is over, and I find myself numb and exhausted. All but a few of our most loyal workers have fled. May the Lord watch over us and give us the strength to face the future.

I felt as if I'd been left hanging by an ambiguous ending to a mystery novel. I wanted to know what happened next. I wouldn't have long to wait. The rest of Rachel's diaries would be back in the archive tomorrow, and I could read the rest of the story, as it were.

I shut down the laptop and got up to put it on the desk in the corner of my bedroom. Back in bed I lay there and stared at the ceiling. Diesel slept on beside me. I dozed off at some point, then was roused by the ringing of my cell phone.

I yawned as I picked up the phone. "Hello, love," I said.

"You sound as tired as I feel," Helen Louise replied. "Long day?"

"Yes, I'll tell you about it later. How was your day? Was business good?"

"Very good," she said. "So good, in fact, I'm thinking about expanding into that empty storefront next door. What do you think about that?"

"That's great," I said. "Congratulations to you for building up such a successful business. You have such a gift, not only for creating the most delicious food I've ever tasted, but also for creating a wonderful ambience at the bakery. It's no wonder everyone in Athena loves it."

"Thanks, love." I could hear the smile in her voice. "I have to sit down with my banker and figure out the finances, but I think it's doable. Going to be a lot more work, though, and of course I don't want to be shut down long for the construction. I need to talk to an architect about that and see what the options are."

"Maybe all you'll need is a door between your space and the one next door. That should be simple enough."

We talked about her plans for several minutes before we both began to yawn. Soon after that we bade each other good night. I promised to come by for lunch again tomorrow.

The next morning I was eager to get to the archive and hurried through breakfast. I didn't know when the diaries would arrive, or who would bring them. I doubted that the person bringing them would show up before nine, but Diesel and I made it there by eight thirty just in case.

Melba's door was closed, but she would arrive soon. Diesel and I headed upstairs. I planned to get a few things done before Melba popped up for her usual visit and before the diaries arrived.

I had neglected e-mail the past few days, and I needed to catch up. I spent half an hour responding to messages, some of which required answering questions about the archive's collections. I also needed to make new archival boxes for the four diary volumes. When I finished that task I decided to act upon a half-formed idea I had when I woke up this morning.

My knowledge of Civil War–era Athena was sketchy at best, and I intended to rectify that. I wanted to know more about what happened here during those dark days, and I figured there might be theses or dissertations that could satisfy my curiosity. I hadn't run across any books on the subject, but students earning degrees might have written about aspects of the town's history.

I also debated going through the Long collection to look for letters that Rachel might have written, but decided that she would hardly have confided plans to poison the Singletary children to a correspondent.

A search of the college library's online catalog yielded several works with the town of Athena as a subject. One of them, *Athena, Mississippi, During the Civil War: A Study of Social and Political Life Under Crisis*, was a dissertation by Catherine Louisa Brooke. The date of the degree was 1987, and according to the catalog the bound item was on the shelf in the library.

I considered my options and decided to ask Melba to watch Diesel while I went next door to the main library building in search of the dissertation. I knew she would be happy to have my cat to herself for a while. "Come on, boy," I said to the napping feline on the windowsill. "Let's go see Melba."

Diesel perked up the moment he heard Melba's name and slid down from the window. He scampered to the door ahead of me and was down the stairs by the time I reached the top of them. I hurried down, and as I neared the office, I could hear Melba already cooing over the cat.

"Morning, Charlie," she said. "I was asking Diesel if he sneaked down to see me on his own." She rubbed her hand along the cat's spine, and Diesel chirped happily in response.

"No, we came down because I wanted to ask you to watch him while I go next door. I want to get a book from the library."

"Of course." She beamed at me.

"One other thing," I said. "Someone will be returning the Rachel Long diaries to the archive today. I'm not sure exactly when, but I was told it would be this morning. Give me a shout on my cell phone if they show up before I get back, okay?"

"Sure," Melba said. "Take your time. Diesel and I'll be fine."

The whole errand took me only ten minutes, and it was almost nine thirty when Diesel and I arrived back upstairs in the office. He got comfortable in his favorite spot, and I sat at my desk and opened the dissertation.

I noted that Professor Newkirk was the student's major advisor and also that Marie Steverton had been a member of her committee. I skimmed the acknowledgments and was not surprised to see that Marie received only a bare mention.

I settled back in my chair and started to read. I was happy to discover that Dr. Brooke had an engaging style and her prose didn't suffer from the usual academic dryness. The opening chapter related the beginnings of the town of Athena in the early 1820s, and I recognized several names as those of our most prominent families: Ducote, Long, and Pendergrast, among others. Then I had the pleasant shock of seeing the name of my own great-great-grandfather, Henry Harris. He had owned a large dry goods store in Athena and was considered one of the town's most prominent businessmen.

The narrative absorbed me, and I lost track of time while I read. A knock at the door roused me, and I looked up to see a man in the uniform of the sheriff's department standing there.

"Please, come in." I stood and motioned for him to enter. He looked vaguely familiar but I couldn't remember his name.

"Morning, Mr. Harris," the deputy said. "Where would you like me to put this?" He nodded to indicate the box he carried.

"Right here on the desk, Deputy Turnbull." He had come close enough for me to read the name on his badge.

Turnbull set the box down and pulled some papers out of the top. "If you'll sign this for me, sir, to acknowledge you accepted return of the books, I'd appreciate it." He put the papers on the desk in front of me.

"Certainly." I sat and picked up a pen. I followed the direction of the deputy's pointing finger and signed as asked.

"Thank you, sir," he said. He gave a sharp nod. "Have a good day."

I thanked him in return and bade him good day as well. My hands trembled as I reached in a drawer and pulled out a pair of cotton gloves. I was thrilled to have the diaries back in the archive.

I stared down at the contents of the box as I pulled on the gloves. Would the diaries yield the information necessary to shed light on the bizarre events of the past few days? I took a deep breath and began to unload the box.

THIRTY

"Well, boy, I have my work cut out for me now," I said as I placed the last volume on my desk and set the box on the floor beside it. I figured the cat would want to investigate the box, and better that it should be on the floor than on my desk.

I turned to the windowsill. Diesel wasn't there.

I had a brief moment of panic, then forced myself to calm down. "Diesel? Where are you, boy? Come here please."

I waited for at least fifteen seconds before I repeated my summons.

No cat appeared. He was probably downstairs with Melba. I stripped off one glove, picked up the office phone, and punched in her extension. She answered right away.

"I was about to call you," she said. "I have a furry visitor, and I'll bet you didn't know he'd sneaked out of the office and come down here."

I felt a huge sensation of relief. "No, I didn't know he'd left the office. I was pretty engrossed in reading, and he got out without my knowledge. Thank goodness he's safe with you, the little demon."

"I thought he might follow Art Turnbull, the deputy who was here a few minutes ago. He stopped in to say a quick hello to me before he came upstairs."

"One of your many admirers, no doubt," I teased her gently. I figured Turnbull for mid-forties, but that was close enough for Melba.

"No, he's married," she said. "But I know his sister Madge real well. You probably don't remember her. She was a few grades behind us in school."

"No, can't say that I remember her. Look, are you okay with Diesel down there? Or do you want me to come get him?"

"He can stay with me for a while," Melba said. "When I get ready to take a break, we'll come upstairs."

"Thanks." I felt relieved but also a bit aggravated with myself. I shouldn't have been so wrapped up in my reading that I missed seeing my large cat slink out of the office. I needed to be more alert.

My heart rate returned to normal, I picked up the discarded glove and put it back on. I figured I might as well take a look at the volume with the missing pages. Each of the volumes lay on its side on my desk, with the bottom pages of the book toward me. I bent closer to them and examined each one.

The volume with the missing pages wasn't hard to spot. There was a slight gap in the pages about two-thirds of the way toward the back of it. I pulled that one forward and opened it with care.

I turned to the place in the book where the pages had been taken out. I examined the area, and it looked to me like Marie had used a razor blade to cut the pages loose. There was no point in feeling anger over Marie's act of vandalism. She had already paid a higher price than I could have exacted.

The date of the entry preceding the gap was August 10, 1863. I turned to the beginning of the diary and found the initial date there: November 1, 1860.

That was odd. This volume covered at least part of the same period as the volume Mrs. Long found hidden in the false bottom of the trunk.

I checked the final entry for a date: June 3, 1866.

This volume *did* cover the same time period. Actually it was a bit more extensive, I realized after a moment's thought. The volume I had read started in March of 1861 and ended in mid-May 1865, a week or two after the end of the war.

Why had Rachel kept two diaries for roughly the same period? The one I read did not use all the pages of the book like this one did. Was the one I read the original diary of the period, and the one on my desk perhaps a fuller version Rachel wrote later? I knew Mary Boykin Chesnut edited and rewrote parts of her diary before the book, *A Diary from Dixie*, was published in 1905. The diary was not published in Mary's lifetime. From what I could remember she died in the mid-1880s and asked a friend to see about getting it published.

Rachel couldn't have known, of course, about Mary Chesnut's diary, but perhaps she had a similar ambition, to see her diary published as a record of her experiences growing up in the South through a tragic era.

Miss Eulalie might be able to shed light on the subject, although I now felt diffident about asking her. There might also, I realized, be information in the correspondence and other papers in the Long collection.

All that could wait. Right now I wanted to delve into this volume of the diary to see what information it might contain that would be in any way relevant to present-day events.

I went back to the gap in the pages. The last sentence before the missing pages read, "Words cannot express the horror and sickness I feel over . . ."

Over what? I wanted to scream. How frustrating. This lead-in told me that there must be something sensational in the missing pages.

I suppressed my irritation and read the first words on the page after the gap. They were just as intriguing as the words preceding the gap: "behind us, never to be mentioned or recalled as long as I draw breath."

I glanced down the page to see the date of the next entry: September 30, 1863.

What had happened between August 10 and September 30, 1863, besides the deaths of Rachel's husband and father-in-law? The Union Army didn't come to Athena until the winter of 1863, in November, I thought.

I would have to do some digging to see what I could find about the summer of 1863 in Athena. Dr. Brooke's dissertation might cast light on it. I closed the diary and set it aside.

A knock at the door caught my attention before I could resume reading the dissertation. I looked up to see Jasper Singletary approaching me.

"I apologize for dropping by unannounced like this, Mr. Harris." He extended his hand, and I shook it. "I took the chance you'd be here and would have time to talk with me about the diary."

"I'm glad to see you." I indicated a chair. "Please sit. I have to tell you I've been curious about your reaction to the information related to your ancestors."

Singletary regarded me in silence for a moment. I couldn't read his expression.

"My first reaction is that Rachel Long was a liar," he said. "She came across to me as a bit self-righteous about her charitable behavior. Just because she didn't admit to anything in that diary doesn't mean she didn't poison the children and their mother deliberately."

He surprised me. I thought the first thing he'd address would the news about Celeste. Instead he focused on his grievance against the Longs.

"I can't deny that," I said. For now, I decided quickly, I wasn't going to tell him about the diary he read being a partial duplicate of another one. I wanted to figure out the reason for its existence before I talked with him or any of the Longs about it. "Rachel could very well have omitted anything that would make her look guilty. You'll have to look elsewhere for your proof that she was a murderess."

"I'm not giving up," he said firmly. He crossed his arms over his chest and regarded me with that enigmatic expression again. "Rachel was also lying about my great-great-grandmother Celeste. Don't you think we would have known before now if she had been a slave before she married my great-great-grandfather Franklin?" He snorted.

"What kind of family documents do you have?" I asked.

The question obviously surprised him. "What do you mean? Are you talking about birth certificates?"

"No, because I don't think they gave them out in the 1860s. I'll have to look that up," I said. "I'm talking about a marriage license, or some proof that Franklin and Celeste married. It was illegal for a black woman—and Celeste would have been considered black even though she was allegedly of mixed race—to marry a white man, and vice versa."

"You think if I have a copy of a license showing they were legally married, that would prove she was white?" Jasper shrugged. "Look, it doesn't matter to me whether she was or she wasn't a slave in the long run. By all accounts she and Franklin had a happy marriage even though they were dirt poor all their life together. I'm not ashamed of my background, but I am curious why nobody in my family, including my great-aunt who's ninety-eight and still sharp, knows anything about this. I asked Aunt Addie this morning, and she laughed. Celeste died when Aunt Addie was fifteen."

"The fact that your great-aunt knew Celeste doesn't rule out the possibility. If Celeste had been a slave, she and her husband would have taken great pains to keep it from the rest of the family."

"Yeah, I get that," Jasper said. "But how come no one ever came up to Aunt Addie or my grandfather and said anything about their grandmother being a slave once upon a time? If Celeste had been a slave, people in town would have known. You couldn't hide something like that."

I couldn't argue with his logic, and I told him so. "That's been troubling me, too. For the moment, let's assume that it's true that she was a slave. If that became public knowledge now, would it have a bad effect on your campaign?"

"I might lose some votes from narrow-minded people." He sounded tired all of a sudden. "Look, people come up with all kind of nutty reasons not to vote for a candidate. They think he has a squint and looks like a crook, or the other candidate is more attractive. If it does turn out to be true, who knows? I could actually pick up support from black voters in this district."

I couldn't tell whether he really believed what he had told me, about not being all that concerned over Celeste's racial heritage, or whether, in typical politician fashion, he was saying what he thought was most expedient in the situation. I hoped it was the former.

Singletary stood. "I've taken up enough of your time, and I've got to get on the road. More campaign stops. I'd also better do what I can to find out if Beck Long and his handlers plan to make this stuff public."

We shook hands again, and out he went. I sat again and stared at the diaries on my desk. On a sudden whim, I got up and went to the storage room next door. I found the fifth volume and brought it back to my desk. I opened it to a random page beside one of the other volumes and began to compare them.

After fifteen minutes I gave up. The handwriting looked pretty much the same to me. The fifth volume had the same binding, the same paper, from everything I could see. Still . . .

I hesitated for a moment, then picked up the phone. I punched in Stewart Delacorte's number on campus and hoped he would answer.

THIRTY-ONE

||||||||||||||||||||||||||||||||||||||||||||||||||||||||||||||

Stewart answered after several rings, and I identified myself.

"Hi, Charlie, how are you?" Stewart asked.

"Doing fine. I'm working on a new project," I said. "I was wondering if you could help me with something."

"Sure," Stewart said. "What do you need?"

"It might be better if I explained in person," I said. "Can I come over to your office sometime today?"

Stewart chuckled. "I'm not in the office at the moment. I have my office phone forwarded to my cell phone. I'm home, actually. How about I come to your office in about twenty minutes?"

"That's fine," I said, "if you're sure you have time."

"I do," Stewart replied. "See you in twenty."

I hoped Stewart might be able to answer the questions I now had about the authenticity of the fifth volume of Rachel's diary. I suspected that it was a fake, and if Stewart could give me some kind of basic evidence of that possibility, I would turn the book over to Kanesha and tell her it needed to be thoroughly tested.

If the diary proved to be a fake, then the question was, who did it?

The most obvious answer was the mayor herself, Lucinda Beckwith Long.

Her motive? To embarrass Jasper Singletary and cost him votes by spreading the news that he was a descendant of a slave who once was the property of the Long family.

The arrogance that lay behind such a plan stunned me. Was the Long family so desperate to put Beck in office that they would stoop to something so preposterous? I suspected they were. I also found repugnant the notion that Jasper Singletary was less *worthy*—I had to struggle for a word—because of the alleged connection to a slave woman. Did Mrs. Long really believe that was such a terrible thing, enough to turn voters away from Jasper?

The man himself didn't seem that bothered by it, and I had to credit him for that attitude if it was, indeed, genuine.

How did the murder of Marie Steverton connect to this? I wondered whether she had known about the faked diary. *Allegedly* faked diary, I reminded myself. Had the mayor run Marie down in cold blood to keep her from giving away the scheme? That was possible, I supposed, but it didn't seem likely somehow.

I kept running these and other questions through my brain while I waited for Stewart to arrive. The frustration from not being able to find answers was building, and I knew before long I would have a headache from the tension.

Stewart's arrival came as a welcome interruption. "Hi, Charlie," he said from the doorway. "Here I am, and I have a companion with me."

Diesel trotted into the room ahead of Stewart and came around the desk to sit by me. He looked up at me and meowed.

"Your companion has been naughty," I said. "He sneaked out of here while I was busy and went down to see Melba."

"Oh, Diesel, you are a bad boy." Stewart chuckled as he made himself comfortable in the chair across from me.

I looked down at the cat and frowned. "You shouldn't do things like that."

Diesel meowed and placed a large paw on my leg. For him, this probably constituted an apology. I patted his head. Reassured, he climbed into the window behind me and stretched out.

I turned to Stewart, who looked as neatly groomed and fresh as always. I wished I knew how he managed to stay that way, even in the heat of a Mississippi summer.

"Thanks for coming by," I said. I waved a hand to indicate the volumes of Rachel Long's diary on my desk. "I need your help with these."

Stewart quirked one eyebrow. "Are they old chemistry books? Otherwise, I'm not sure I'd be of much help."

"They're not," I said, "but it's your expertise in chemistry that I need." I tapped the suspect volume lightly. "I think this one is a fake, and I'm hoping you can tell me if I'm right."

"What are they?" Stewart asked.

"I'm getting ahead of myself," I said. "These are diaries written by Rachel Afton Long around the time of the Civil War."

"Long?" Stewart said. "As in our esteemed mayor's husband's family?"

I nodded. "Yes. Mrs. Long brought four of the diaries to me on Monday. She found them in a trunk in the attic and wanted them added to the Long collection here in the archive. Later she brought me a fifth one." I held it up. "She said she found it in the same trunk, but hidden in a false bottom."

"What makes you think it's a fake?" Stewart asked.

"The contents," I said. "From what I can see, the paper, the ink, and the handwriting are similar. But the time period covered in this volume is also covered in one of the original four Mrs. Long brought."

"Tell me the whole story," Stewart said. "I've got time, and before I get involved with this, I want to know what's really going on."

That was a fair request. I gave him the salient facts as I saw them. When I finished, he shook his head. "The Longs have always been snobs, but this really takes the *gâteau*." He shifted in his chair. "Do you think the mayor ran Marie down, then?"

"I don't know," I said. "I'm really not sure how the murder fits into this mud-slinging scheme. Unless Marie managed to figure it out and threatened to expose it."

"I'll leave that up to you and your buddy Kanesha." Stewart grinned. "Have you told her yet that you think you've got a fake on your hands?"

"No, I haven't. I wanted to have some kind of evidence before I tell her and suggest she send it for a more thorough investigation."

"And that's where I come in." Stewart looked thoughtful. "I'm sure you don't want me to do anything to harm the integrity of these books. Probably the easiest thing would be for me to examine the paper and ink with the microscope."

"What would that tell you?" I asked.

"I can compare the fibers in the paper, to start with," Stewart replied. "Then I can look at the ink, see how it has bonded with the paper, for example. If one was written back during the Civil

War and the other one only recently, there will be noticeable differences."

I forestalled him before he launched into a more technical explanation. "If you do find these differences, then I'll feel more confident about calling Kanesha and telling her what I suspect. When will you be able to do it?"

Stewart smiled. "I don't have class this afternoon, so I can work on it now. I'll take the suspected fake and one of the others and compare them."

"Thanks. I really appreciate this," I said. "I've got a box here you can take them in." I put the suspected fake and the final volume of the four original ones into the box for him.

"I'll bring them back when I've finished," Stewart said. "Shouldn't take too long if I can get into one of the labs and find the appropriate tools available. This time of the semester the labs are pretty full."

Diesel warbled and trilled a good-bye as Stewart left. He called a farewell to the cat before he disappeared into the hallway.

I turned in my chair to regard the cat. Diesel gazed sleepily at me. He meowed, and I rubbed his head.

"I can't stay mad at you for long," I told him. He purred and pushed his head against my hand. "I'm going to have to pay more attention, though."

Diesel settled down after a bit more love, and I tried to focus on what I needed to do next. I had to keep busy or else I'd be staring at the phone every other minute, silently urging Stewart to call.

My glance fell on the diary volume with the missing pages, and my thoughts homed in on the time period of those pages. What had happened in the summer of 1863 in Athena?

I picked up the dissertation. Too bad it didn't have an index, I thought. Instead of looking up pages where any of the Long family was mentioned, I'd have to read or skim through the text.

After the chapter on the early history of Athena, the author of the dissertation focused more tightly on the years of the war and its aftermath. I started skimming, looking for mentions of the Long and Singletary families. After fifty pages or so, I found what I was looking for.

Tragedy befell the Long family twice in rapid succession in the summer of 1863 with the deaths of both Andrew Long Senior and his son, Major Andrew Long Junior. The major, badly wounded during the Battle of Gettysburg in early July, and no longer able to serve, somehow managed to make it home to Bellefontaine by mid-August. He remained secluded there with his wife, son, and father until his death. Several of the town's prominent citizens called upon the family to welcome Major Long home, but were turned away by his wife, Rachel. The major's wounds were so disfiguring, she told them, the major refused to see anyone.

The footnote to this paragraph cited the letters of one Josiah Rhodes, who was evidently the Longs' banker. The author of the dissertation went on to say that word reached the town in late September of 1863 that the major had succumbed to a fever, and shortly after, his father died as well. Mrs. Long was left with her young son and a few servants at Bellefontaine.

I had seen photographs of the carnage wrought by the Civil War and the grievous wounds borne by the soldiers who survived. I could understand that a proud man might not care to be seen and pitied by anyone other than his family. The Battle of Gettysburg had the highest casualties of any battle during the war, with more than twenty thousand of them from Lee's Army of Northern Virginia. Meade's Army of the Potomac sustained a similar number.

I put the book aside, my question about the death of Major Andrew Long answered. Time now to focus again on Rachel's diaries. Ordinarily I would have started at the beginning, but because of the questions I had regarding the diary I thought was fake, I started with the volume with the missing pages. There might be clues in other parts of the diary that could be helpful.

For the next forty-five minutes I read steadily, and I paused every few minutes to make sure Diesel remained on the windowsill. I also cast a few glances at the phone, wishing Stewart would call, but I had no idea how long it would take him to examine the paper and ink. I hoped he had been able to find the equipment he needed and hadn't had to wait for it to become free.

The office phone rang while I was standing and stretching in front of the desk. I snatched up the receiver.

"Charlie, I've got an answer for you," Stewart said without preamble. "Based on my analysis, I'd say this one volume is definitely a fake. The inks don't match, though the paper does."

THIRTY-TWO

|||||||||||||||||||||||||||||||||||||||||||||||||||||||||||||||

Stewart continued before I could respond. "I used Raman spectroscopy, which basically gives a fingerprint of the ink. The paper, too. It's a fast test and noninvasive as well."

"Noninvasive is good," I said.

"Now, about the ink," Stewart said. "I did a bit of research on nineteenth-century inks before I did the tests. You probably know about iron gall ink already, so I won't bore you with the details. I found spectra online for iron gall ink. There has been a fair amount of research on it related to historical documents. For one thing, it's corrosive over time, and it leaves telltale evidence of that.

"When I looked at the spectra for the ink in the two volumes, I could see that the spectra were similar in a couple of respects. The forger obviously tried to duplicate the iron gall ink but the formula wasn't the same. The other giveaway is that the ink hasn't caused corrosion in the forged diary."

My head buzzed a bit with the details, but the result was clear.

The fifth volume of the diary was a forgery, and I was certain I knew the identity of the forger: Lucinda Beckwith Long.

"Thanks, Stewart," I said. "I'm going to call Kanesha right away and tell her about this. I need to get the diaries back, though. Shall Diesel and I walk over and retrieve them?"

"No, I'll bring them back to you," Stewart said. "I'll be heading home anyway. Got a hot date tonight to get ready for, and you know it takes me simply ages to look my best."

I had to laugh because I couldn't remember ever seeing Stewart look less than his best. "I appreciate it."

Before I called Kanesha I wanted to organize my thoughts. One in particular intruded, and I was irritated by it. The mayor obviously thought I wasn't experienced enough, or smart enough, to catch on to the forgery. Maybe she thought I would believe the diary was real simply because she said it was. The Longs, I guessed, were so accustomed to being respected and obeyed, she thought I would just toe the party line, as it were.

I felt my temper rising, and I had to keep it under control. I would have to guard my tongue if I encountered Mrs. Long anytime soon. I couldn't afford to let her know I knew the one volume was forged.

Kanesha answered her cell phone almost immediately.

"I've got big news for you," I said. "One of the diaries is forged. I think you should send it off for a complete forensic examination, because you're going to need expert proof."

Kanesha didn't waste time with questions. "I'll be there in about fifteen minutes. Keep those diaries locked away until I get there."

I didn't have time to tell her that I didn't have the forged one, but I figured Stewart would have it back in my office before Kanesha arrived.

Sure enough, Stewart turned up ten minutes later with the box. I thanked him again, and he grinned. "Glad to do it. Made for a nice little puzzle this afternoon. I wish I could hang around but I have a lot to do today." He ran his fingers through his thick, dark blond hair. "For one thing, I have to get this shaggy mop tended to. I'm starting to look like a Yeti."

His hair was a bit longer than I was used to seeing, but it wasn't anywhere near long enough to qualify as a mop of any kind.

"Have fun tonight," I said.

Stewart bade Diesel and me good-bye and vanished through the door.

A few minutes later Kanesha arrived and strode into the office. She greeted me and stood in front of my desk. "Tell me about this forgery."

"Please, have a seat," I said. "My neck will cramp if I have to sit and look up at you like this."

Kanesha sat and leaned forward in the chair. Her laser stare focused on me, and I knew I'd better start talking. "There were things in this one volume—the one the mayor brought after the others were stolen—that weren't adding up. I talked to Jasper Singletary this morning, and he says the family has never heard anything about his great-great-grandmother Celeste being a freed slave. He wasn't particularly upset about it, just puzzled."

Kanesha nodded. "Go on."

Diesel had climbed out of the window to greet her, and she gave him a few rubs on the head while she listened to my explanation. When he'd had enough attention, the cat went in search of his water and food bowls, along with a litter box, that I had stowed in a corner of the room.

I explained the duplication in time coverage between the forged volume and one of the original four. "I'm not sure what the forger was thinking. It would have been smarter to keep back the volume from the same time period and substitute the forged one for it. I might have been slightly less suspicious if she had done that."

"She?" Kanesha asked. "Do you think the mayor is responsible for the forgery?"

"I think it's the most likely answer," I said. "And if she didn't do it, then someone in the family or closely connected to the family did it on her orders."

"The reason for the forgery?" Kanesha said.

"To embarrass Jasper Singletary and help Beck Long win the election."

Kanesha shook her head. "Strange way of going about it, if you ask me. Politics makes people crazy sometimes, although I don't know why the Longs are so afraid of Jasper Singletary. Beck Long was ahead by a mile in the polls until recently, and no one could have produced that forgery in a few days. It would have taken several weeks, don't you think?"

Point to Kanesha. I hadn't considered that, but she was right. "Yes, it would have taken more than a few days. The planning had to take some time as well before anyone sat down and started to write."

Diesel reappeared, his errands done, and chirped at me before he climbed into the window.

"What about the handwriting?" Kanesha asked, seemingly oblivious now to the cat. "Did it look like the same person's writing to you?"

"I wasn't able to compare them until today," I said. "Remember, the four real diaries were missing when I received the forgery. I didn't get the real ones back till this morning, but when I did compare the writing, it looked close enough to me. A handwriting expert could—and will, I'm sure—find discrepancies."

Kanesha gave me a grim smile. "This is going to get nasty. I'm sure you realize that."

I nodded. "That's why I wanted you to know right away, so you can take care of getting these analyzed before the mayor knows they're gone."

"I'll do my best," she replied. "I'm still trying to figure out how this ties into the murder of Dr. Steverton."

"I have no idea, either," I said. "Did your men ever figure out where Marie hid the diaries?"

"Yes, because they were a lot more thorough than the first time," Kanesha said. "Dr. Steverton had an old chifferobe with a hidden compartment. They found it this time because it hadn't been closed completely, and they also found tiny flakes of leather that matched the bindings. No sign of those boxes you had them in, either. I'm figuring she must have discarded them somewhere on campus."

"Marie must have been careless and in a hurry," I said. "Did they find the missing pages in the compartment?"

"No, it was empty," Kanesha said. "We're still looking for them but I'm out of places to try." She stood. "I'd better get these on their way to the crime lab. In the meantime if you come up with any ideas on where we should look for those pages, let me know." She picked up the box and headed for the door.

If the pages still exist, I thought. I hoped they hadn't been destroyed, but depending on their contents, it might have been the safest thing for the killer to do.

Who was the killer? I asked myself.

Because I was so certain the mayor created the forged diary, she had to be at the top of my list. She had a lot at stake, especially if she was willing to go to such absurd lengths to help her son win a state senate race. She couldn't afford to let Marie get in her way. Lure Marie out into the street in the early hours of the morning, run her down when the neighbors were sound asleep, and Marie was no longer a problem.

That was cold-blooded, I thought. I had never thought of Lucinda Long as a ruthless person, but I didn't really know her. She had married into a family that was used to commanding respect and wielding power—political, social, and economic. Her own family, the Beckwiths, were also wealthy and well connected.

Did they think they were above the law? I wondered.

The only other candidate for murderer that I could come up with was Beck Long, but it was possible his father was involved. I didn't know either Beck or his father, although I had seen Beck twice recently and observed him in action. He was less than impressive intellectually, but I could see him acting on impulse and aiming a car at someone who was causing him trouble. Whether he had the temperament to act so rashly, I didn't have a clue. It might have been an accident, but it wouldn't do for a rising political star to be caught at the scene of a hit-and-run. That could compromise his career pretty quickly.

Time to stop all this woolgathering. I had work to do, and I should get on with it. I went back to the diary volume I was reading earlier, the one with missing pages.

Most of what I read was not particularly interesting, at least to me. Rachel spent a lot of time on the minutiae of clothing and her criticisms of the neighbors. One example of the latter I did find amusing:

Andromeda McCarthy (and what a pompous name that is, makes her sound like a bluestocking, and she is just a sweet girl of ordinary intelligence who doesn't care for reading) wore a gown of the most unfortunate peach satin today during the call she and her mother made here. Andromeda does not have the complexion for peach, being far too pale, but I fear it is her mother who insists upon such insipid colors.

This Rachel came across as more frivolous than the Rachel in the forged diary, and I began to wonder whether the forger had bothered to read the original volumes at all. The section I was reading was for the months before the war began in earnest, and I supposed that Rachel, like many at the time, did not think the war would last long. Perhaps after she experienced the terrors and privations of war, Rachel became more mature and thoughtful.

I was tempted to skip to the second half of the volume to see whether I was correct about a change in Rachel's outlook, but I decided against it. It would be more interesting, if Rachel did change, to see it as it happened.

I set the book aside a few minutes later to give my eyes a rest and to check on my feline companion. Diesel was in his place, and I closed my eyes and leaned back in my chair. I was enjoying the quiet until, a few minutes later, Melba startled me from my half doze.

"Charlie, what are you doing taking a nap up here?" Melba laughed.

I glared at her. I didn't like to be startled like that. Then I noticed she had a large stack of mail in her hands.

"What's that?" I said. "For your information, I was only resting my eyes."

"Okay," Melba said as she approached my desk. "I hope your eyes are rested, then, because you've got a pile of mail to get through." She set her stack in the tray on my desk. "When was the last time you checked your box in the mailroom?"

"Last week," I muttered. "I do remember to check it at least once a week, sometimes twice, but this week has been anything but normal." I reached for the pile, picked it up, and set it on the desk in front of me.

Melba made herself comfortable in the chair across from me while I sorted through the mail. "Anything new on the murder you can talk about?"

"No, not really," I said.

There was one large campus mail envelope, and I pulled it out of the pile. I checked the front and saw that the envelope had last been used to send something to a history faculty member. These envelopes were multiuse and traveled across the campus and back many times.

I opened the envelope and reached in to extract the contents. Felt like several pages bound together with a paper clip. When I had them out of the envelope and on the desk in front of me, I nearly fell out of my chair from the shock.

THIRTY-THREE

|||||||||||||||||||||||||||||||||||||||||||||||||||||||||||||||||||||||

I recognized the handwriting and the paper itself. These had to be the pages missing from Rachel Long's diary. I stared at them for a moment before I realized there was a handwritten note paper-clipped to the pages.

"What is it, Charlie?" Melba sounded slightly alarmed. "You're white as a sheet." She had a hand on Diesel's head. I hadn't even heard or felt him get down from the window and go around to her.

I took a deep breath to steady myself. "These are pages that were taken out of the diary. They've been missing, and we had no idea where they were." My eyes skimmed the note attached to them. "Oh my Lord, this is a note from Marie Steverton."

"What does it say?" Melba asked.

" 'You'll know what to do with these' is all it says, along with her initials." I shook my head, still a bit in shock. What had compelled her to send the pages to me?

Melba shivered. "That's creepy, getting a letter from a dead woman. What are you going to do with them?"

I had trouble focusing my thoughts for a moment. The first thing I wanted to do was start reading the pages to find out why Marie had removed them from the diary. I realized, however, that they constituted evidence, and my first duty was to inform Kanesha of their return.

I picked up the phone and called her. This time, however, I had to leave a message. I made it terse and urgent.

For some reason I felt tense and almost panicky. Diesel picked up on that. He came around to me and put a paw on my leg. He meowed loudly several times, and I forced myself to breathe deeply and relax to keep from upsetting him.

"Charlie, you don't look good. Are you sure you're all right?" Melba got up from her chair.

I waved her back before she could come around and start fussing over me. "I'll be okay, just a little concerned about all this. We can't let anyone else know I have these pages."

"You're acting like they're going to explode any minute," Melba said. "Maybe you'd better go lock them up next door."

"They do need to be put somewhere safe," I said. I began to feel a bit calmer, thanks to her pragmatic suggestion. "I'll do that right now." I put the pages carefully back into the envelope. "You stay here with Diesel and answer the phone."

Melba nodded, and I hurried to the storeroom next door. I would feel better once the pages were locked away in a more secure place. I didn't know how long it would be before Kanesha could come back or send one of her men to retrieve them. Until I could safely turn them over to the sheriff's department, I wanted them out of reach of anyone who might come into the archive.

"Mission accomplished," I told Melba and Diesel when I returned to my office.

"Good. Maybe you can relax now," Melba said. "You had me worried there for moment, like you were going to pass out on me."

"Sorry about that," I said as I resumed my seat behind the desk. "Getting those pages out of the blue like that was shocking."

The phone rang and startled me. I picked up the receiver, praying that Kanesha was returning my call.

Thankfully for my nerves, it was her. I didn't give the chief deputy a chance to speak. "I've got the pages locked up in the storage room next door. Please come get them right away."

"One of my deputies is on the way there now," Kanesha said. "Here's what I want you to do. Handle them with extreme care, but scan those pages. Ordinarily I would take them right away, but I want to have a backup copy. Wait until my deputy is there, though. When you're done with them, he'll bring them in to the sheriff's department."

"All right," I said. "I can do that."

"Thank you," Kanesha said. "Send me a copy of the scan. You have my e-mail. Go ahead and read the pages and I'll do the same as soon as I get the file."

"Will do," I said and then ended the call.

I didn't know why I was so jittery, but talking to Kanesha helped me feel calmer. I didn't expect the mayor to come to my office, waving a gun around, threatening me unless I turned the pages over to her. I was simply on edge because of the events of the past few days, I decided.

I relayed the news to Melba. She nodded vigorously.

"Good, the sooner all this crazy mess is settled, the better."

She stood. "Unless you want me to hang around until that deputy gets here, I guess I should get back downstairs."

"Thanks, but I'll be okay," I said. "The deputy should be here any minute."

"All right. See you later." Melba gave Diesel's head one last quick rub and headed for the door. Diesel meowed after her and watched for a moment before he came back and climbed onto the windowsill.

I looked up and Melba was back in the office. "You've got company," she said in an undertone, "and it's not the deputy."

She had no chance to explain further. Behind her I saw Beck Long and a strange man pause at the door. Long knocked and smiled.

"Sorry to interrupt you, Mr. Harris, ma'am." He took a couple of steps into the room. "I really need to talk to you for a few minutes, if you have time."

I wanted to tell him to go away, that I was far too busy, but I knew I had no choice. I hoped I could get rid of him and his companion before the deputy arrived.

"Come in, Mr. Long." I rose and came around the desk to shake his hand. I introduced Melba, and they shook hands.

Long nodded to indicate his companion. "This is my associate, Daryl Kittredge. He's a member of my campaign staff."

Melba and I shook hands with Kittredge. He was short, verging on plump, with dark hair and eyes, a definite contrast to tall, blond Beck Long.

I glanced over at the windowsill, and Diesel remained there. He was watching the proceedings, however. I wondered why he hadn't come over to greet the visitors. Perhaps he had picked up on my unsettled state and was keeping out of things.

Melba quickly excused herself. She paused in the door to mime something. I thought she was trying to tell me she would hover nearby in the hall in case I needed help. I gave her a slight nod.

"What can I do for you, Mr. Long?" I didn't ask them to sit because I didn't want to encourage them to hang around.

Long didn't seem to notice the lack of invitation. He smiled, exposing a set of perfectly formed, dazzlingly white teeth. "My mother shared with me the contents of the diary. Daryl and I would like to see it for ourselves. He's going to take a few shots of the pages for a press release."

Exactly *not* what I needed to hear. My hopes of keeping the mayor from finding out I suspected the diary was a fake were fading quickly.

In as bland a tone as I could manage, with my heart suddenly racing a mile a minute, I said, "I'm sorry, but that won't be possible." My mind raced along with my heart as I tried to come up with a plausible excuse for denying their request without revealing I didn't have the diary in my possession.

Long's brow furrowed. "Why not? It will only take a few minutes."

"It's not the time," I replied. Inspiration struck. "Or rather, it *is* the time. Your timing, I guess I should say. The binding of that volume has some problems, and it's in the process of being repaired. These problems had to be addressed immediately to insure the integrity of the binding for the future. I'm sure you understand. I know you wouldn't want such an important resource to be damaged; nor would your mother."

I cut the babbling off as Long's eyes glazed over. I wasn't sure he understood what I was telling him; he looked so blank. His associate, Kittredge, however, caught on quickly.

"That's too bad," he said. "I suppose we'll have to go with the scans." He reached in his jacket and pulled out a leather business card holder. He extracted a card and handed it to me. "If you could e-mail the scanned pages to me right away, I'd appreciate it."

"No problem," I said.

Long frowned at his associate. "I don't see what the big deal is about letting you take a few pictures. That's not going to hurt an old book."

Kittredge looked slightly exasperated but then cleared his expression.

"That's the problem," I said quickly. "Until the binding is fully repaired, you can't open the book wide enough to take good pictures without damaging it."

"We understand," Kittredge said. "How long before the repairs are completed?"

"A week, I suppose." I shrugged. I prayed that this would all be over well before a week passed.

Kittredge nodded. He shook my hand. "Thanks for your time, Mr. Harris."

Long looked sulky as he in turn shook hands with me. "Yeah, thanks."

I watched them leave with great relief. I went back to my chair and sank down. Diesel meowed and tapped my shoulder with a paw. I turned to face him. He meowed again, and I rubbed his head. "Everything's okay, boy. No need to fret."

Diesel and I sat quietly for a couple of minutes, until I heard another knock at the door.

Deputy Turnbull walked in. "Morning, Mr. Harris. Ms. Gilley alerted me that Mr. Long was here, so I waited down in her office until he and his associate left the building."

"I'm glad to see you, Deputy," I said. "It's been a bit nerve-racking the last half hour or so. If you'll come with me, I'll retrieve the pages."

He nodded and then followed me next door to the storage room. I picked up the envelope with the pages inside, and we went back to my office.

"It won't take me that long to scan these," I told the deputy. "Please have a seat if you like."

Deputy Turnbull shook his head. "Thank you, sir, but I'll stand here in the door to keep an eye out for potential visitors."

"Good idea," I said. While I readied the scanning station, Diesel got down from his spot and walked over to the deputy. He sat at the man's feet, looked up, and meowed. Turnbull grinned and said hello to the cat. He rubbed Diesel's head, and that apparently satisfied my boy. He left the deputy and came to sit beside me.

I felt tense as I worked on the pages. The cotton gloves I wore made the process a bit slower as I took each page and scanned both sides. I was sweating by the time I finished. I reassembled the pages but did not paper-clip them. The paper clip could damage the pages. I advised Turnbull of this when I gave him the envelope. Then I remembered I should let Kanesha know what I'd told Long and Kittredge about the diary volume they wanted to photograph. "Sorry to load you down with messages for Deputy Berry," I said when I finished.

"Not a problem, Mr. Harris. I'll pass it all along to her when I give her the envelope," Turnbull said. He smiled briefly before he left the office.

Before I shut down the scanning station I e-mailed the file of the scanned pages to myself and to Kanesha.

I returned to my desk, where I collapsed in my chair, Diesel by my feet, and mopped my sweaty brow with my handkerchief. My rampant curiosity about the contents of the missing pages made me want to start reading right away, but my brain needed time to relax from the tensions of the morning.

"I don't know about you, boy, but I'm ready for lunch," I said to the cat. "Let's go home." A good meal in the quiet of my house was what I needed right now.

Diesel meowed loudly to indicate his approval, adding in a couple of the odd trills he made sometimes.

Downstairs we stopped by Melba's office to let her know we were going home for lunch.

"I'm about to head out myself," she said. "I'm going over to the bakery to meet a friend for lunch. Y'all want to tag along? I know Helen Louise would be happy to see you. As hard as she works, I reckon she doesn't have a lot of free time."

Hearing Helen Louise's name gave me a guilty start. Hadn't I promised her last night we would come to see her at lunchtime today?

I *had* promised her, I decided. "Thanks, we'd appreciate the ride," I said. "Saves me from going home to get the car."

About fifteen minutes later Melba found a parking space on the square across from the bakery. We crossed the street, and I opened the door for Melba. The ever-tantalizing scents from the bakery filled the air.

"There's my friend," Melba said, nodding in the direction of a lone woman seated at a nearby table. "Y'all enjoy your lunch, and we'll head back in about forty-five minutes, okay?"

"Sounds good," I said.

Diesel and I made our way to our usual spot, the table near the cash register Helen Louise always kept reserved for us when we were expected.

I didn't see Helen Louise and figured she was in the kitchen. I sat, and Diesel stretched out under the table near my feet. We settled in to wait for Helen Louise.

"Mr. Harris," a voice called out over the low hum of conversation in the bakery. "I was hoping I'd find you here."

I looked around to see Kelly Grimes advancing toward my table.

"Hello," I said when she stopped about three paces from me. "What can I do for you?"

She smiled. She held out a slim book. "You can read this and tell me what you think."

I accepted the book and glanced at the cover. The title read: *A Memoir of Mrs. Rachel Afton Long of Athena.*

THIRTY-FOUR

"Where did you find this?" I had almost forgotten about Angeline Long's reminiscences of her grandmother-in-law.

Kelly Grimes pulled out a chair and sat. She set her briefcase on the floor beside her. Once she was settled, she reached over and pulled the memoir from my hands.

"In a place that no one else remembered to search." She regarded me coolly. "Marie Steverton's carrel in the college library. I found it there several days ago. The day she was run down in the street, in fact."

I held my hand out for the book, but she shook her head. "No, I think I'll hold on to this until we can come to an agreement."

"An agreement on what?" I said, irritated. I couldn't believe the nerve of the woman.

"I want an exclusive interview with you," she said. "Because after you've read this, you can help me prove that the story about Jasper being descended from slaves is a lie."

I stared at her. She couldn't possibly know that Stewart had determined the diary was a forgery. Then I focused on something she'd said. *After you've read this,* meaning the memoir. "What's in the memoir that disproves the story in the diary?"

She shook her head again. "Are you going to give me the interview?"

I didn't have a choice, I supposed. Although I could call Kanesha and she would probably be able to take the book as evidence in the case. I didn't tell Ms. Grimes this. At the moment my curiosity had too strong a hold. I had to see what was in the memoir that made Ms. Grimes so certain of her position.

I was about to reply when I thought of something. "I spoke to Jasper Singletary this morning, and he didn't say anything about this. Surely you've told him you have this so-called proof that the story is a lie."

She looked disconcerted for a moment. "He's been too busy the past two days, and I only read the memoir last night. I wanted to be certain before I told him."

I wasn't sure I trusted her, but I wanted to get my hands on that book. There had to be a reason Marie had hoarded it away, and why someone had taken Miss Eulalie's copy.

"Okay, then, I'll give you your interview," I said. "Once I've read that memoir. And when the murderer has been identified. Not before."

"Fine." She held the book out to me. "I think you'll find the contents interesting."

"Contents of what?" Helen Louise asked. I looked up to see her standing behind the writer. Kelly Grimes started and half rose from her chair.

"Sorry if I startled you," Helen Louise said.

The writer gave a polite smile. "Not at all. Mr. Harris and I are done for the moment. I'll hear from you soon, I hope." She picked up her briefcase and stood.

I nodded. "When we agreed."

She stared hard at me for a moment before she turned and walked away.

During that interchange, Helen Louise and Diesel were greeting each other. Once Ms. Grimes was out of earshot, Helen Louise slid into the chair next to mine. Her hand still on the cat's head, she said, "What was all that about?" Her glance fell on the book I held. "Something to do with that?"

"Yes." I explained about the memoir as much as I could. I couldn't discuss the diary's claims about Jasper Singletary's great-great-grandmother Celeste. "I'll tell you the rest of it as soon as I can."

"All right." Helen Louise smiled. "I bet it's a doozy of a story. Now, how about lunch?" She glanced around the room. "I'm shorthanded today, so I'm not going to be able to eat with you."

"I understand," I said. "Don't worry about us. I'm sure you've picked out something wonderful as always."

She leaned over to brush my cheek with her lips. "I'll be back in a minute."

Diesel watched her go, then turned his head to look up at me and meow.

"She'll be back with food," I told him. "You're going to get your treat like you always do. You're not going to expire from starvation for another sixty seconds or so."

He regarded me solemnly for a moment before he positioned himself to watch for Helen Louise's return.

I had to confess to Helen Louise later that I couldn't remember what she served me for lunch that day. My brain was so focused on the memoir, Rachel Long's diary, and the murder of Marie Steverton and how they all connected, I couldn't process much else.

When Diesel and I both finished and Melba came to collect us for the drive back to campus, I at least remembered to wave good-bye to Helen Louise. She was busy with customers but gave me a quick wave back.

Melba chattered about something she and her friend discussed over lunch but I barely heard her. Diesel warbled a few times from the backseat, and Melba laughed.

"At least one of you is paying attention to what I've been saying." She pulled her car into her parking space in the library lot and turned to grin at me.

"Sorry." I had the memoir clutched to my chest like a favorite teddy bear. "I didn't mean to ignore you; I'm just really preoccupied right now."

"No kidding," Melba said as we got out of the car. "It's okay. I know you. Go on up to your office and start reading."

"Thanks, and thanks again for the ride to the bakery and back." Diesel and I followed her into the building through the back door, and we parted ways in front of the stairs.

"Come on, boy." I jogged up the stairs, but Diesel made it up to the office door several seconds ahead of me. He thought I was playing, and he liked to race me on the stairs. Sometimes he acted almost like a dog.

After I let us into the office, I locked the door behind us. I didn't want to be surprised by any other visitors this afternoon while I dug into both the memoir and the missing diary pages.

While Diesel got comfy on his windowsill, I sat at my desk and mulled over which one I should read first. After several moments of going back and forth between the two, I finally opted for the memoir, even though there were fewer diary pages.

I picked up the memoir and opened it. The book had a frontispiece, a portrait-style photograph in black and white of Rachel Afton Long, taken near the end of her life. She would have been around seventy at that point.

I studied the picture. Rachel's rather stern gaze in partial profile made her look like a formidable old lady. I could tell from her bone structure that she had been a beautiful woman in her youth, though she did not seem to have aged well. Her mouth had a slightly petulant twist to it, as if Rachel resented being old. Perhaps it was simply the result of the tragedies of her life, the losses during the war and their effect on her.

The book was published in 1911, the fiftieth anniversary of the beginning of the Civil War. By then Rachel would have been dead for about fifteen years.

I turned the page to the foreword from the author, Angeline McCarthy Long. The book was based on "reminiscences of the life of a Southern gentlewoman during times of great strife and their aftermath." That sounded typical for both the time in which the book was written and for the intent of such a memoir. Angeline Long went on to say that she had the privilege of knowing her husband's grandmother intimately only the final two years of her life, but had been so in awe of Rachel's experiences and character she wanted to share her love and admiration with others. She stated that she had first written the memoir three years after Rachel's death in 1896 but had waited until the anniversary year to see it published. She ended the foreword by writing, "I know all the citizens of Athena will join with me in celebrating the life and contributions to our wonderful town and, indeed, our great state of Mississippi, as we remember those sad years of the war. From Rachel Afton Long may we all take inspiration for the future and model ourselves upon a woman whose charitable works enriched us all."

I couldn't help but feel a bit cynical at the cloying sweetness of Angeline Long's words. She made Rachel Long sound almost like a candidate for sainthood rather than a flesh-and-blood woman. Once I had time to read the complete diary, I thought it would be interesting to come back to the memoir and read it again after making my own assessment of Rachel's character.

The memoir was brief, only seventy-eight pages, and the print was good-sized. It wouldn't take me long to read. If the rest of the book was as sickly sweet as the foreword, I'd be glad of the brevity.

I plunged in and quickly discovered that the memoir consisted mostly of Angeline's retelling of stories told to her by Rachel. The first of these was the tale of Andrew Adalbert Long, Jr.'s courting of Rachel Afton.

Upon first glance Rachel knew that she was destined to share her life with this dashing young man. Though it meant leaving her family in Louisiana to head north to Athena, she went willingly. "He was everything most gallant and handsome," Rachel once told me. "The epitome of every manly virtue with none of the vices that bedeviled so many of his acquaintance."

Angeline went on to share certain details of the actual courtship and its successful conclusion, resulting in the couple's wedding. Then she moved quickly forward to Rachel's stories of life at Bellefontaine during the war. Some of the incidents sounded vaguely familiar, and I realized I had read about them in the forged diary.

That was interesting. I wondered whether this book was the chief source the forger used.

The more I read, the more convinced I became that I was right.

When Angeline launched into the story of Rachel's charitable acts—and in particular those involving the Singletary family—I no longer doubted it. The phrasing sounded very similar, and I knew if I compared some of the passages, they would be word for word the same.

The story of the pitiful appeal from Vidalia Singletary on behalf of her children was identical as was Rachel's response. Then I hit upon one detail that was significantly different from the story in the forged diary.

According to Angeline Long, the girl Celeste was not a slave from the Afton plantation in Louisiana. Instead she was the daughter of the overseer there and had been sent north at her father's plea to keep her from making an unsuitable alliance with a poor white farmer's son there. Celeste did work for the Longs— as a seamstress.

No wonder Miss Eulalie's copy of this little book disappeared, I thought. Lucinda Long couldn't afford to let anyone get hold of it.

Then another question struck me. What had prompted Marie to take the college library copy and hide it in her carrel?

THIRTY-FIVE

||||||||||||||||||||||||||||||||||||||||||||||||||||||||||

I remembered that Marie Steverton knew about the diaries from
the mayor before Mrs. Long brought them in. Marie had made
her interest in them plain to me. She was evidently determined
that Rachel Long's diaries would finally help her earn tenure at
Athena College, after failed attempts at other schools. So, my reasoning ran, she took the memoir from the library collection and
hid it. Then she went to the circulation desk and told them it was
missing. After a quick check by one of the staff—that was the
usual procedure—the library declared it lost.

On a hunch I decided to call the circ desk and talk to the head
of the department, Lisa Krause. She answered right away.

After the preliminaries were out of the way, I said, "I know
circulation information—who checks out a particular book—is
confidential, but that's not what I need to know. Here's the situation. On Monday a book had its status changed to lost, and I

wanted to double-check the procedure on that. At what point is the status actually changed?"

Lisa said, "That's easy enough. A student or professor comes to the desk and says, *I can't find such-and-such book. It's not on the shelf.* We ask them to fill out a search request, and then it gets passed on to one of the student workers, who will go into the stacks to look for the book. About half the time the book is simply mis-shelved somewhere nearby, and a diligent search is all that's needed." She laughed. "Professors in particular are usually in too much of a hurry to look beyond the spot on the shelf where the book is supposed to be."

"I can imagine," I said, thinking of my own experiences as a volunteer at the public library in Athena and in the days when I was a public librarian in Houston. "How long is it after a person fills out a search request that the student actually goes and looks for it?"

"That depends," Lisa replied. "Usually they do it in the evenings. Most students are studying, and the desk isn't that busy. Sometimes, if the person requesting the book makes it sound urgent, I'll have a student go right away to look for it."

"That's really helpful," I said. "What I am about to ask next needs to be kept in confidence for now. Are you okay with that?"

"Certainly," Lisa said. "Is it anything to do with the murder of Dr. Steverton?"

"Yes," I said, and before I could pose my question, she continued.

"Dr. Steverton came to the desk on Friday afternoon—I'll have to check with the staff, but I'm pretty sure it was Friday—looking for a book. She wasn't too happy it was missing, but then, she was never happy about anything. I can't remember the title, but maybe the staff member she talked to will know."

"That's okay," I said. "I'm pretty sure I know the title. *A Memoir of Mrs. Rachel Afton Long of Athena.* Was that it?"

"Yes, that was it," Lisa said. "How did you know?"

"Because I have the library copy on my desk right now. I think what happened is that Marie took it herself and then hid it. For some reason she didn't just want to check it out. Instead she wanted it to look like the library's copy was missing or lost."

"How strange," Lisa said. "She was a strange woman, poor thing."

"Just to make sure I have all the details," I said, "when did the student actually look for the book? Do you know?"

"I can't say for sure without checking, but it was probably over the weekend. Once the student finishes the search, he or she marks the search form accordingly; then it goes to one of the full-time circ assistants who changes the status in the online catalog."

"In this case, the status was changed on Monday."

"That sounds about right, for a search request placed on a Friday afternoon," Lisa replied. "Is there anything else you need? I promise I won't tell anybody about this."

"Thanks," I said. "That's all for now. Someone from the sheriff's department may want to verify all this with you later, though."

I put the receiver down and stared at the little book. My mind kept hopping from one thought to another. Was there any significance in the fact that Marie reported the book missing on the Friday before she was murdered? How long had she known about the diaries?

The latter was a question I really wanted to put to Lucinda Long, but at this point I couldn't. I ought to keep track of my questions, though. Accordingly I pulled out a notepad and pen to start jotting them down. I preferred writing to typing at times like this, because something about the physical act itself seemed to help clarify my thought processes.

After further reflection, I added a few more questions to my list. Did Marie assist the mayor with the forgery? Was that the motive for her murder? Did she threaten to expose the scam?

I recalled that Mrs. Long mentioned a phone call she had from Marie the night she died. Mrs. Long said Marie had been drinking heavily and was asking questions about the monetary value of the diaries. What was the figure the mayor mentioned? Fifty thousand dollars—yes, that was it. Was that conversation Marie's way of letting the mayor know she wanted fifty thousand dollars to keep quiet about the forgery?

That made no sense. Why would the mayor tell me about the conversation if Marie had been trying to blackmail her?

Maybe the mayor did it to blacken Marie's character. Mrs. Long might also have assumed that no one would figure out the one volume was a forgery, so she thought it safe to mention the conversation with Marie.

I put the pen down for a moment because my hand started to cramp, trying to keep up with all the questions and thoughts streaming through my head.

Back to the memoir, I decided. I'd read the rest of it instead of coming up with more questions I couldn't answer. Then on to the removed diary pages—from the real diary. I might find some answers there.

I didn't spend long on the remainder of Angeline Long's overblown prose. I recognized several incidents from the forged volume. Whoever the forger was, she had clearly used this memoir to include authentic-sounding details. Even to the extent of the green tarlatan fabric that Rachel gave to Vidalia Singletary for herself and her children.

The final few paragraphs offered a pious summation of Rachel's life of charitable works and extraordinary goodness. Her "piety and Christian love for all those around her was noted by all who met her." I had to wonder what Rachel herself would have thought of this ersatz encomium. I repeated those two words to myself. Yes, I thought, they described this little tribute well.

Before I started on the diary pages, I thought I ought to call Kanesha and give her an update. She needed to know I'd discovered the source of the information in the forged volume. I was about to pick up the phone when another, all-too-obvious question struck me.

Why had the forger used Angeline Long's memoir of Rachel rather than Rachel's own diaries? Had the forger even *read* the original diaries?

Every question I posed seemed to make the whole situation more impenetrable. I couldn't follow a straight line of logic more than a point or two before hitting a dead end. This was beginning to drive me mad.

It was all too complicated to get across in a phone call. Instead I decided to send Kanesha an e-mail. Then I would send a text message to alert her to the e-mail.

For the next fifteen minutes I typed. I went through the message three times before I was satisfied that I'd included enough details along with the important questions I had. When I finally hit Send I was about ready for a hot shower followed by a couple of stiff shots of whiskey.

Diesel warbled, and when I glanced at the windowsill, I saw him on his back contorted in a position that looked painful, with his head nearly under one shoulder and his chest thrust out at an angle. This was my signal to rub his belly and scratch his chin, and being the well-trained servant I am, I complied.

After a couple of minutes of cat therapy I was ready to tackle the formerly missing diary pages. I located the file in my e-mail, saved it to the computer, then opened it. I increased the size by about 20 percent to make it easier to read.

I picked up the volume from which the pages had been cut and opened it to the gap. I wanted to get a running start, as it were, on the scanned pages.

The entry before the gap was dated August 10, 1863.

This day began like so many before it, with prayers to our Lord to deliver us from the evil in which we daily found ourselves. The war drags on, and there are constantly rumors that the Union Army is about to descend upon us. Then there came to us what at first looked like the Lord's blessing, a wonderful gift.

Words cannot express the sickness and horror I feel over the acts of betrayal perpetrated by one so dear. The blessing became a curse, one which we must keep to ourselves. The shame, if the truth should ever be known, is unthinkable. Already Father Long looks ill, and I fear that his heart cannot withstand this. Already weakened by the loss of his wife, my own dear mama-in-law, he cannot sustain such a blow. I can write no more for fear that my tears will soak the ink from the very page.

The entry ended there. Rachel sounded as if she were upon the point of utter despair.

What terrible thing could have happened? I wondered.

The phone rang and startled me, and I uttered a word I thought I had excised from my vocabulary.

THIRTY-SIX

I sounded none too cordial when I answered the phone. I could have screamed in frustration at the interruption.

"Catch you at a bad time?" Kanesha said coolly into my ear.

"Sort of," I said. "Sorry if I sound grumpy, but I'm reading the pages that were missing, and I was just about to find out something important when you rang."

"Sorry about that," Kanesha said. "I haven't had a chance to get to them yet. I did, however, read your e-mail. I wanted to alert you to the fact that I'm sending Turnbull to your office to pick up that library book. I am also trying to track down Kelly Grimes. I think it's time I had another chat with her."

"Did I sound like a rambling fool in the e-mail?" I asked a bit nervously. "I gave you more questions than facts, I think, but this is the screwiest case I've ever seen."

"I was able to follow it," Kanesha said. "It is a screwy case, but I'm beginning to see my way clear. As soon as you've finished reading those pages, call me." She disconnected.

She was beginning to see her way clear, she'd said. I wanted to bang something on the desk. That meant she was pretty sure she knew who killed Marie Steverton. I knew I couldn't really expect her to confide in me before she was ready to make an arrest, but still, it was annoying.

I shrugged that off and went back to the computer. I scrolled down until the beginning of the next entry, dated three days later, was at the top of the screen.

I have been far too heartsick, and too worried about the state of Father Long's mind and general health, to sit and write. I have no one in whom I can confide, for we cannot allow anyone to know what has befallen us. Though my heart at first rejoiced to have my husband returned to me, and whole of body, if not of spirit, it soon thudded painfully in my breast when my husband confessed his actions.

My eyes went back to that phrase *whole of body*. According to Angeline Long, Major Andrew Long had been so grievously disfigured by his injuries he would allow no one to see him.

The explanation came in the next paragraph.

Andrew told us of the horrors of the battle that took place in early July near Gettysburg, which is in the Union state of Pennsylvania. The carnage, the bloodshed, the noise, the cries of the wounded and dying, he made them all seem much too real to us. I know Father Long was moved by this recital, and by Andrew's sobs. The horror of it clearly overwhelmed him,

and that I could understand, for what he described to us was
a veritable Hell upon earth. Andrew had his own horse shot
out from under him, but he was able to roll free and thus not
be pinned beneath the dying beast. Andrew said he does not
really remember what happened next. At some point he found
himself away from the battlefield. How he came to be there
he cannot, or will not, say, but he turned his back on his men
and General Lee and walked away.

Poor Andrew, I thought. I could not imagine the horror of that
battle. Simply reading descriptions of it made me sick to my stomach. Gettysburg was truly the stuff of nightmares. I was not surprised that Andrew had walked away from it, but of course I
knew his family and his fellow soldiers would not see it that way.
I understood Rachel's reaction, but my sympathy was with
Andrew.

I resumed reading although I wasn't sure I wanted to know
much more.

Andrew begged his father for forgiveness. "You cannot imag-
ine the demons that live inside my head," he said. "All I knew
is that I must find my way home again, in hopes the demons
would leave my dreams, my every waking thought."

Father Long could not speak during Andrew's confession.
When Andrew fell to his knees before him, Father Long
turned away from him. "No true son of mine would dishonor
his name in such a cowardly fashion." He walked from the
room, and Andrew turned to me. I wanted to comfort him,
but I did not know how. I too was stunned by his betrayal of
his country and of his family, though my tender woman's

heart ached to see my beloved husband brought to such a state.

Old Mr. Long's reaction to his son's desertion didn't surprise me but it certainly saddened me. Dereliction of duty was a serious thing, and I couldn't approve of desertion in wartime. I did, however, have compassion for Andrew. I understood the stress that drove him to walk away from the hell of war.

I read on. Rachel's entries after this one confided more of her distress over Andrew's state of mind and his desertion from the Confederate Army. Mr. Long remained obdurate and refused even to speak to his son. Rachel came up with the idea to tell people that Andrew had been seriously wounded and had come home to convalesce. She also told them he did not want to be seen until such time as he felt he could face his friends and neighbors with composure.

Rachel wrote several times of the nightmares that terrorized her husband and kept her from sleeping through the night. Andrew's mental state deteriorated, along with his physical condition. Finally, one night when Rachel was sleeping soundly, Andrew slipped out of their bedroom, found some rope, and hanged himself from the rails of the staircase. Mr. Long found him, and the shock caused the stroke that led to his own death only three days later. Rachel was devastated.

This double loss is almost beyond bearing, but I will trust my faith to see me through. I must remain strong for the sake of my son who is, I pray, still too young and innocent to understand the magnitude of his father's actions and to feel the shame of them. I pray that Andrew is at peace with Our

Lord, despite his taking of his own life, and that the demons that beset him are finally banished. Henceforth we shall put these tragic events behind us, never to be mentioned or recalled as long as I draw breath.

With that entry I reached the end of the torn-out pages and had to consult the book to complete the final sentence. I closed the computer file and turned away from the screen.

I stared at the diary on the desk in front of me. At the moment I did not have the mental energy to read further. Nor the emotional energy, I realized. Rachel's recounting of the family's shameful secret and its tragic consequences affected me deeply, even though the events occurred a century and a half ago.

Once my head cleared a bit from the pathos of what I had just read, I found one thought going round and round in my brain.

Lucinda Long obviously hadn't read these diaries, or she would never have put them in my hands. The family wouldn't want this made public. The fact that Major Andrew Long had deserted and come home only to commit suicide would constitute a huge embarrassment for a family that for generations had prided itself on its public service and attention to duty.

If either candidate lost the election based on the contents of Rachel's diary, it would be Beck Long, not Jasper Singletary.

Why wouldn't the mayor have read the diaries before she allowed someone outside the family to see them? The fact that she hadn't done so baffled me. I couldn't understand, then, why she went to the trouble of creating the forgery and making copies of Angeline Long's memoir unavailable.

Maybe Mrs. Long read the memoir and assumed that the story Rachel told Angeline was the truth, that Andrew had died of his severe wounds. Not a particularly intelligent assumption, but given the pride in their ancestry exhibited by the Longs, the mayor probably never dreamed that the truth was so radically different.

She was a busy woman and didn't have time to read through the whole diary. It would have been slow going for her, I imagined, to read Rachel's handwriting straight out of the diaries. I was able to read it more easily because I could increase the size of it on the computer. Also I had more experience reading documents like the diaries and quickly adapted to the cramped nature of Rachel's penmanship.

Could the answer be that simple?

Maybe.

My thoughts turned to Marie. Had she suspected that the diary held secrets that could embarrass the Long family? She had torn out the pages that revealed Andrew's desertion. What had she intended to do with them?

The obvious answer was blackmail. She could have threatened to make them public, knowing she had the mayor over a dangerous barrel. The Longs were reputedly worth millions, and Marie could have named a high price.

There was something else she wanted badly, I realized. Tenure, and the respect that came with it.

Professor Howell Newkirk, a power in the history department, was a great friend of the Longs. If Lucinda asked him to support Marie's bid for tenure and told him it was vital that he do so, he might have done it. Marie would then have had the status she had desperately sought all throughout her academic career.

I knew that would sound ridiculous to anyone outside the halls of academia. I thought, however, that Marie would have wanted both tenure at Athena as well as a nice sum of money from Lucinda Long.

Another memory surfaced. Marie told me, in our first conversation about the diaries, that the mayor would do what she wanted and make sure Marie had exclusive access. She implied that the mayor didn't dare say no. Why? I wondered.

Perhaps because she already knew about the forgery. I had come up with that thought earlier, but now it seemed more likely to be the truth, or close to it.

Or, I thought, Marie could have taunted the mayor with the story of Andrew Long's desertion.

I was going in circles. There were too many holes in my scenarios.

One thing was clear, however. Lucinda Long had the strongest motive for killing Marie Steverton.

THIRTY-SEVEN

I hated to think of our mayor as a murderer, but this wouldn't be the first time a politician had gone off the rails and done something criminal and downright stupid. Was it truly that important to the Longs and their identity as a respected family to get Beck Long elected to office, no matter the cost?

Time to call Kanesha back, I decided. I had done everything I could, and it was her job now to sort through it all and make a case against the killer.

She answered right away.

"I've finished reading the pages," I said. "Have you had a chance to look at them yet?"

"No," Kanesha said. "I've been following up a promising lead on the car that struck down Dr. Steverton. What have you got for me?"

"The fact that Andrew Long—Rachel's husband—wasn't the war hero everyone thought he was," I said. "He deserted at the

Battle of Gettysburg and came home. He committed suicide, and Rachel covered it up. Everywhere except in her diary, that is."

"I wonder why she didn't destroy her diaries at some point," Kanesha said. "Surely she wouldn't want to risk having someone read them after she died."

"Good question," I said. I should have thought of that myself, but I was too caught up in the tragedy to consider it. "Perhaps she meant to and put them away and then forgot about them."

"Possible, I suppose," Kanesha said.

"Are you ready to make an arrest?" I asked.

"Not until I get the details on the car," she replied. "Then I'll move forward."

"Do you know who the killer is?" I asked. I didn't figure she'd tell me, but I decided to ask anyway.

She surprised me. "No, not yet. I'm still trying to sort out a few details, but what you've told me about Rachel Long's husband helps."

That was the most I'd get from her at this point. "I see. I don't have the mental energy to read any more of Rachel's diary today. Besides, I think we've found the part that's pertinent to this case."

"I agree," Kanesha said. "Why don't you go home and relax? I appreciate all you've done so far, but I think it's time for you to bow out."

"Gladly," I said. "But my curiosity is going to be rampant until I found out whom you've arrested."

That got me a rare chuckle. "I'll keep that in mind." She ended the call.

"Okay, boy," I said to Diesel. "Let's go home. I've had enough of this office for today." I restored the one diary volume to its new archival box, then transferred all three to the storage room where they would be safe until I was ready to go back to reading.

A few minutes later we stopped downstairs to say good-bye to Melba. I was happy to see she was on the phone, because that meant Diesel and I could get away without an extended conversation. I waved, and she waved back. Then Diesel and I made for the front door.

The afternoon heat made me uncomfortable, and I was thankful that the walk home was a short one. I knew Diesel would be ready to get back inside with air-conditioning, too. We had gone only two blocks, however, when a car pulled up to the sidewalk a few feet ahead of us. Mrs. Long stepped out of the car on the driver's side.

"Good afternoon, Mr. Harris," she said. "I was on my way to see you. Could we go back to your office and talk?" She was already getting back in the car before I had a chance to respond.

"I guess so," I called after the car as it headed up the street to the library. I did not want to have to talk to her right now, but I really had no choice.

I pulled out my cell phone, though, and speed-dialed Kanesha. The call went straight to voice mail, and I wanted to shout in frustration. Instead I left a terse message. "The mayor is here to talk to me. Please get to my office as soon as possible."

I ended the call and stuck the phone back in my pocket. "Come on, boy," I said to Diesel. I knew that my turning around and going back toward the office confused him. "Let's get this over with."

I hoped like anything I could get away from the mayor without giving away what I knew about the forged diary and the family secret. I also hoped Kanesha would arrive quickly, or at least send one of her deputies. I no longer trusted the mayor, and I didn't want to be alone with her.

I walked at a slow pace back to the building. For one thing, it was blasted hot outside, and I didn't feel like hurrying. I also wanted to delay this meeting as much as I could.

Mrs. Long frowned when Diesel and I met her at the head of the stairs near my office. "I began to think you ignored me and walked home, Mr. Harris."

I flashed her a smile. "Oh, no, it's so hot outside I had to take it slow so Diesel didn't get overheated." As if on cue, the cat meowed. "With all his hair this weather can be hard on him. If the walk home weren't so short, I'd use the car to get to work." I fumbled a bit with the lock. A covert glance at the mayor's face told me she was not happy with the delays. "Please come in," I said as I unlocked the door and opened it.

Mrs. Long strode in while I turned on the lights. She made for the chair in front of my desk and sat. Diesel and I walked at a normal pace to my desk. I removed his leash, and he climbed onto the windowsill. I sat and faced Mrs. Long. "What can I do for you, Your Honor?"

"I want to know why you refused to let my son and his aide take the pictures they wanted earlier today," she said, her tone becoming more heated with each word. "I know perfectly well the binding of that diary was just fine, and the pictures Mr. Kittredge wanted to take would not have damaged the book in any way."

"That was my decision to make, Your Honor," I said, hoping to stonewall her until Kanesha or a deputy arrived. "When you signed the deed of gift and handed over the diaries, you basically gave the right to make decisions about their care to me."

"That deed of gift can be revoked," Mrs. Long said sharply, "as can any future donations to this college. I don't appreciate your interference, Mr. Harris."

Miranda James

"I regret that, Mrs. Long," I said. "I don't see why Mr. Kittredge and your son can't use the scans of the pages instead." The moment I said it, I had the guilty feeling I had forgotten to e-mail the file to Mr. Kittredge. "The scan isn't any different from a digital photograph. In fact, it might be better, depending on the camera's resolution."

"You neglected to send the file to Mr. Kittredge," the mayor snapped. "Really, I don't understand this obstructive attitude of yours."

"I apologize for forgetting to send the file," I said, "but I have been busy today. I simply got distracted and forgot. I'll send it right now, if you like."

She glowered at me. "Yes."

I turned to the computer and switched it on. "This will take a couple of minutes."

She did not reply, but I could feel the heat of her gaze on me. While I waited for the computer to boot up, I found the card Mr. Kittredge had given me earlier. As soon as I could open the e-mail program, I prepared the message, attached the file, and sent it. I swiveled my chair to face the mayor. "There, it's done." I longed to tell her that if her son and his campaign staff made use of the contents of that diary, they would only be embarrassed, if not sued. But I couldn't.

"Good," the mayor said. "Now I want to see that diary. I want to assure myself that it wasn't damaged after I turned it over to you. You might as well show me the others as well. My husband and I expect these diaries and anything else given to the archive to be handled with the utmost care."

The more she said, the harder I found it to hold on to my own temper. If I wasn't careful, I'd let something slip in anger, and Kanesha would have my hide if I did that. If only Kanesha would walk through that door. I was trying to think of a way to stall the mayor, but I wasn't sure I could keep lying and doing it convincingly enough.

"Good afternoon, Your Honor, Mr. Harris." Kanesha spoke from the doorway and almost made me jump out of my chair. Thank goodness the cavalry arrived in time.

Mrs. Long twisted in her chair. "Deputy Berry, I didn't expect to see you here, but it's just as well that you've come. Mr. Harris is not cooperating with me, but perhaps you can persuade him, if I can't."

Kanesha regarded the mayor coolly. "Not cooperating? In what way?" She advanced farther into the room.

"I asked him to show me the diaries that my husband and I donated to the archive, and so far he is refusing to do so." The mayor shot me an angry look.

I didn't try to defend myself. Instead I waited to see what Kanesha would say.

"Mr. Harris, I really think you should let the mayor see the diaries," Kanesha said in a gently chiding tone. When the mayor turned to give me a smirk, I saw Kanesha wink.

"As you wish," I said.

Diesel had remained quiet so far, and that didn't surprise me. The tension in the room was palpable, and I knew he was uneasy. Before I left the room to retrieve the three diary volumes from the storage room, I rubbed his head and told him everything was okay.

Mrs. Long and Kanesha waited in silence while I went next door. When I came back, diaries in hand, they didn't appear to have moved. I set the archival boxes on my desk and carefully began to extract each book. When they were all on the desk in view of the mayor, she got up from her chair and moved closer to them.

"Please, if you intend to handle them," I said, "wear these." I pulled a pair of cotton gloves from the drawer and handed them to her. I took a pair for myself as well.

"Very well," she said as she accepted them. She frowned. "There are only three volumes here. Where are the other two?"

"We can get to those in a moment," Kanesha said smoothly. She joined the mayor in front of my desk. "Why don't you go ahead and check these three first?"

The mayor looked puzzled, but she did as the deputy suggested once she had her gloves on. I had placed them so that she would be able to open them properly, and she opened the one in the middle first. That happened to be the one with the missing pages, and I wondered how long it would take her to notice the gap.

I glanced at Kanesha. She had her eyes on the mayor.

Mrs. Long carefully flipped pages until she reached the gap. "What is this?" She glared at me. "Someone took pages out. How could this have happened?"

"It happened when they were taken from this office," Kanesha said. "I'm pretty sure that Dr. Steverton is the one who stole the diaries and then cut out those pages."

The mayor shook her head. "Why would Marie do such a thing? She was so excited to work on them. I can't believe she would deliberately damage them."

"She might if the stakes were high enough," Kanesha said. "Tell me, Mrs. Long, did you ever read the diaries? All five volumes?"

THIRTY-EIGHT

What was Kanesha's strategy here? I couldn't figure out where she was headed with this particular gambit.

The mayor evidently found it strange. She handed me the volume she was holding and turned to face the deputy.

"What does that have to do with Marie vandalizing Rachel Long's diaries?" the mayor asked. "If you must know, I only read a bit of the first one. The handwriting gave me a headache, and I didn't have time to read further. What I did read seemed interesting enough to be of potential historical value. That's why my husband and I decided to donate them to the archive."

"I see," Kanesha said. "And the fifth volume? The one you found in a false bottom of the trunk. Did you read any of it?"

"I fail to see what you expect to accomplish with these questions," the mayor said, her tone increasingly frosty. "I don't have time for this."

"Could you please answer my question, Mrs. Long?" Kanesha said.

The mayor stared hard at the deputy, but then Mrs. Long's glance fell away. "Well, I might have looked at a couple of pages, but the handwriting was too small and cramped, as I've said. I was as surprised as everyone else when Mr. Harris told me about that slave woman getting involved with a Singletary."

Mrs. Long seemed uneasy to me, and I was surprised. She was an experienced politician, and I would have expected her to maintain a calm, poker-like demeanor. Perhaps she didn't handle guilt well, I thought.

The mayor pointed to the volume I now held. "Have you found the missing pages? If you know Marie took the diaries, surely you know what she did with them."

"We do have them," Kanesha said. "Because they're evidence, though, they will remain in the custody of the sheriff's department until it's determined whether they will be needed for the trial."

"Yes, I understand," Mrs. Long said. She turned to me. "Did Marie remove pages from any other volume?"

"No, the others are all intact," I said.

"I would like to see the other two to reassure myself of that," the mayor said.

"I'm afraid that won't be possible," Kanesha said. "I've sent the fifth book you found along with one of the others to the state crime lab for testing."

"Testing?" Mrs. Long said. I thought she suddenly looked a bit pale. "Whatever for?"

"We suspect that the one you found in the bottom of the trunk is a forgery," Kanesha said. "I want to know how recently it was done. Do you have any ideas about that?"

The mayor laughed, a shaky sound. "Now, why would I know about such a thing? It can't be a forgery."

Kanesha looked at me, and I realized this was a signal for me to talk.

"I'm certain it is," I said. "I asked one of the chemistry professors here to compare it to one of the original four."

"Why would you do that?" The mayor stared hard at me.

"I began to suspect, because of the contents, that something wasn't right with it," I said. "The story about Rachel Long's slave getting involved with the present Jasper Singletary's ancestor didn't hold water. I spoke to Mr. Singletary after he'd had a chance to read that volume, and he was puzzled by it. He thought it odd that, if Celeste truly was a slave, no one in the family knew about it."

The mayor laughed harshly. "It's hardly the kind of thing one would pass down to one's family. Apparently she was light enough to pass for white, and that's how they fooled everyone."

"I don't think they could have gotten away with it," I said. "Celeste might not have interacted with the people in town, but the other slaves would certainly have known she was one of them. I don't think they would have been quiet about her marrying a white man once she was free. It was illegal for blacks and whites to marry then."

"Well, I think you're wrong," the mayor said. "I think they did get away with it."

I glanced at Kanesha, and she nodded again.

"There is other evidence," I said. "I found a copy of Angeline McCarthy Long's memoir of Rachel and read it."

The mayor did pale visibly this time. "How did . . . But Marie said . . ." She fell silent, obviously horror-stricken over what she let slip.

"I'm sure Marie told you that she had taken care of the library's copy of the memoir, and I imagine you visited Miss Eulalie Estes and *borrowed* her copy," I said. "Someone found the copy Marie had hidden and brought it to me. I read it. Angeline Long states very clearly that Celeste was white. She was the daughter of the white overseer on the Afton plantation in New Orleans. Rachel wouldn't have written that Celeste was a slave when she clearly wasn't. Therefore that volume of the diary is a forgery."

Mrs. Long sank into the chair behind her. She looked back and forth from me to Kanesha twice. I knew my expression was every bit as stony as the deputy's.

"Did Marie Steverton play a role in creating the forged diary?" Kanesha asked. "Before we go any further, Your Honor, I will read you your rights, unless you waive them."

The mayor stared down at the floor. Behind me I heard Diesel stirring, so I set down the book I was holding and reached behind me to pat him for reassurance. He stilled under my touch.

"Well, Mrs. Long?" Kanesha said.

"I'll waive them, and Mr. Harris can be your witness." The mayor sighed. "Marie did all the work, actually. At my request."

"What did you promise her?" I asked. "To make sure she got tenure?"

Mrs. Long's head jerked up. "Yes. How did you know?"

"It was pretty common knowledge around campus that she was desperate to get it," I said. "She had tried and failed at previous colleges, and this was her last shot before retirement."

"I see. It was mostly her idea," the mayor said. "I found Rachel's diaries several months ago and told her about them then. She kept pestering me to let her have them, but I refused to do it. I didn't trust her with them."

"How did you hit upon the scheme to forge a volume of the diary?" Kanesha asked.

"Jasper Singletary was gaining ground in the campaign against my son, and his campaign manager was worried that unless something drastic happened, Singletary would overtake Beck and win." The mayor shook her head. "I love my son, but he is not a natural politician. He is handsome and charming, but he doesn't have the oratorical gifts his opponent has; nor is he as quick on his feet. My husband refuses to see that, however, and is determined that Beck will be elected. He's too proud to believe Beck isn't going to win.

"So I came up with a scheme to help influence the election," Mrs. Long continued. "I'd read that memoir of Rachel, and I remembered the story Angeline told about aiding the Singletary family. I thought it would be a good story to adapt to suit my purposes. I knew Marie had some skill with forgery, because she learned how to write like me when we were at Sweet Briar together. She was very good at it."

"Did Dr. Steverton see the real diaries before she created the forged one?" Kanesha asked.

"No," the mayor said. "I promised she would be able to use them once the forgery was complete. She wanted me to give them to her personally once she finished the job, but I told her they would have to go to the archive, and she could access them through it. I couldn't turn over valuable family documents to her, but of course she had a fit."

"Did she at any time threaten you?" I asked. "You told us about a phone call the night she was killed, when she asked you about the monetary value of the diaries?"

"She couldn't threaten me," the mayor said. "She would expose

261

herself if she exposed me. She didn't dare. She was roaring drunk when she called, and she didn't make a lot of sense when she drank that heavily. She asked me several times if I thought the diaries were worth fifty thousand dollars and I told her I didn't know."

"Did she give you any indication why she was asking?" Kanesha said.

The mayor frowned. "There was something about *interested parties* but I could never get her to tell me what she meant." She shrugged. "I finally told her to quit drinking and go to bed."

"Are you sure that was the extent of your conversation with Dr. Steverton that night?" Kanesha asked. "She didn't bring up anything else?"

"No," the mayor said. "Of course, I had no idea she'd stolen the diaries from the archive, and she didn't tell me. If I had known, I would have driven right over and taken them home until they could be returned to the archive."

She looked from Kanesha to me and back again. "Now it's my turn to ask a question. What was in those pages Marie tore out? Obviously something important, or I doubt she would have vandalized a historical document."

I glanced at Kanesha, and she nodded at me. I decided I'd rather be sitting when I delivered the blow to the mayor, and most likely, to Beck Long's hopes of being elected, if this ever got out to the public. "This won't be pleasant, Mrs. Long, but there is no way to sugarcoat it."

Mrs. Long took a deep breath. "Go ahead."

I told her the story of Major Andrew Long's desertion and its aftermath. I kept it short, and she grew paler by the syllable. When I finished, I thought she might keel over in a dead faint.

Kanesha and I waited for Mrs. Long to respond to what I'd related to her. She gazed wildly at me and wet her lips a couple of times. "My dear Lord," she said, "this will kill my husband if it ever gets out. He's always been so proud of his family, and his distinguished lineage. You can't let this be made public. You simply can't." Her voice rose on the last three words to nearly a shriek.

"I don't intend to tell anyone," I said. "I give you my solemn promise on that."

The mayor turned to Kanesha. "Will it have to come out?"

"I don't know, Your Honor," Kanesha said. "The pages had to be taken into evidence because of the seriousness of the crime. It will be up to the prosecutors to decide whether it's relevant to the murder. If they deem it is, then it probably will come out."

Mrs. Long nodded wearily. "I'd like to go now, if you don't mind. I have to tell my son he can't use that story about the slave woman before it's too late. Singletary would turn him into a complete laughingstock."

"Let me walk you down to your car," Kanesha said. "I'll be back, Mr. Harris."

I stared at her. I couldn't believe she was letting the mayor go. Wasn't she going to charge her with the murder of Marie Steverton?

I was stunned. I was sure the mayor was responsible, but I began to realize that if Kanesha had the evidence to make the charge, she would have. There were obviously pieces of the puzzle still missing, at least officially.

Diesel climbed from the windowsill into my lap, and I hugged him against me. He purred, and I knew we both felt better. We snuggled until Kanesha returned about three minutes later. Then Diesel wanted to get back into his spot in the window.

"That's one thing settled," Kanesha said as she sat across from me. "I know you're probably wondering why I didn't charge her with the murder."

"Yes, the thought did cross my mind," I said wryly.

"I couldn't," Kanesha said. "She didn't do it."

THIRTY-NINE

||||||||||||||||||||||||||||||||||||||||||||||||||||||||||||||||||

"If Mrs. Long didn't run down Marie, then who did?" I asked. "Was it Beck? Or maybe that man Kittredge?"

Kanesha shook her head. "No, Beck Long and his associate Kittredge both have alibis. They were down in Jackson that evening, meeting with a public relations specialist until around one in the morning. They couldn't have driven back to Athena in time."

"Why are you so sure Mrs. Long didn't do it?" I still thought the mayor was the most likely candidate for murderer.

"We checked her car, her husband's, her son's personal vehicle, even their housekeeper's car," Kanesha said. "None of them had any kind of damage, and we know that the car that hit Dr. Steverton had at least minor scratches to the blinker on the front passenger side. Also, preliminary evidence on the paint residue on Dr. Steverton's clothing didn't match the makes or models of any of those cars."

That sounded pretty conclusive. Then another possibility

occurred to me. "What about rental cars? Couldn't one of them have rented a car just for the purpose?"

"We're checking rental car agencies in a hundred-mile radius," Kanesha said. "The Mississippi Bureau of Investigation is helping with that. If necessary we'll extend the radius farther. I'm hoping for a report from them sometime today."

"So it's still possible that Mrs. Long or her husband could have rented a car and used it to run Marie down."

"Yes, it's possible," Kanesha said, "but I don't think either of them did that. Renting a car takes time and effort, and unless Mrs. Long had planned in advance to do it, I can't see where she had the time to arrange for and pick up a rental, even with her husband's help." She leaned forward. "Look, we know from phone records that Dr. Steverton didn't call the mayor until close to midnight that night. We're checking into calls from Dr. Steverton's office in the history department, now that we know she must have gone there at some point in the afternoon or evening in order to put the diary pages into the campus mail."

I took a moment to digest all that, and I had to agree—albeit somewhat reluctantly—that Kanesha was right. The mayor seemed to be out of the picture as the murderer. Given the mayor's reaction when I shared with her the contents of those pages, I believed she had not heard any of it before. Clearly Marie hadn't disclosed it to her at any point. The mayor had been far too shocked to be acting, despite her years on the political stage.

"Did Marie call anyone else that evening?" I asked.

"Not from her home phone," Kanesha said. "That's why we're checking on her office phone. I have the feeling that she must have called someone else. I am pretty sure I know who she did call."

"Let me guess," I said. "Jasper Singletary."

Kanesha nodded. "That's the only answer that really makes any sense. With those pages, she had political dynamite. If she was as drunk that night as the mayor claims, she might have called and offered the pages to him."

I frowned. "That would defeat her purpose, wouldn't it? Singletary wouldn't have the pull to get her tenure, not the way Mrs. Long would, through her connection with Professor Newkirk."

"True," Kanesha said. "That's the sticking point in this scenario."

"There's another point that has to be considered," I said. "The return of the diaries to this office. Doesn't it seem reasonable to assume that the murderer returned them?"

"I believe so," Kanesha said. "I can't see another person getting into the middle of this, finding the diaries at Dr. Steverton's home, and then returning them. We're trying to determine exactly when they were returned, but it's difficult. There are no security cameras in this building, and the two doors in and out of the building have locks that are very easy to bypass." She shook her head. "Chief Ford is going to take this up with the president, but it's too late to help us in this investigation."

"Campus security didn't see anything suspicious during their rounds?" I asked.

"No," Kanesha replied. "As I said, we have nothing really to go on for the timing of the return. We know that they were taken while you and Ms. Gilley were both out of the building for lunch, but that's all."

"What about Kelly Grimes?" I asked. "Are you considering her as a possibility?"

Kanesha shot me a repressive look. "Of course. Her car doesn't have any damage, either. Neither does Singletary's nor those of any of his campaign staff."

"Could the damage have been repaired before you got around to all of the vehicles?" I asked.

"No, because I made sure that was done the first day of the investigation."

"Surely by now the car will have been repaired," I said.

"It could have been," Kanesha said, "but if it was a rental, there will at least be a record of it. With that and paint residue, we should be able to make an identification and go from there."

"Frustrating," I said.

"Yes, but not unusual," Kanesha replied. "We'll get there; it's just a matter of time and persistence. We'll identify the car, and then we'll know the killer."

Another point occurred to me. "Singletary's car wasn't used, nor those of any of his staff. Kelly Grimes's car wasn't used. What about alibis for them?"

Kanesha smiled briefly. "Neither Mr. Singletary nor Ms. Grimes has one after midnight. They left Athena together around six thirty p.m. and attended a fund-raiser in Charleston and another in Enid that evening. Mr. Singletary dropped Ms. Grimes at her place around midnight, then immediately went to his home. The timing is about right, because we know approximately when they left Enid. Both of them say they went to bed right away, but neither one has an alibi for the rest of the night."

"There's at least a possibility," I said. "Surely it has to be one of them."

"Yes, I'm pretty sure it is. One more piece of information, and then I have to go. Kelly Grimes lives in a duplex. Her neighbor has a car, but the neighbor is out of town. Ms. Grimes said he left on Tuesday but doesn't know where he went. I want to verify that he left on Tuesday and not early on Wednesday. We're trying to trace him and his vehicle."

"You think she could have borrowed her neighbor's car?" I asked.

"Yes, as long as he didn't leave until Wednesday," Kanesha said. "We're checking with neighbors to see if anyone remembers seeing his car in the driveway on Tuesday and how late. Nothing so far, but we'll keep digging." She stood. "Thanks again for your help. Now it's going to be down to routine investigative work."

"Good luck," I said. "I hope this gets resolved soon."

She nodded and raised a hand in farewell.

I turned to the cat. "Come on, Diesel, let's go home. And this time we're going to get there."

He perked up right away. I glanced at the wall clock and wasn't surprised to see it was already a few minutes past five. Definitely quitting time. This had been a strange day, not to mention emotionally and mentally exhausting.

On the walk home through the oppressive early evening heat, I tried my best to think of other things. Kanesha was right. Routine police work would achieve a solution to this.

The harder I tried to think about another subject, the more my mind stubbornly refused to cooperate. I was thinking about Kelly Grimes as the murderer when I unlocked the front door. I kept thinking about her in the kitchen while I was pouring myself a glass of iced tea.

I sat at the table and slowly sipped at the tea. Diesel disappeared and then reappeared to settle near my feet. He dozed while I continued to think about the various things I knew about Kelly Grimes and the events of the past few days. I began to piece together what I thought, in the end, was a plausible scenario for what happened.

The diaries were the catalyst. Marie Steverton wanted them for scholarly research and had agreed to forge a fifth volume in return for help getting tenure at the college. Kelly Grimes wanted them because she wanted to help her boyfriend find evidence that Rachel Long was a cold-blooded murderess.

I witnessed the unpleasant incident between the two women and their obvious dislike for each other. Neither one would be happy if the other got her hands on the diaries first. Marie insisted that Mrs. Long make sure she had exclusive access to them, but that apparently wasn't good enough. Marie sneaked into my office while Melba and I were both out of the building for lunch and took them.

I was pretty sure Kelly Grimes was keeping an eye on Marie, and I speculated that she saw Marie with the diaries. Or she found out somehow that Marie had them. She decided to steal them from Marie so she could have access to them first. She didn't have time to do it in the afternoon before she had to go with Singletary to the two fund-raisers in Charleston and Enid. Besides, doing it in the early hours of the morning when Marie would presumably be asleep would probably make it easier.

Okay, that all seemed plausible so far.

Next step. Kelly helped herself to her neighbor's car and drove to Marie's house. I figured she probably parked down the block. Then she made her way to Marie's and let herself in, either by picking the lock or finding an open window. Given Marie's inebriated state that evening, she might even have left a door unlocked.

Kelly got into the house and located the diaries. Marie would not have had them hidden away at the point, I figured, because the cops had come and gone without finding them and weren't likely to search again. Kelly grabbed the diaries, stuffed them in the bag, and started to slip out. Something woke Marie, maybe Kelly stumbling against a piece of furniture or knocking something off onto the floor, and Marie saw what she thought was a burglar. Maybe she even recognized Kelly.

Marie went after Kelly to try to get the bag with the diaries back. Kelly ran for the car, Marie hot on her heels. Marie caught up with her and tried to snatch the bag. Somehow the diaries got dumped out of the bag. Kelly scooped them up, got in the car, started it, and tried to drive off. Marie stepped in the way, and Kelly hit her, knocking her to the ground and killing her. Then, perhaps terrified over what she had done—on purpose or accidentally, I wasn't sure—she took the diaries to the archive instead of taking them home with her. Unaware the whole time that pages were missing from one volume.

Then Kelly went home, put her neighbor's car where it belonged, and went to bed. The neighbor got up early for his trip, not noticing the damage to the blinker on the front passenger side, and off he went, destination unknown.

I thought about my scenario a little while longer. I finally concluded it was possible, but until Kanesha found evidence, it was only a theory.

FORTY

"That was pretty much the way it happened, as it turned out." I paused to have a spoonful of the delicious lemon sorbet Helen Louise had brought for our Sunday dinner.

"Was the hit-and-run an accident?" Frank Salisbury, my son-in-law, asked.

"According to Kanesha, Kelly Grimes claimed it was. She panicked and drove off," I replied.

"Do you believe her?" Laura asked.

"I'm willing to give her the benefit of the doubt," I said. "When Kanesha confronted her with evidence linking her to her neighbor's car, she went ahead and admitted it. Insisted that it was an accident, though."

"Where was the neighbor during all this?" Helen Louise asked. "Did Kanesha tell you?"

"Oh, yes," I said. "He was at Enid Lake, fishing with a couple of friends. One of them has a cabin nearby, and he finally turned up Friday evening. Had to be at work Saturday apparently."

"So Kelly Grimes lied about when he left, obviously," Sean said. My lawyer son always liked to nail down every detail.

"Yes, he got up at four and left half an hour later. He didn't spot the damage to the blinker until he got home Friday. Of course, one of Kanesha's deputies was waiting for him. They hadn't been able to find him, but luckily he turned up sooner rather than later."

"What's going to happen to the diaries?" Stewart ladled more sorbet into his mouth and smiled. "Helen Louise, this is heaven on the tongue."

"Thank you," Helen Louise said. "I'll give you the recipe if you like."

"I like." Stewart grinned. "Now, Charlie, about the diaries. I kept quiet like you asked me to, but I'm burning to find out the whole story."

"I'm really not sure," I said. "A lot will depend on how much of the content of them factors into the trial. Kelly Grimes has been charged with vehicular manslaughter and failure to stop and render aid. The contents of the diaries might not enter into the prosecution's case."

Since Beck Long and his campaign manager had been stopped before they used the false information about Jasper Singletary's heritage, Singletary didn't seem inclined to make an issue of it. He could change his mind, however, because the forged diary might figure into Kelly Grimes's defense somehow. I couldn't share any of this with my family, however, because none of it was public knowledge yet. I had promised the mayor I wouldn't tell people about the forgery, and I would abide by my word.

"I wish you were able to tell us more about what's in those diaries," Alexandra Pendergrast, Sean's girlfriend and law partner, said. "They must be pretty hot stuff to be the cause of so much activity."

"There are a lot of interesting details in them," I said. "If you're really curious, you can read some of Rachel Long's story in the memoir of her written by her granddaughter-in-law, Angeline McCarthy Long. The college library's copy isn't available at the moment, but Miss Eulalie Estes has graciously donated her copy of it to the archive. The only other copy known to exist is one belonging to the Long family."

Miss Eulalie had colored slightly when she offered me her copy of the memoir on Friday afternoon. "It turns out I was mistaken, Charlie. I found my copy after a more thorough search at home, but now I think it belongs in the archive."

I thanked her, well aware that both of us knew that Lucinda Long returned it after having stolen it in the first place. I wasn't going to embarrass Miss Eulalie, and since I had promised the mayor my silence, I simply took the book and added it to the Long collection.

"Can't you tell us some of the stories, Dad, without our having to read the book?" Laura asked with a big smile. "As much as I like to visit you in your office, I don't have a lot of time this semester."

Diesel, back beside my leg from one of his periodic treks around the table in search of handouts, warbled loudly. Everyone laughed because the cat always seemed to know just when to speak up.

"I suppose I can, especially since Diesel has asked, too," I said. I thought about what to tell them, and I decided to recount the story of Rachel Long and the Singletarys. Though it was sad, it illustrated what a strong and charitable woman Rachel had been.

I had since read more of her diaries—they were still in the archive, pending a decision by the Longs to ask for them back—and had come to admire her.

"Rachel was an admirable woman," I said. "She, like everyone in Athena, had difficult times during the war. Food and other supplies became increasingly scarce, but she was willing to share what she had. One example from the first year of the war is the Singletary family."

"Jasper Singletary's ancestors?" Sean asked.

I nodded. "Yes, the same family. The head of the family at that time was also Jasper, and he had a son, Franklin, by his first wife. She died, and when Franklin was around ten, Jasper remarried, a young woman named Vidalia. They had three children, one right after another, and they were all under six in 1861. Franklin was sixteen, I think."

I paused for the final spoonful of sorbet. "Times were hard for the Singletarys. Jasper had a heart condition; plus he was around sixty by then, and couldn't work. Franklin, though much younger, had similar heart problems. Their only hired hand left to enlist in the war. Jasper didn't condone slavery, you see."

"Good for him," Laura said. "I like him already."

"They didn't have enough food, but Jasper refused to ask for help, particularly from the Longs. He hated them, and Rachel's father-in-law wasn't too fond of Jasper, either. Vidalia, on the other hand, couldn't stand seeing her children go hungry. Without Jasper's knowing about it, she went to Rachel and begged for food. Her children also needed clothes. Rachel, being a compassionate woman, gave Vidalia food and bolts of some material she had but had never used." I paused, trying to remember the name of the cloth. I had meant to ask Laura about it.

"That was kind of her," Alexandra said.

"She was a good woman," I said. "Green tarlatan, that's it." I looked down the table at my daughter. "That was the name of the cloth Rachel gave Vidalia. I'd never heard of tarlatan before, and I've been meaning to ask you about it."

Laura's nose wrinkled. "I've heard of green tarlatan, Dad. It was actually poisonous."

"What do you mean?" I was stunned, and, I could see by their expressions, everyone else except Frank was equally taken aback.

"It had arsenic in it," Frank said. "Arsenic was used in many things in the nineteenth century. In wallpaper, for example, and in cloth."

"It helped fix the dye in the cloth," Laura said. "But it was deadly. There were cases of people getting really sick and even dying from it because of the fumes it gave off."

"I read somewhere recently that they examined some wallpaper produced by William Morris," Frank said. "It still had enough arsenic in it to be deadly, even after more than a century. I'd never heard of it, but Laura and I were doing some research on nineteenth-century clothing and stumbled across it. We're thinking of putting on a stage version of *Little Women*."

"What happened to the Singletarys, Dad?" Laura asked with a frown. "Were they affected by it?"

"Yes, they were, sadly." I paused for a breath to steady myself. The unintentional tragedy of Rachel's charitable act upset me. "All three of the little children and Vidalia died several months after Rachel Long gave them the cloth. The winter was harsh, and I suppose the children were already weak from malnutrition. Vidalia probably died from heartbreak as much as from exposure to the cloth herself."

No one spoke when I finished. Even Diesel was silent.

To think that Jasper Singletary and his family had been right all along. Rachel Long did kill Vidalia and the children, but never knew she had.

Helen Louise reached out and placed her hand on mine where it lay on the table. I curled my fingers around hers, glad of the warmth and the loving concern in her touch. I looked around the table at my family, and I could see they were all deeply affected by the tragedy, even though it took place a hundred and fifty years ago.

Laura pushed back her chair and came to put her arm around me. She gave me a brief squeeze, and I looked up into her loving and beautiful face.

"I'm so sorry, Dad," she said. "I know you had no idea about that cloth. It was a terrible tragedy, and I know we all feel sorry for those poor children and their mother." She paused and glanced over at Frank. He gave her a slight nod.

"Frank and I have some news that will cheer you up, though," Laura said, tears starting to form in her eyes. "In about seven months, you're going to be a grandfather."

I stood, unable to speak, and pulled my daughter close, tears now streaming down my face. Diesel meowed loudly, and the rest of the family noisily gave their congratulations to the parents-to-be.

I would never forget Rachel Long or Vidalia Singletary and her children and how an act of charity brought about so much sorrow. I would say a prayer for all of them later. Now, however, I looked to the future and the expansion of my own family and was grateful to be so blessed.

||||||||||||||||||||||||||||||||||||||

See how it all began!
Turn the page for the never-before-published
bonus short story . . .

WHEN CHARLIE
MET DIESEL

||||||||||||||||||||||||||||||||||||||

I looked out the kitchen window at the wet, gray November morning, and I wanted to go back upstairs and climb into bed. Surely they could get along fine without me today at the Athena Public Library. I was only a volunteer, after all.

On days like this I sometimes wondered whether I'd made the right decision a little over a year ago to leave Houston—my home for twenty-five years—and move back to my hometown in Mississippi. With my wife gone—thanks to pancreatic cancer—and my two children grown and out of the house, suddenly what had been a happy home felt more like a prison. Though loving memories abounded in that place, I no longer felt that it was home, with only one person to occupy it.

Not long after my wife, Jackie, died, my dear, sweet aunt Dottie, my father's sister, also passed away—ironically, from pancreatic cancer. She left everything she had to me, her only surviving relative. That included her beautiful old house, a place I loved with all my heart. Along with the house came a surprisingly large amount of money, and that meant I could afford to retire from my job in the Houston Public Library system and move home to Athena.

That's what I did, and most days I didn't regret it. Other days I felt mildly depressed—all part of the grieving process, I knew, but recognizing that didn't help much. Volunteering at the public library once a week got me out of the house, as did a part-time job cataloging rare books at the Athena College library three days a week.

"You need something, Mr. Charlie?"

The voice of my housekeeper, Azalea Berry, broke into my melancholy thoughts. I turned away from the window to face her. She set a basket of laundry on the kitchen table and regarded me, her head tilted to one side.

I offered her a faint smile and shook my head. "No, I was only looking at the weather. Trying to talk myself into getting out in it and going to the library."

"That'd be better than moping around here like a dog done lost his favorite bone." Azalea didn't mince words. I didn't think she meant to be unkind, but a year's experience had taught me that she didn't believe in mollycoddling, either. I also realized, guiltily, that Azalea had had to come out into this same weather to take care of the house. "Miss Dottie sure wouldn't like to see you dragging your tail-feathers."

Azalea had worked for my aunt for many years, and on the day I moved in, Azalea told me she would stay on because Aunt Dottie made her promise to look after the house—and me. I hadn't argued because I knew a superior force when I met one. Besides, Azalea took such good care of the house—and of me—that I had quickly grown used to being looked after and fed delicious South-ern food. My expanded waistline attested to that.

For a moment I fancied I saw my aunt standing right behind Azalea and nodding her head at what her housekeeper had said. I blinked, and the image faded. This wasn't the first time over the past year that I'd had these hallucinations—if that was indeed what they were.

"You're right." I nodded. "I won't melt. Guess I'd better get a move on."

Azalea picked up the basket and nodded. "I'll be gone by the time you're home again. I'm going to bake a casserole for you. It'll be in the oven."

I thanked her before I went into the hall to grab my raincoat from the coatrack. When I walked back into the kitchen on my way to the attached garage, I heard her singing in the utility room, along with the sound of water filling the washing machine.

The drive to the public library took only a few minutes. Nothing was far from anything else in Athena, a fact over which I marveled frequently after so many years in Houston. I parked my car in the lot beside the building. The front end touched the low hedge that bordered the lot on three sides. As I stepped out of the car, unfurl-ing my umbrella as I did so, I thought I saw something moving in the shrubbery. I shut the door and stood for a moment, watching, but then decided I must have imagined it. There was no further movement in the dark areas beneath the shrubs on this murky day.

I headed into the library to get out of the rain and into the warmth. The cheerful faces of two of the library staff members, Lizzie Hayes and Bronwyn Forster, greeted me, and my spirits began to lift. Really, I was lucky to have such nice people to spend time with, and I ought to be more grateful for that. Besides, I knew they appreciated the help I gave them.

I spent a couple of hours cataloging and processing new books, interrupted by the occasional short burst of conversation with either Lizzie or Bronwyn. Teresa Farmer, the chief reference librarian, popped her head into the office to say hello, and we chatted for a moment. Teresa asked if I could work the reference desk from two to three today, and I said I'd be happy to. After that I would be done for the day.

The time passed pleasantly enough, though slowly. Few people made it into the library, probably due to the weather. When I finished my stint at three, I bundled up again, bade everyone good-bye, and headed to my car, umbrella over my head.

As I neared my car, I saw a longish, dark shape dart out of the shrubbery and run under the car. I stopped a few feet away and squatted awkwardly as I tried to keep the umbrella over me. I thought I saw an animal of some kind behind one of the rear wheels, but the afternoon was so gray that I had difficulty discerning anything clearly.

My knees protested as I stood, and I remained in place. What kind of creature was under my car? Could it be a possum or a raccoon? They turned up in people's yards all the time. The last thing I wanted was to be attacked by a wild animal. No, I decided after a moment's reflection. The way the creature moved, it had to be a cat. Probably a family pet that had strayed away from home.

I took a couple of steps toward the car and knelt again. "Hello there, kitty. Don't be afraid. I'm not going to hurt you. Come out where I can see you better." I repeated my words in a croon, over and over, and although my knees ached, I kept it up until finally a dark head with two large ears appeared from behind the rear tire.

"Well, hello, kitty," I said. "You look wet and unhappy. How about you let me come closer? Would that be okay?" I kept up the soft patter as I moved clumsily forward in a crouch.

The cat didn't run off. Instead he—or she—watched me intently. I got as close as three feet from him, and still he hadn't moved. I stopped and held out my hand.

"Why don't you come over and say hello? I'm not going to hurt you, I promise. I bet you're really wet and cold by now, and I've got an old towel in the backseat of my car. I can wrap you up in that and you'll be all nice and warm. How does that sound?"

The cat regarded me for a moment, and I had the strangest feeling he understood every word. He meowed, rather loudly, and took a couple of steps toward me. I held still, but kept murmuring to him, and finally he came close enough for me to touch his head gently.

His bedraggled coat dripped water, and he looked to be a year or so old. He must weigh a good ten pounds, I reckoned. I couldn't see a collar, and I wondered whether he had gotten loose from a nearby house or if someone had dumped him here. The latter thought made me angry, because I despised people who abandoned their pets. If they couldn't care for them for some reason, they should at least have the decency to turn them in to a shelter. I knew Athena had a no-kill one.

I shouldn't be so pessimistic, I realized. He was probably only lost. If that were the case, perhaps an ad in the local paper would help locate his family.

The cat rubbed his head against my hand and then looked up at me with sad eyes. He chirped at me—at least, that was what it sounded like. I'd never heard a cat make such a sound before. When my children were young, we'd had a pair of cats, littermates. Both of them were chatty, but I'd never heard either of them chirp.

What should I do next? I wondered. Should I try to pick him up and put him in the car? Or open the car door and see if he would jump in? I might scare him off if I tried to pick him up. I certainly didn't want to get clawed. My coat would protect my arms, but I didn't have gloves with me.

While I debated what to do, the cat solved the dilemma for me. He turned toward the car and put a large paw on the rear door. Then he stretched up on his hind legs and touched the handle.

I was so surprised I almost lost my balance and fell back on my rear on the wet pavement. This was one smart cat, I realized. I steadied myself and got to my feet, wincing at the stiffness in my knees.

"Okay, kitty, I'll open the door and you hop in, okay?" I unlocked the doors, and the cat moved back to allow me to open the rear door. I closed my umbrella and stuck it on the floorboard. The cat jumped inside, and I leaned in to grab the towel I kept there and wrap him in it. I rubbed him with the towel, and he rewarded me with a deep, rumbling purr.

"You sound like a diesel engine." I laughed. He kept up the purring while I continued to dry him with the towel. By this time the back of my raincoat was dripping, and I decided I had better get in the car myself. I left the towel around him, shut the door, then opened the front door and climbed in.

I twisted in my seat to look at the cat. He chirped at me again, all the while keeping his eyes focused on my face.

"What should we do now?" I said. "You don't have a collar, so I have no idea where or to whom you belong." I thought for a moment. "Maybe you have one of those microchips. I'll need to take you to the vet to find out."

The cat meowed, then started licking his right front paw. Had he just agreed with me? I wondered.

I pulled out my cell phone and tapped the icon for the browser. I did a search for veterinarians in Athena, and the first one who came up was a Dr. Devon Romano. Her clinic wasn't far from the library, so I decided to head there.

A few minutes later my passenger and I pulled up in front of the clinic. There were three other cars in the parking area. I hoped I wouldn't have to wait long. I still felt damp and chilled, and I was ready to get home for a hot bath.

Deciding that trying to handle the umbrella and the cat at the same time would be a recipe for disaster, I resigned myself to a wet head. I climbed out of the car and opened the back door. The cat eyed me with what seemed to be a suspicious glare as I stuck my head and shoulders inside the car.

"Everything's going to be okay," I said in a soothing tone. "We're going to go inside and talk to the nice people here, and they're going to help us find out who you belong to, and then you'll get to go back home and be warm and dry."

As I talked, I reached toward him, and for a moment I thought he was going to slap at me with one of his large front paws. He held still, however, and let me check to make sure the towel was secured around him. He shivered suddenly, but then seemed content to let me pick him up and tuck him close to my chest.

I looked down at his face, and he stared up at me. His eyes seemed to be saying, "I trust you, human. Don't let me down." I got a funny feeling in the pit of my stomach. Then I decided I was simply imagining things. I shut the door and locked the car. Then we dashed for the clinic.

The only person in the waiting room was a redheaded woman who had a rabbit in her lap. She smiled at me, and I smiled back. I stepped up to the receptionist's window.

"Good afternoon, sir." The young woman at the desk gave me a brief smile. "How can I help you?"

"I found this cat in the parking lot at the library. He doesn't have a collar, and I wondered whether y'all could check to see if he's been microchipped."

"Why don't you have a seat, and I'll let Dr. Romano know you're here. Your name, sir?"

"Charles Harris," I said.

"Thank you, Mr. Harris," she replied.

I nodded and turned away. The cat had been calm all this time, and I glanced down at him. He appeared to be asleep. He certainly was a trusting creature.

I took a seat opposite the lady with the rabbit. We exchanged smiles again. Before I could speak to her, however, a young man in scrubs opened a nearby door and took a step into the room. "Mrs. Kendall, the doctor is ready for you."

The redhead rose from her chair, the bunny in her arms. "Good luck with your cat," she said.

I started to reply that he wasn't my cat, but she had already turned away and walked toward the door. The young man ushered her inside, and the door closed behind them.

Once again I looked down at the cat cradled in my arms, still snug in the damp towel. My arms were tiring from the weight. I settled him gently on my lap. His eyes opened, then he yawned and began to purr.

"Don't get too cozy with me," I said. "I'm betting that you'll soon be back where you belong. Although I can't say I think much of someone who would let you get loose in weather like this."

The cat made a sort of warbling sound, almost like a bird, and

I blinked at him. What kind of cat was he, to make all these odd noises?

The clinic waiting room was nicely heated, so I decided to unwrap the towel. The cat should be warm enough without it now. I examined him when he was uncovered. He was dark gray and white, with some black markings. A tabby with tiger markings, I guessed. The fur around his neck was rather thick, no doubt part of his winter coat, and there were little tufts of hair sticking out from the points of his ears. He was a handsome fellow, and he had an uncanny way of looking at me as if he knew exactly what I was thinking.

"Mr. Harris, Dr. Romano is ready for you."

I looked up to see the young man in scrubs standing in the doorway. I got up from the chair, the cat in my arms, and walked through the door.

"Exam room number three, please," the young man said. "Just up there to your right."

I preceded him a few feet down the narrow hallway to the room he indicated and stepped inside. He followed me in and moved around to the other side of a stainless steel examination table.

"Let's have him up here." The veterinary assistant patted the tabletop.

I set the cat down, the towel under him, and the assistant began to examine him.

"Seems to be in good shape," he said after a moment. "He's been eating regularly. Where was it you found him?"

"In the shrubs at the public library," I said. "He darted under my car when I was about to leave. I got him into the car and dried him off the best I could with the towel, and then I brought him here."

The assistant nodded. "He's lucky you did before he got run over, poor guy. Dr. Romano will be with you in a couple minutes." He disappeared through a door behind the examination table.

I sat in the chair next to the table and eyed the cat. He stood still, gazing calmly around. He made that chirping noise again, then it turned into a sort of trill. His eyes fixed on mine, and he seemed to be asking me, "What next?"

"I don't know," I said. Immediately I felt foolish, but this cat had an odd effect on me. Perhaps I was running a fever and letting my imagination get the best of me. I felt my forehead with the back of my right hand. It was cool and dry. No fever.

A young woman of about thirty-five, dressed in scrubs with a white coat over them, stepped into the room. "Good afternoon, Mr. Harris. Tell me what you know about this big fellow."

I stood hastily. "Afternoon, Dr. Romano." I explained the circumstances.

The veterinarian nodded. "Good of you to catch him and bring him in." She turned away to the cabinets behind her. She opened a drawer and extracted a device about twice the size of her hand. "We'll find out in a moment whether he has a chip. Let's hope he does, so we can get him back home where he belongs."

She stroked the cat's head and spoke soothingly to him for a moment. He remained calm, stretching his neck to push his head against her hand. She held the device over his shoulders, and, after a moment, she shook her head. "No chip, I'm afraid."

I felt oddly relieved, and that surprised me. I had no plans to adopt a pet, so why should I be happy this cat had no chip?

Dr. Romano laid the microchip reader aside. She examined the cat while I watched.

When she finished, I asked, "How old is he? He looks like he's at least a year old because of his size."

Dr. Romano smiled and shook her head. "No, he's only about eight to ten weeks old, still very much a kitten."

"He's pretty big for a kitten, isn't he?" I looked at the cat, who continued to sit calmly on the table between the vet and me.

"Not for his breed," Dr. Romano said. "He's a Maine Coon, and they are larger than most domestic cats. They reach maturity around three years, and adult males on average can weigh about twenty-five pounds." She pointed out the distinguishing features, some of which I had already noticed: the tufts on the ears, the ruff around the neck, and then the hair between the pads on his feet. His tail was fluffy and long, now that he was completely dry.

"They make wonderful companions," the vet continued. "They're intelligent, loyal, and loving. They also tend to be mellow around children and other pets, even dogs."

"You sound like a salesperson." I smiled to remove any sting from the comment.

Dr. Romano grinned. "He's going to need a home if you can't find his owner. I don't know of anyone in Athena or the surrounding area with Maine Coons, and we haven't seen this handsome boy here before."

"Maybe someone passing through town dumped him near the library," I said. "That makes me angry even thinking about it."

"I know," the vet said. "Sadly, though, it happens a lot. People sometimes adopt pets without realizing the responsibilities that go with adoption. Then when they feel they can't cope, they abandon the animals to fend for themselves." She shook her head. "Sometimes when people move, they don't take their pets with them. It's totally reprehensible, especially when there are shelters to take them."

I nodded. "I'd like to reserve a special place in hell for people who mistreat animals."

"No argument with that here." Dr. Romano sighed. "The question is, what are we going to do with this fellow?"

The cat, obviously aware we were talking about him, meowed loudly, then began to chirp. He turned toward me and walked to the edge of the table next to me. He held out a paw in my direction and chirped again.

"I think he's telling you he wants to go home with you." The vet laughed. "He seems pretty determined about it."

I stared at the cat. I didn't really feel up to the responsibility of a pet, and the good Lord only knew what Azalea would say if I brought a cat home. But there was something in those eyes, an intelligence perhaps, that made me think the vet was right. This cat had decided I was the person to take care of him, and that was that.

I shook my head. "I guess I don't have much choice. He needs to be checked out, I'm sure. Aren't there tests you need to run?"

Dr. Romano nodded. "We ought to check for feline AIDS and feline leukemia. The tests are relatively easy, and we can check for other problems as well by taking a look at his kidneys and urinary tract. If you don't mind waiting about twenty minutes, we'll take the samples we need, and then he can go home with you."

The cat kept staring at me. Then he began to purr, that deep rumble that reminded me of a diesel engine. The way he looked at me made me feel he knew how lonely I was. My instincts were telling me that I needed to have this cat in my life.

I also thought he might be telling me that he needed me, too.

"Very well," I said after a deep breath. "Let's do it. My housekeeper may have a fit, but he needs a home. I'll ask around and put an ad in the paper. I want to make sure no one else is going to claim him."

"What about a name?" the vet asked.

I smiled. "Diesel."

The cat warbled loudly, and Dr. Romano and I both laughed.

I stroked Diesel's head. "I guess he approves."

So did I, I suddenly realized. My heart felt lighter, and my depression had lifted, at least for now. I would have sworn Diesel smiled at me just then.

I hoped fervently that no one would come forward to claim him, because I was already quite attached to my new friend.

Luckily for both of us, no one did.